Books by Joseph Rosner

Public Faces in Private Places

The Hater's Handbook

THE HABITS OF COMMAND

 THE

JOSEPH ROSNER

HABITS of

Harcourt Brace Jovanovich HBJ New York and London

COMMAND

Library of Congress Cataloging in Publication Data
Rosner, Joseph, date
    The habits of command.

    I⟩ Title.
PZ4.R8223Hab [PS3568.08419]   813'.5'4   74–22406
ISBN 0–15–138330–8

First edition
B C D E

TO MAGGY

● THE PLACE

The wealthy lady who built the place had chosen her site with care. This remote and mountainous area, far up in the wooded Idaho panhandle, was guaranteed to keep the world at bay. All her consultants agreed on that. The most cunning and fanatic intruder, they assured her, even should he learn of the place, would face extraordinary problems reaching it. They heartened her with the fact that supplies, mail, and even the occasional visitor could be brought in only by helicopter.

Done.

It gave her great pleasure to read her beloved Henry James over and over in an atmosphere of triumphant inaccessibility. But in time it became less and less rewarding. Despite every precaution, outside unease had found a path to her door. What to her meant security and peace, to the staff meant only an isolation that bordered on imprisonment. Extravagant wages and a beguiling pension plan, it became clear, were not enough. Even the movies available three nights each week in the private screening room served only to emphasize the life of denial. In the outside world projected by the film, joys appeared to lie everywhere.

So, after three years, she had made a gift of the place to the government. Her lawyers persuaded the appropriate parties of its value as a bird sanctuary, and a suitable tax deduction was worked out. The lady then went off to another hilltop in another country. There she was sheltered from the unease of the present and the untidiness of the future by a national tradition of order and service. And there official rebuke was immediate for ideas that might be uncongenial.

Her bequest was put to the uses of men.

In the beginning, airplanes were not permitted to fly within fifty miles of the place. At a military field in Montana, three pursuit planes were kept on special alert to warn away any intruder. That was necessary in the first months because, despite the dense woods, portions of the buildings could still be seen from the air. But the speedy artifice of landscapers on a crash program soon shut out the sky. Then, closed off from any possibility of even aerial view, the place was assigned an APO number.

● THE PROBLEM OF LEADERSHIP

A group of assorted scholars was convened for a week at a prominent California thinking facility and given the problem as a hypothetical one:

Conceive of such and such a situation. In that situation, conceive of such and such a group. What personal qualities, then, would best serve the needs of the guiding intelligence of such a place and such a group?

The resources available to the security agencies could not produce the name of any man in a federal uniform who combined all those powers of brain and personality— they bordered on the occult—that the scholars agreed were essential. The ideal was then edited slightly, and three cards fell from the machines:

A submarine captain on temporary leave was briefly considered, but rejected on suspicion of strange pleasures. Modes of self-indulgence that might be condoned in the enforced solitudes of the conning tower could easily prove disruptive here.

An artillery major seemed to satisfy many of the requirements, but he was only thirty-four, and too obviously young to convey an appropriate sense of presence and command among statutory betters. The fact that Alexander the Great had lived to be only thirty-three was dismissed as an unsatisfactory argument. When publicly routed in an exchange of opinion, it was noted, he had been licensed to kill.

A three-star general, in many respects exceptionally qualified, was turned down for the most awkward of reasons.

It was clear to those on the Selection Team that in a brief enough time he was almost sure to become one of the Guests.

The computers were then turned loose on the far larger army of Americans not in uniform. The man finally selected was the Executive Editor of a prominent magazine empire. He displayed every faculty essential to the assignment. Equally important, he was willing to step away from the imperial rewards of his public position. He was drawn by something more than the plea of national emergency, the challenge and the secrecy of the project. He saw the certainty of a unique place in history. However, in less than a month's dry run—Test by Ordeal, the Selection Team called it—those qualities that had rewarded him with such success on high civilian levels of confrontation proved inadequate. When his mind failed, prudent explanations were offered to his wife on behalf of a grateful government. He was then transported (Top Secret) to the special attentions of a small government psychiatric hospital in northern New Mexico. There his remarkable stories of mad admirals and lunatic generals could be judged for exactly what they seemed to be—the fouled effluent of a brilliant but overburdened modern mind.

● NO INTRUDERS

All through this early selection period, the low-lying original buildings were being refurbished and added to by a battalion of Army engineers. The rumor was put among them that they were constructing a debriefing retreat for exceptionally important foreign defectors to the American way of life. The original plan, to build a single narrow road, many miles to the nearest railhead, was soon discarded. Roads produce cars, which produce intruders. And intruders ask questions. It was decided at the highest level that all supply and traffic, in and out, would be by Army helicopter. Even the most meddlesome Senate committee would never dare to question *this* expense.

Two hundred yards apart, three barbed-wire fences encircled the compound. Long stretches of the wire were invisible amid the covering trees. Because an experienced infiltrator would never choose to enter in so primitive a fashion, only the middle fence was electrified, and only enough to stun and discourage, rather than kill, the rare and inquisitive backpacker. There was no break, no visible entrance through the fence. A single sign, placed at random on the outer shield of wire, was considered adequate to warn away roving innocents: PRIVATE CLINIC. In a week, the sign was removed and altered. The noun was dropped, the far-ranging adjective left alone as warning.

The hand-picked platoon of Green Berets on constant patrol was more than equal to the infrequent trespasser. In their government-issue cowhand uniforms, they instantly conveyed the cool-eyed authority of forceful loners, dividend of half a century of Western films. To them, the place was known as the Ranch. It was because of this casual fact, picked up from the bug secreted in their barracks bathroom, that the place was soon given that cover title. The chapped and booted major who was their commanding officer, hedged in as he was by many other necessary secrecies, was then officially designated Ramrod.

● TEACHER

The Army Intelligence team responsible for discovering the all and everything about Dr. Bosca found him a most puzzling case. Why, for instance, would a psychiatrist have his office in Long Island City? Could it be only an indifference to professional rental chic? Or, perhaps worse, could it be because apartments were cheaper across the river from Manhattan? And why did he seem almost to hide behind the modest and ambiguous "Doctor" when his more lustrous credentials from Prague and elsewhere were quite in order? Also, his caseload seemed remarkably light for a time when one of the most widely used of four-letter words was *Help!* In fact, each of his clients had apparently jumped or been pushed from some other doctor's couch. When approached for information about Dr. Bosca, each of three separate patients (two male, one female) promptly attempted physical attack on the interrogator. This mode of inquiry was then discontinued.

Bits of fact about him were strewn all over the map of Europe. A few bread crumbs on a square mile of flypaper. Born in Bulgaria to a family of on-the-cheap aristocrats. A place and an age in which owning four goats could confirm a peerage. Ran away. Much movement, many cities. Although small, every evidence of fine health, and yet never tapped for service in any Continental army. Undersized? Overbrained? Somehow a medical degree. Also psychiatry. Then to Vienna for special study. Freud unavailable, so a member of the second team had to serve. Frictions. Cashiered from all professional associations for "ideas unbecoming." Odd event in Italy. (Thrown out the door, there, for something concerning a cabinet minister. Sex? Politics? A case of "Doctor, you know too much"? Mystery.) Came to U.S. in 1938. Spent 1947 among Eskimo of Cape Dorset, studying "leadership and power problems." On return, confided to a colleague that he had a "refreshing time" there, and had put on seven pounds. Weight now about 140. Occasional writings in professional journals. Usually cushioned by disclaimer: "The views of Dr. Bosca do not represent those of the editors." Two books—total sales less than a thousand copies. Both apparently rocks through important windows. Disavowal all along the line. Marriage around thirty, but wife died after two years. No children. In affairs, preference for dancers, lady acrobats, and guitar players. For the past ten years or so, nothing.

ITEM:

Recent summers, instead of usual vacation of his profession (the Cape, the Hamptons) he superintended private reform academy (Maine) for affluent young layabouts with personality problems. (The father of one of these, highly placed in security apparatus, was impressed, even startled, by effects of the Bosca treatment. Why not look into *him* for the Ranch?)

ITEM:

The lieutenant in Psychological Warfare who was assigned to read and report on the Bosca writings and theories came to certain conclusions almost immediately. It was easy to understand why the man had been practically outlawed by most of his own peer group. He had declared war on the conventional assumptions of modern psychology. He struck out at all prevailing judgments of the stress and disarray that might crack the seismograph in the interior universe. According to Bosca, all was determined by a man's capacity for belief. (Hmmm) Commitment to an idea, an ideology, a hero or whatever —it did not matter. A driving inner steam could arise from almost anything, if only it was deeply believed. And from that steam came power. (Hmmm)

As far as could be seen, through the mist of language and idea, he seemed to be saying that power shaped reality, but one's view of oneself shaped the view of reality, and *that* made (or unmade) power. (Hmmm) In some manner, he seemed to use REALITY (usually spelled that way) as a form of shock therapy, to jolt the patient back to a functional point of view. According to him, most people were like planes that flew swift and straight on automatic pilot, but in the wrong direction.

Had not others, before him, said something like this? Yes. In one form or another it was by now a kind of din. But Bosca declared war on them too. The word, he wrote, must be made flesh. (Hmmmmm) All philosopher's stones, foreign and familiar, were reduced by him to gravel.

An explainer? A shaper, arranger, manipulator? A Director?

The lieutenant, reading on, found all of this fascinating, much of it perplexing, some of it disturbing. He thought deeply before writing his report, and included an unusually strong and perhaps too personal commendation of the doctor's ideas. "Prophet without honor" was one of his careful throwaway descriptives. The lieutenant then put in a request for a leave of absence. He wished to move from Washington to Long Island City temporarily. Reason: to sign aboard with Dr. Bosca as a student, or, barring that, as a patient. (Request denied.)

ITEM:

At the preliminary meeting with the panel in mufti, at Pershing Artifacts, Inc., a cover office in the Empire State Building, the flow pattern was soon reversed. Dr. Bosca spent much of the time probing the interviewers.

a. General M confessed to climbing through window of Delaware schoolhouse, as a boy, to read the love letters his teacher kept in her desk (all from a lawyer in Pittsfield, Massachusetts). The doctor claimed to have, still, similiar letters taken from schoolhouse outside Varna, in the country of his birth.

b. General L presented problem of his eighteen-year-old daughter, currently dating author of embarrassing off-Broadway battle pageant (*Twilight of the Honky*). Dr. Bosca made a useful suggestion (Paris).

c. Other men, other problems. And other suggestions. By the time they got around to asking the ultimate question, they seemed to present it almost on their knees. A few elusive facts were embedded in precautionary foam-rubber detail. Suppose. If. In such a case. Would he? The large brown-bald head nodded in its cloud of cigarette smoke. Yes. Absolutely. Unlike those born here, he had become an American by choice. Had selected this country after much experience with others. Proud to perform such a service for such a country. Besides, he detected a rare opportunity for science.

ITEM:

All tests were passed without difficulty. The Test by Ordeal, so disabling to the first candidate, seemed to affect Bosca not at all. It was extended an extra week to permit additional stresses. Two members of the Selection Team had to be withdrawn because of emotional exhaustion, but in Bosca there was no change.

ITEM:

Because he was a naturalized citizen, one more safeguard was invoked, and it produced one more surprise: the GSR (galvanic skin response) line of the polygraph ran straight, without waver, down the entire chart. It was thick and broad, as if the needle had pressed with a special affirmation to cry out the honesty of this man. The technician in charge, head shaking, repeated several times the word "Unbelievable!" In his written report he indicated several possible explanations. Subject was either
1. devoid of nerves and normal internal rhythms;
2. operating at some incredible level of personal honesty;
3. a psychopath;
4. a combination of above.

Before writing the report, the technician examined the machine carefully for evidences of defect. (None.)

Dr. Bosca was finally cleared, finally and fully briefed. Given the nature of the assignment, he was told, it had been decided that his function would best be served by cloaking his professional self under some high-visibility evidence of caste, status, power. He would bear, at the Ranch, the assimilated rank of a major general in the United States Army.

No.

"Actually, gentlemen, it is not necessary. In time, they will learn to call me 'Teacher.' "

● THE NEW SHERIFF

The first security chief was a retired general, briefly minister to a Central American country. A man of resourceful graces, he spoke four languages, could tell the difference between a pavane and a gavotte and subscribed to unusual and even questionable magazines. He played chess, bridge, the piano, and was full of indoor charms that could soothe the natives wherever he might be. For the first uncertain months of the Ranch he was the ideal security chief (code name: Sheriff). But when the crisis hit, it was clear that a different kind of man was required.

Colonel Kilburn had never been to West Point. He was one more grudging expedient of a modern Army threatened by forces too new, too raw, to yield to the traditional norms of civilized warfare. All his judgments, modes, and graces moved in straight lines, and they were confined to one language. He had time for a single overriding consideration: following orders.

ITEM:

As a Green Beret officer in San Francisco, he had supplemented his regular training with a private judo course, paid for with his own money. At the first lesson the Japanese instructor had explained the philosophy of the ancient art. It did not celebrate aggression, he pointed out. One learned it only "to be able to run with confidence."

"I don't run," the student said.

The helicopter that brought him in was first spotted at eleven minutes past noon. It sent a ripple of combat alertness through the guard unit, because the regular plane, at 5:00 P.M., was always preceded by a coded message. Very briefly, there was time to wonder if the sound overhead meant that *they*, ever pressing, had at last discovered the Ranch. Were they now sending in a KGB suicide unit, atomic warhead and all, to blow the place into the classified archives?

For the three long minutes in which the security chief tried to figure out how to defend from air attack an installation never designed so to defend itself, he felt almost angry at being put in a position of such obvious futility. It was only when Sergeant Yost wondered aloud how a helicopter could get this close to the Ranch without disturbing the local radar pattern that the general felt a sudden calm. Of course. Any ruffling of that pattern would have brought in pursuit planes, and since there were none about, the meaning of the unexpected plane became less unnerving.

The general went out to the landing pad personally to wait. Despite the soothing force of logic, there was still the possibility of having guessed wrong, the possibility, still, of ugly incident. Much more than an incident, perhaps. In that case, combat initiative would provoke the casual circle of Wranglers who ringed the pad to open fire on the plane with carbine and pistol. Crack shots all.

The moment Colonel Kilburn stepped on the ground he walked directly to the chinoed, tin-starred general. He handed over a sealed envelope stamped MOST SECRET— EYES ONLY and said, "You'd better read that right here, sir."

The message on the single sheet of paper was brief. The general was being replaced. (With honor? Without honor? There was no hint.) The plane would leave in exactly one hour and he must be on it. Anything he could not carry with him would be sent along later. A jet transport was waiting for him at Great Falls, Montana, and it would fly him directly to Washington.

Perhaps he would find some answers there.

For approximately half of the next hour the two men were together in the quarters of the security chief. The incoming man was opening and unpacking his two bags, the outgoing man packing and closing his four. It was a situation that might produce in some men a few words, a sudden action, of personal understanding, if not uneasy warmth. Perhaps mutual reflection. Perhaps the usual wry review of the brusqueness with which the Army so often had to perform its necessary acts.

The colonel said nothing as he moved through his own necessary acts. He was taking off his uniform and putting on the carefully rumpled chino pants and shirt he had brought with him. The general left his own cover uniform on a chair. There was no use for it where he was going. Wherever he was going. Despite the calm and ungiving gray-eyed efficiency of the colonel, the general chanced a question.

"I don't suppose there's any point in asking you what this is all about, Kilburn?"

The lean head of sandy hair, early white at the temples, shook in a single No. By then the general had noticed that his replacement had not bothered to pin the Sheriff's badge to the breast pocket of his shirt. Perhaps the man felt that the obvious toughness of the long, large-boned body was badge enough. He had the look of a mechanical soldier, a man of portable roots. Well, the Army had need of such officers, too. And it certainly must have discovered a special need for this one. He seemed barely out of his mid-forties, and already he wore an eagle on his shoulder.

Hurrying to the waiting plane, the general felt a twinge of melancholy. There was no time for good-byes. He would have liked at least a last word with Daniell. And certainly with Bosca, that charming man. He regretted that the doctor would probably find in this hasty departure yet another example of the curious ways of men in uniform.

At the plane he saw Bosca waiting with a smile. The wrinkled hand was warm and firm in its good-by. As the general stepped aboard he felt much better.

● SEX

The darker needs of the flesh had not been overlooked.

There were almost fifty men at the Ranch. Most of them were still young enough to find sex a pleasure and consider it a right, not worn enough to recall it as a memory or serve it as a duty.

To ignore the problem was to pretend that a live bomb did not exist in the trunk of one's car. The situation was far more explosive than for men on submarine duty. Such men might be away for months, but every volunteer at the Ranch had slammed the door shut on America for a minimum of two years.

While the Ranch was being hurried through its blueprint stage, a panel of specialists met for three days at a well-known institution in Topeka, Kansas, to study this problem. Sociology, psychology, and medicine were represented, each man a scholar of caprice and desire, need and behavior, a respected calibrator of human breakdown in all degrees of refinement. The problem was presented to the panel as a hypothesis, a *maybe,* an exhilarating *suppose.* Given the need to maintain for some reason, in some place, in such and such a situation, a maximum of security, national as well as emotional, then:

1. What would be the advantages of providing a strictly supervised Love Clinic, or brothel, on the premises?

   Answer: Negative.

   Men frequently say things in bed that are meant to enhance their sense of power. Telling a fact they knew would obviously endanger security. Telling as a fact something they did not know might endanger it more. The artfully dressed lie, unstructured from above, could be at least as perilous as the naked fact.

2. Would there be benefit in scheduling brief, occasional leave to some supervised adjacent facility, for release of irrelevant tension?

   Answer: Negative. See reply to Question 1.

3. What recommendation would the panel make to ensure maximum military security along with minimum sexual insecurity?

   Answer: a. Celibacy.

   When accepted as a necessary article of faith, in advance of service, it was likely to strengthen the will and fortify individual and group conception of goals and methods. Those who fell from grace would be likely to do so discreetly, resorting to the traditional consolations of male quarantine.

   b. A single female at such a place might serve a variety of psychological and even necessary ends, defusing the negative and infusing the positive. *Recommended type:* Desirable yet chaste. Should dispense personal services profoundly intimate yet obviously innocent. Mature, mythic mother-whore surrogate, with institutionalized unattainability. Should be about thirty-five, above average in looks and figure (but not too much). Authority with warmth. Perhaps a nurse and/or dietitian. (So ordered.)

● MARRIAGE

It had been decided the very first day that all their meetings would take place in her room, adjoining the small Dispensary.

1. It was comparatively easy for him to get through her door without being seen.
2. Even should he be spotted slinking into the room of the only woman at the Ranch, it would probably be considered normal behavior for any Army sergeant who respected his responsibilities as an American.
3. His room was in a more frequented area, and she would be far more noticeable going there. Such notice might arouse ideas and actions that could cause trouble.

All these arguments were ticked off by Sergeant Yost with a kind of Blackstone-at-the-brief logic. And besides, he pointed out, limiting their meetings to a single room would cut in half their efforts to find the predictable bug.

It was two weeks before he discovered it. It was woven cunningly into the wicker netting of the government-issue wastebasket at the head of the bed. (The one in his own room—four days of only casual searching—was tucked in the crotch of the southwest bedpost.) In the two weeks before its discovery, all their comment was in sign language and penciled notes. Even after they had made love that second time in the small clothes closet, its door shut, no voices were raised in the resulting fight. Hand signals and heavy breathing did the work, until she grabbed a pencil and one of the large yellow pads he used for his homework, and began to scribble fierce arguments. His written answers were more sober, as usual, grounded more firmly in the imperatives of the possible.

But even with the bugged wastebasket tucked safely away from the zone of action, they were careful to pursue their love-making with a wary rapture. As if they were characters in a suburban farce, with her husband or his wife snoring blissfully in an adjoining bed.

The fact that they were married made the situation more exasperating. In those two weeks of enforced connubial calm it was only the thought of the larger goal, a reward far beyond the possibilities of that room, that reined in her need to cry out in mid-passion, to the surrounding world, a sudden fierce and disinhibiting "Fuck you!"

It was the money that had attracted them.

For him, as a sergeant, the special bonus would come to $1,000, over and above his base pay, for each of the two years. Added to that was the equally special "overseas pay differential" plus the "combat bonus" for this assignment. For her, as a captain, double his special bonus for the same period, in addition to those other compensations proportionately handsomer than his own. All that extra money was a neon sign in gold, too attractive to resist. It spelled out a more stable footing for a new life and a freer one.

So they had volunteered.

In his special position in the Intelligence unit that proc-
essed the applications, he had performed an unmilitary
act. He had withheld from final consideration by the review board the records of the four Army nurses who might
have been judged more eligible than Susan.

He was surprised by how much each of the candidates re-
sembled her. They were all in their mid-thirties, all were
blond, and all were within an inch of five feet six. From their
photos, each of them even looked something like her. None
had Susan's helmet of bobbed hair, but each had the same
strong, clean-featured face, the same calm expression. Each
seemed exactly the kind of woman that a man would want
to see somewhere in his own lifeboat. It made him wonder
what he might be letting her in for.

He thought deeply about the violation of his oath to the
Army. But had he not seen the higher brass make exactly
such left-handed judgments to favor friends and the sons of
friends? Yes. Had he not seen them withhold earned favors
because of personal prejudice or spite? Yes. But he had
done what he had done not out of whim or casual impulse.
The grandness of a vision could confer a special sanction,
he assured himself. Besides, he decided, he had not actually broken the law so much as bent it slightly to meet the
needs of justice. He was going to become a lawyer.

From the Special Bonus Table, stamped, along with the
other briefing materials, with the rarely used U.S. (Ultra-
Secret), he sensed the bait for an obviously unpleasant
assignment. But he had deduced that any part he might take
in this mysterious project could not possibly be on the combat level. His years as an Intelligence clerk had been spent
in specialized civil routines. And there was another relieving

clue: the roster called not for a medical corpsman, but for the more passive nurse/dietitian. Anyway, in that early period when he worried about withholding the cards of those other nurses—dietetics experience far superior to Susan's—he knew that even if his act had been discovered there were plausible excuses he could offer. His record of almost twenty years was immaculate, so the immediate jury was almost sure to believe his case.

When it was official that she too had been selected, they traveled separately, out of uniform, to a small town in Maryland where, with the license they had taken out weeks before, they were married by a justice of the peace. In the weeks that remained for them in Washington, they avoided seeing each other in daylight and in public. That sacrifice, too, they were willing to make for the foreseeable and measurable reward. To reveal their marriage, especially on such an assignment, would be to provoke immediate separation. Each had been in the Army long enough to know that God and man do not always march to the same drummer.

The wastebasket, secret listener, was behind the closed door of the bathroom. It was put there whenever he was with her. So they could speak freely now, though careful to keep their voices under sensible control.

She turned the light on.

"I feel a little better." She patted his knee.

"You're supposed to." Lying back, he lit a cigarette.

"But I don't know if I can stand it much longer."

"You'd better get used to it. We still have a lot of this ahead of us."

"You know what I mean." She got up from the bed and went off to the bathroom. They said nothing while she was there. Sudden silences were a reflex by now. When she emerged, shutting the bathroom door behind her, he could see by her expression that there would be questions.

"What was all that excitement today? What's it all about?"

"No messages, no warning, no nothing." He shook his head in frowning wonder. "But they don't make a change like that, in a place like this, without a lot of important people being up all night thinking about it."

"He'll tell you what it's about—the new Sheriff—won't he?"

"I hope so. Hardly anyone's seen him, and the place is crawling with some pretty interesting lies about him already."

"If he tells you, you'll tell me—at least a hint—won't you?"

"Come on, Susie. Don't start up with that again. Whatever he's here for, it's not just to rearrange the files. This could be bigger than that thing with the hydrogen bomb. Remember—they threw a two-star general out of here today. Like he was behind in his rent."

"Well, we can talk about it when you know a little more."

"Thanks. In law, we call that a reprieve."

Alongside him on the bed once more, she was now smoking too.

"Anyway, I wish they'd get a regular doctor in here."

"Not a chance," he said. "You know what Doctor Bosca says. You do that and you'll have the men staying awake nights, dreaming up complaints. Besides, anything too serious for a nurse, he can handle. Until the next plane, anyway."

"I suppose so," she sighed.

"And even if they were all big Christian Scientists, like Secretary Wadlow, they'd still want someone around here like you—just to make them feel good. A touch of the female." He patted her belly.

He got out of bed, lifting himself over her body to do it, and put on his shorts and then his pants. He went to the table that served at times as a desk. "I brought over a little homework I had left from the last mail," he said. "Torts."

In another moment she had a nice view of the back that he bent over the Law.

"I love you, Norm," she called idly from the bed.

"I'm not against it. Just don't let any of them get you down. Play it easy." He did not turn to underline the words with a look.

"I wish I'd known it was going to be like this."

"Nobody knew. And even if we did, we couldn't afford to push it away."

"I'm not so sure we could afford to accept," she said.

Still bending over his papers, he waved a hand in the direction of the shelf of books that ran along the wall. "Read something for a while," he said.

"This place is a jailhouse. And we're just as much prisoners as the Guests are. Sometimes, I feel like handing in my resignation. Then I could run right out of here. In any direction I want."

"Great." Still ungiving over his work. "You want to run away. Remember, Captain, your husband is only a staff sergeant. They don't let an enlisted man quit on a thing like this. Besides, he's got to put in his time if he wants his pension. You want to spend all those nights out there by yourself? You want to wait a year and a half before your husband can come home from the office and lay a hand on you? Is that what you want?"

"All right, Mr. Lawyer. I won't bring it up again."

"Sure you will. And I'll still be telling you the same old story. We're working on a nest egg, so we can march out of our uniforms in style. My pension will bring us three hundred and fifty clams the last day of every month, for the rest of my life. Stop shaking the mailbox."

"You won't be too old to practice law?" Family joke.

"Nobody's too old for that. They could *wheel* me into court and it wouldn't make any difference. I'll still be strong enough to throw briefs all over Arizona. When Clarence Darrow was forty-one he wasn't such a big shot yet, either." For the first time he turned to look at her on the bed. "You always like to move furniture." Deadpan. "Is there some big decorator you want to be?"

"I want to be Mrs. Norman Yost," she said. "Out loud. Then, after we get that settled, I'd just like to be myself. But meanwhile, I hate this place."

"You haven't been keeping it much of a secret. General Winkler complained to the office. You're still throwing too much fish on that menu."

"Americans eat too much meat," she said.

"O.K. Let's not get into all that again." One side of the sun-tanned face crinkled in a smile. "You've already filed that brief about those big, strong ancestors of yours, back in Iceland."

"I don't feel so strong."

Her hand moved slowly in the air as she beckoned to him. He turned his head back to Torts.

"We'll have to wait for that, too," he said. Then a quick smile at her. "But keep the oven warm. It'll only be a few more minutes this time."

● CLASS

At the front of the large, carpeted room, the blackboard framed the upper half of the shrunken body as Dr. Bosca bent forward. The skin hung loosely from the browned and rutted made-in-Europe armor of a face, as if he had drawn a uniform one size too large from nature. Under the tattered brows, the almost-black eyes flashed an electric summons to attention.

Cigarette smoke billowed from his mouth as he tapped his pointer twice at the desk beside him.

In the club chairs, the men in chino shirts and pants continued to murmur among themselves. It was not that their attention had been lulled by the combined warmth of the radiators and the crisp September sunlight that struck through the windows. Considerable power lurked under the anonymous chino: three generals, one admiral, a former Secretary of State, and a cashiered staff officer in a legion that could trace its victories back—some said—to the Sicily of the eleventh century. Such men were capable of poor discipline in all temperatures.

"Students. I will have to have your attention. All of it. If you are to profit from our studies here. Otherwise, the course may have to be extended for some of you. And for such bad pupils there may even be more immediate penalties."

A sudden quiet fell among them.

"I'd like to do a little punishing myself around here." White-haired, firm-jawed General St. John, hero of a thousand miles of headlines ("He's three inches taller than Napoleon!"), bit down on the unlit cigar butt fixed on the left flank of his mouth. It was the focus of a million photographs ("He *never* smokes!"), a public badge more awesome than rows of ribbons.

"You have already advanced and been forced to withdraw that point several times, General. Please learn to accept the unavoidable. Here, only I have the power to punish. And he who has the final right to punish, he rules the world. Any world, including the next one. What you are thinking of, General, is fantasy. Here we deal only with reality. And if you enjoy the reality of your privileges, you will not object to paying for them with a little attention. Otherwise, no sauna, no movies, no billiards, bridge, liquor, or cigars for a week. Not just for you, General, but for the rest of the class as well. I will let you decide—a command decision for you all."

Random fire from among the club chairs:

"Quiet, St. John!" Reasonable General Winkler.

"For God's sake, close your ass!" Forthright Admiral Byngham.

"We used to get guys like that. All belch. A ball bat right across the mouth, just once—then they get smart." The deep furrows in the Cadetti face remained at peace, the thin mustache without tremor. He rarely displayed emotion, except when announcing yet another omen of his progressive physical decay.

"Thank you, Mr. Cadetti," Dr. Bosca said. "A useful point."

"This man's background, his vocation, and his ideas are foreign to every American concept, and yet you choose to encourage him. I wonder why." Secretary Wadlow's eyes were more bleakly accusing than ever. The blunt nose and chin that cried out for sandpaper seemed to clamp more firmly at the cheerless mouth.

"Only those things that cause *me* to wonder will be discussed here, Mr. Secretary," Bosca said.

Now all fell silent, looking up toward him. His smile was approving.

"Good. I think it will help us all to understand today's problem much more quickly if we conduct the class as a kind of interview. As on certain television programs. I will be the interviewer. I will represent the people's right to know. We will call our little program 'The Public as Enemy.' They're full of curiosity out there. Searching, endlessly searching. Each one of them a Parsifal in quest of the grail that can be discovered only in the mouth of some public figure. One of yourselves, for instance. And as we all know by now, the wrong word in the wrong place can be very dangerous."

"I think—"

Swack! went the pointer on the desk.

"No thinking for the moment, General Winkler." The large brown-bald head shook slowly in gentle disapproval. "There will be ample opportunity for that soon, and I hope you will take every advantage of it."

"Amen." General Daniell's casual seal of approval was barely heard. The at-ease angle of the slim, extended body, the crossed arms and legs, emphasized his usual unconcern.

Winkler's nod signaled quick acceptance of sensible terms. The relentlessly amiable features were now screwed into a pattern of earnest attention.

"Keep your powder dry, Winkler." St. John's mouth took a firmer purchase on the cigar.

"All right, then. I will ask the questions, and each of you will answer as best he can. You are excused as usual, Mr. Cadetti."

"Yeah. Sure. But I got this pain, Doctor. You said you'd have a look at it. Like it's a golf ball down in my liver."

"You know the rules, Mr. Cadetti. None of your medical bulletins during class—unless you wish to forgo your next examination."

"Gee, I'm sorry, Doctor. Yeah, I forgot."

"Now, students," the doctor said, "please remember that all questions addressed to you in today's class will seem troublesome and embarrassing. There is nothing inadvertent in that. They are designed to be unpleasant, to test each of you in the fire. I need hardly say that if you can learn to deal on your feet with the questions I will ask, then you should have nothing to fear from any of the specialists in public embarrassment that you will run into when you leave here. Please believe me, gentlemen, there is nothing any more personal here than there is in a well-run Marine boot camp. We will all learn by doing."

The pointer went out, drawing a bead on one of the men.

"We begin with you, Admiral. For the purposes of our seminar we will assume a network prime-time program. Audience of ten million people. Each one restless and hungry for that final answer that will solve all their problems. Our first question for you: how could a man of your experience have succeeded in making the mistake of sinking the world's largest oil tanker?"

"I'll tell you how." He lumbered to his feet. The heavy gray brows radiated *battle stations* as they joined fiercely above the bridge of his nose. His voice almost cracked in his eagerness to straighten out the world yet again. "It was because of that goddamned fog they had over there. It was impossible—"

The pointer smacked an interruption.

"So you have been explaining for some time. And watch your language, please. Children may be listening. The taxpayers of the future."

"Because it's the truth, that's why it's always the same. Facts are facts. They don't change. If this was some kind of a lie, an excuse I was handing out, then it would change every once in a while. But you look at the record—"

"The record is quite clear, Admiral. As commander of a major fleet force, you were provided by the American people with every facility for distinguishing between friend and enemy. You had the use of every cautionary device that a rich and zealous ingenuity could provide. But despite these safeguards, you were able to expose very quickly the limitations of mere mechanical perfection. You sank the world's largest, newest, and most expensive oil tanker, the pride of a friendly nation. Tell us why you chose, Admiral, to carry vigilance quite so far."

"It was a tense situation. The whole world was jammed with crisis right then. You can look it up. I didn't invent any of it. I was carrying out orders. When in doubt, you just don't sit on your ass in a situation like that. You strike. And that's exactly what I did. It was the fog that made a difference, that's all. By the time I knew our radar was spelling out a tanker, it was too late. But suppose I had waited that extra minute or so—and suppose it actually had been one of *theirs*—what do you think would have happened then? For all anybody knows, you and I and the rest of us here would be holding this meeting, probably, somewhere in a shack in Siberia." The crew-cut head, almost beautifully square, seemed to brace itself against an oncoming storm.

"Let me see if we understand you, Admiral—and I use the national 'we.' You plead a state of crisis. You claim not to have invented any of it. You were a mere instrument carrying out orders. You speak of being in doubt. You bring up fog, which caused in you grave indecision. Even your striking at this so-called enemy was not a decisive act but one based on a guess. It had the authority only of executive delirium. You use words like *suppose*. You imply a big *if*. Yours is the worst kind of response, Admiral. It lacks every distinction of authoritative judgment. Every one of your answers is an error, showing a total misunderstanding of what the average listener wants to believe—what in fact he *must be made to believe* if you are to discharge your responsibility to the public need. How many more times must this be explained to you?"

"I'm giving you the facts. If you want a fairy tale, then you should have told me."

"First law of command relations with the public: If you can't help your own case, then don't say anything."

Winkler: "We used to teach them that the first day, in the Air Corps." The hair-trigger smile flared in remembered glory.

Daniell: "A man can't say anything right until he knows

what he's doing." Cool, offhand, the tone of a barely listening Caesar.

Wadlow: "How do we really *know* there wasn't something fishy about that tanker? What about *them?*" Large-boned face bent forward, narrowed eyes demanding the Ultimate Answer.

The pointer tapped against the desk.

"Enough, gentlemen. I will make all the significant comments."

St. John: "The trouble with Byngham is, he goes around asking everybody to forgive him. That—"

"General," Dr. Bosca broke in, his head bent even farther forward, to give his gaze a fuller play over the opposition, "I asked for quiet."

"I didn't finish what I was going to say. About his command attitude. I—"

"General—shut up," Dr. Bosca said.

"Wait a minute." The lean and chinoed form rose as if bugled from the chair. "Nobody speaks to me like that." The frosty blue eyes popped, crackled, and snapped.

"Someone already has, General. I said, very clearly, 'Shut up.' "

The general began to walk to where the doctor stood. A felt stillness quickened the room, as if a long-deferred war had suddenly broken into being.

The doctor put a hand to the underside of the desk top, and in a moment the door to the room flew open. A pair of Wranglers entered, and the doctor nodded them in the direction of the general. The two men, clean-cut and blank-eyed, fell upon him instantly with a calm yet brisk efficiency. They held his arms pinned to his sides, his head bent back on his neck, as they began to remove his pants. He kept up a running fire of curses, threats, assorted rages piling past the intact cigar, but their muscles overrode all protest. When he kicked furiously to make the removal of his pants more difficult, one Wrangler struck harshly with the edge of his palm at the general's knee. There was a snort of pain.

"Please, gentlemen," the doctor said. "Dignity."

"Do they have to do that?" The question rang out from Winkler.

"That's a four-star general, Doctor." So said Daniell.

Very distinctly, Secretary Wadlow was heard to say, "Of all the teachers they might have chosen, we were given a Bulgarian. I wonder why."

Dr. Bosca paid no attention to them. Half seated on the edge of the desk, he puffed at his dark-brown cigarette as he watched the men pull the pants over the general's loafers. After the pants lay folded on the desk, and the men looked at the doctor for their dismissal, he pointed at the general's shorts. They began to remove those too.

Around the room, all the men jumped to their feet, with the exception of Mr. Cadetti, who sucked calmly at yet another pill from the new bottle of placebos with which Dr. Bosca had recently provided him. The men yammered, each in his own way, at the spectacle.

"The minute I get out of this place, I'm nailing that man's balls to the mast!" Byngham.

"Shame! Disgrace!" Wadlow.

"I'll kill you for this, you foreigner son of bitch!" St. John.

The shorts gave way with a tearing sound as they came over the shoes.

"Please, gentlemen," the doctor said, "always, with discipline, there should be a little dignity."

The general's threats were now hoarse, frustrated, vulgar, with separate portions of the doctor's person coming in for detailed and colorful attack.

"You may take your hands off him now," Bosca said. But the moment the Wranglers disengaged, the general leaped for the doctor, who did not flinch from his casual seat near the blackboard. It was as if he knew that no harm could come from a man who stood before him like that, naked from the abbreviated tail of his shirt down to the tops of his heavy white golf socks. Or at least he knew that the two Wranglers would grab the general as quickly as they did. Each held an elbow with quiet tenacity.

The doctor nodded toward a nearby corner of the room. "Stand him there with his back to us."

"If you think I'm just going—" The cigar quivered.

"We must have quiet, General," Dr. Bosca said, as the Wranglers adjusted their man into position. "You will stand like that for the next five minutes. Should you choose to give any more trouble to the class, you will have to stand *facing* them from that corner for ten more minutes. And if that does not persuade you, you will be marched around the buildings here, in exactly that condition, for the next half hour. We will follow behind you, then, conducting the class on the march."

From the corner, his back to them, the oddly white behind seemed almost to tense in anguish.

"Do you understand, General?"

No answer.

"All right. Turn him around to face the students," Dr. Bosca instructed. The general, however, his back to them, shook off the Wranglers' hands. His voice came out of the corner, the bitter words barely audible.

"Never mind. I understand."

"Excellent. Socrates would approve, General. If sin is only ignorance, then already you have taken an important first step toward the good."

He told the Wranglers to return to their posts outside.

"All right, students," he said, "we can now proceed with our lesson."

"Doctor," the iron voice of Mr. Wadlow called out, "why was it necessary to do a thing like that to a man like General St. John?"

"A good question, Mr. Secretary. And you can all learn from the answer. First, the social lesson: Because a man is very important, it does not mean that everything he says or does is very important. It could be that some of these things are not the result of wisdom, of philosophy, of special vision or thought. What we are seeing and hearing may be only a temper tantrum. Second, the military lesson: Never a frontal attack in the face of superior fire power. But the practical lesson is perhaps the one most relevant to our morning's theme, 'The Public as Enemy'—Beware of overexposure."

The large browned head leaned forward, the smile cool, the dark eyes narrowed into a torpedo fix on Byngham.

"And now, Admiral"—a plume of cigarette smoke shot from him like a signal—"let us proceed with your interview."

● GENERAL

As soon as the boy was born—fourth child, only son—all the resources of professional genealogy were sent charging into the bush of ancestral fact, hint, and legend. There was much reconnoitering, much hot pursuit of even the most fugitive evidences of a warlike past. The boy's father, Mr. St. John, had always admired men of action. If not for his bad back, it was well known, he might himself have acted more.

The genealogist returned from his mission with ambiguous trophies. There were deficiencies in earlier modes of record-keeping. The custodians of the past were sometimes very sloppy in discharging their responsibilities to the present. The alertness of the tracker, however, had been unsparing. Like a miner's lamp, his imagination beamed through the darkness with which the facts were covered by the inefficient spelling of our forefathers. And he extracted marvels from the tendency of some warriors to hide their glories under false names. (In this part of the report, Barbarossa marched with Robin Hood, the Scarlet Pimpernel with the Swamp Fox.)

Success.

In games at West Point he compensated with creative ferocity for the deficiencies of a small though wiry body. He became notorious for the number of players (some, certainly by accident, on his own side) that he put in the hospital. He was on the rifle team, and if there had been a team that entered competitions for the firing of cannon, bazooka, or flame thrower, he might have tried out for those too. In the judgment of the men who watched over him, he was a born leader.

After a dutiful marriage that produced two dutiful daughters, he was able to advance upon World War II. But promotion brought paradox. The higher he rose, the greater became the distance between him and the visible enemy. In time, as his energies became exiled to impersonal violence, he was reduced to suffering through our wars, barely able to contain his anger at the restraints that curbed the essential dream.

His patriotism was uneasy in the bridle of the larger national purpose. On the way to his four stars there were "incidents." But he was too popular with the press, too necessary a public hormone, to be denied a few private and eccentric side effects. Ugly specifics were played down as "hearsay," "rumor," and "exaggeration."

All went well until a liberal magazine, shrill butcher-paper crybaby, printed a piece about his punching the British military attaché at a Washington reception. (Headline: "Each Man Is an Ireland—") Soon other magazines and then even an occasional newspaper began to breach the silence that had hidden his exploits as a freedom fighter at war with the Geneva Convention. By the time he struck the Secretary of the Navy over the ear with a brass globe at a meeting of the Joint Chiefs of Staff ("I wish it was *ten* stitches—that weak-kneed civilian bastard"), it was already too late. He had by then won too many public victories over too many important people. (Among others: three columnists—two of them syndicated—one senator, the second secretary of a major embassy, and the chief bellhop of a very fashionable hotel.) Even the Sunday newspapers were finding it increasingly hard to exult in his behavior. The tiger of so many American triumphs was no longer baring his fangs only to certified enemies.

The review board considered early retirement and rejected it. His unruly temper, fired by a sense of real injustice, might cause special problems. There was the painful example of that unstrung, retired brigadier general out on the coast. Until his recent death he had served as military affairs editor of a widely read radical scream sheet that erupted regularly from an ecology-crazed commune in northern California. *His* treacheries were still drawing blood, and he had not known a hundredth of what an out-to-get-the-Chief General St. John would know.

A recommendation for psychiatric attention was rejected. Any close-up attempt to soften the Spartan décor of his interior life might result in a murder.

An offer of a vice-presidency (sales) with a major war contractor was arranged. He turned it down. A desk was anathema, emblem of the dark world of civilian ritual and other restraints.

At three o'clock one morning, a major in Counterintelligence, accompanied by two carbine-carrying lieutenants, presented himself at the door of the general's home in Fort Myer. Sealed orders instructed him to proceed with his visitors, within the hour, on "emergency assignment." He was to be flown forthwith to a place unnamed, and must ask no questions until his arrival there.

The Ranch.

● THE PROBLEM

Dr. Bosca was only slightly surprised when the colonel, a moment after introducing himself, suggested that they do their talking while strolling outside, among the surrounding trees.

"Security."

The doctor recognized the mana in the word. Official magic. It sprayed a film of wisdom over the oddest actions.

"Colonel Kilburn," he said, "this entire place was designed to be the most enemyproof in the world. If my office is not safe, then how can we assume that the trees around here are not wired as well?"

"We can't. So we'll keep our voices low while we're talking."

The doctor shrugged. He could already tell a few things from the firmness not only of the jaw but also of the shoulders and the pelvic circle. Most of all he could tell it from the absence of that Sheriff's badge. He could see that he was talking to a man who did not play bridge, read few books, and was probably equally suspicious of light talk and heavy ideas. A rule-abider. An enforcer. The doctor shrugged again.

As soon as they began to walk among the great quiet pines, the colonel made a point. He was confiding in the doctor, he said, not because he wanted to, but because he had been instructed to do so. It was Washington's idea. Bosca, an expert in the study of human nature, had been on the scene for six months. He might have noticed something. Kilburn seemed almost anxious to convey that if it had been up to him, he would not have taken the doctor into his confidence.

"On a thing like this you trust nobody," he said.

"Well, then, Colonel, why can't *I* begin then by not trusting *you?* I've never seen you before. You come in here on an unannounced plane—no prior warning—"

"That should tell you something about how serious Washington considers this."

"That is only one way to see it. Another way might be to congratulate you on your cleverness in fooling us. For all

I can tell, even getting your predecessor out of here so quickly is just one more feather in your cap. There may be an Order of Lenin in this for you, for all I know."

"Don't run away with yourself, Doctor. Just hold your mind still for a minute, while I tell you what we're up against."

The Problem: Only three afternoons before, in London, a certain man had presented himself to the American embassy and asked for asylum. He was in England ostensibly to attend an international scientific congress, and his credentials as a correspondent for a boys' poultry journal in his own country were in order. He was not an especially high official in the secret apparatus of his government, it appeared, but he had given the original debriefing unit one piece of information that was puzzling, astonishing, and perhaps priceless. It was transmitted immediately to Virginia HQ in the rarely used Brown code. Word came back within minutes to get the man to this country, and seven hours later he was in Washington.

It was a dark moment for America, the darkness perceived clearly by the enlightened few. Not only did *they* know about the Ranch, but they had somehow infiltrated the place. The defector, despite every inducement, could not remember—if he had ever known—what was the grand design of the infiltration. To convince us of his ignorance he had volunteered his mind to the usual amenities of hypnosis, polygraph, and truth serum. Nothing. A stranger was somewhere about, and he had penetrated beyond the most skillfully contrived shield. That was very bad. But not to know precisely *why* he was there was even worse. There were a number of possibilities.

1. The Ranch represented a blue-chip storehouse of national

securities. Every Guest was a walking repository of important secrets. Except, of course, for Mr. Cadetti. And every one of them was in a state of questionable stability. This was the big reason, in fact, why each of them was there. A kind word, a casual question, even the mere presence of some other person, might be enough at some informal moment to jar into play subtle machineries of strategic revelation. Out might pour a barrage of crucial reminiscence and miscellaneous data that would keep the computer banks of the enemy spinning happily for years.

2. They wanted to copy it. In the past, whenever they had special problems with their own prime commanders, solutions had come with quick efficiency: the firing squad or the insane asylum. Either of these solutions is useful *only* when prime commanders abound. Besides, grumbling could now be heard from down below. Their officer class was beginning to express dissatisfaction with the traditional solutions. It could be that they saw sense in the American way. Having copied so many other things that had once been exclusively ours, it would be only logical for them to try to steal the plans of the Ranch too. Such imitation was more than flattery. As with their Xeroxing our original atomic bomb, it could be one more candid evidence of mass-homicidal intent.

3. They would blow the place up, and blast permanently out of action some of the keenest minds on the free world's side of the barricade.

4. They were out to exterminate a single precise target in the Ranch community. A Guest perhaps—but which one? Or was it Teacher? (Shrug: "We cannot always

choose the way in which our contemporaries will seek to honor us.") Mr. Cadetti? Unlikely. True, his former friends had set a million-dollar price on his head, good until his appearance next month before that Senate committee. After that the price would come down by half. But of what interest could such a man, such a fact, be to *them?* And then a more sinister *but:* wasn't that the same kind of question people had asked before Hitler and Stalin hopped into bed together in '39? Anyway, to assume the marriage of their world aims with those of the Mafia was still premature. Was General Daniell, perhaps, the target? His memory coils would provide years of important secrets. But they could have kidnaped him at any time during his long European service.

5. Most ominous were all those possibilities that anyone thinking of the situation might happen to dream up. In this world the boundaries of probability have been pressed farther and farther outward. Therefore anything that could be thought of by one man—one of us—might just as easily be thought of by some other man—one of them. And if one of them could think of it, then the national security demanded the assumption that they might find a means to profit from it.

Dr. Bosca said very little as the colonel, murmuring rather than talking, expounded on the possibilities. Soon the evening wind began to rustle among the trees, and the two men, as if by agreement, turned their steps toward the main building. The problem was clear: a mysterious Who? was abroad in this most secret and well-defended of hideaways, and he aimed at achieving an equally mysterious What?

To the direct question, Dr. Bosca explained that he had no

helpful ideas, hints, or clues that might suggest a quick path to the enemy. For a few moments after he spoke, the unswerving gray eyes remained fixed on him.

"All right," Kilburn said. "Just remember, Doctor, I don't want to give you any wrong ideas. To Washington you're one of the good guys, but until I'm sure, you're still one of the possibles."

"I have no objection at all, Colonel." The doctor smiled agreeably. "Every profession has its caste marks. In 1931, in Munich, I wrote a paper on—please forgive the expression—'the monks of power.' Men who have taken the vows of austerity, violence, and national security. Such men are usually steeped in the ambiguities of the obvious. They often see things that escape the rest of us. My paper had so many useful points to make that nobody wanted to publish it, much less read it. It's an old problem in philosophy, Colonel—when an idea is put forward, and nobody hears it, then does it exist?"

"There's something around here that exists, Doctor, and my job is to find it."

"Of course. And I will certainly do what I can to help. And now, just to satisfy an old man's professional curiosity, do you mind if I ask a question perhaps unrelated to our topic?"

"Go ahead."

"Why do you not wear the Sheriff's badge, as you have a precedent and a right to do?"

"Because I won't need it."

"Thank you. I hope, no matter what happens, that you will enjoy your stay here."

"Don't worry about me, Doctor. I like my work."

"In many cases, Colonel, the first sign of a healthy mind."

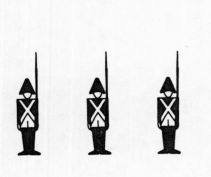

● SHARING

The moment he shut the door behind him and turned the
lock, he hurried to the wastebasket. The bug, so cunningly
sewn into the woven artifice of the fibers, was gone. At least
he could not find it. It was hard for him to believe that so
shrewdly placed an object could have been removed—and
so soon—without disturbing the neatness of the twining
pattern. But then, they had probably substituted a new bas-

ket, this time an innocent one. "They," of course, would be that closemouthed tech sergeant over in Message Center.

When Susan saw him examining the wastebasket, and making no attempt to carry it into the bathroom, she waited until he looked at her. Then she let her eyebrows ask the question.

"It's O.K.," he said.

"What's O.K.?" Her voice was even lower than his.

"The bug is gone. He told me it would be."

"Who told you?"

"Colonel Kilburn. The new sheriff. He just had a talk with me. He looks tough, but I think he'll be all right."

"What did he say about the bug?"

"He doesn't need one in here. He's going to have to depend on me a lot, he says. He knows about us seeing each other. But he didn't say we should stop."

"Does he know we're married?" She only mouthed the last two words.

He shrugged, unknowing.

"Before he came he ran a vacuum cleaner over the whole staff here. He says he knows everything about everybody. Whatever that means."

"But he won't send one of us away?" Only her first three words were spoken, the others barely breathed.

He went to the table that served him as a desk and quickly penciled an answer on the yellow pad there: *He never mentioned it.* Under that he wrote: *Hope he doesn't know about holding back on those other nurses.*

She took the pencil from him and wrote, under his words, *My God!!* Casually, her voice asked, "Why is he here?"

"You know I can't tell you."

"Sure you can—if you really wanted to."

"There're rules about things like this. I can't go telling you everything that happened at the office, like it was some nine-to-five job. Does a CIA man do that with his wife? What are you going to do when I'm practicing law? Are you going to want to hear everything a client tells me?"

"This is different. We're both in the Army. I'm your superior officer. Tell me."

He almost laughed, but stopped himself. It would only annoy her more.

"Come on, Susie," he said. "Don't get so personal about it. You *know* there are some things they won't let me tell you, not even in bed."

"All right, then. But he said the bug is out of here now?"

"*Two* of them. He said we always had two in here."

Her green eyes widened.

"Two?" She ran a hand slowly through her bobbed hair.

"That's right. All the time we were keeping so quiet, with the wastebasket locked in the john, there was another bug in here somewhere. And for all I know they might have been picking us up on video. We were practically on network here."

"Then they've known about us all along, haven't they?"

He nodded.

"They could even be listening to us right now, couldn't they?"

A laugh would have helped, but he couldn't manage one.

"He said he was taking out the other bug too."

"Do you believe him?" The words did not sound as fierce as she looked.

For a moment he did not answer. Then, "Yes, I do." But he shook his head deliberately as he spoke.

"Well," she said, "then I don't think it makes any difference what we say in here any more. They already know the worst about us."

He smiled, although a part of him wondered what he had to smile about.

"I wouldn't call it the worst," he said. "We've had six months already, and I still kind of like it."

"You know what I mean. If they needed any kind of information against us at all, then they've got it by now. I'm not going to lower my voice any more in here for anybody. This is my room. My home. And if they don't like the way I talk, then they can go to hell with themselves."

"Come on, take it easy," he said.

"I've been taking it easy for too long." Her mouth and jaw set themselves into an announcement of defiance. "Now, I'll ask you once more—what is this all about?"

"What is what all about?"

"Don't run around in circles with me, Norm. This is your buddy, sharing the foxhole with you. I've been spending my honeymoon at a hotel for Peeping Toms. I'm entitled to know what's got this whole place agitated all of a sudden."

"Nobody's agitated. I don't know what you're talking about."

"I can always tell when you're lying. One side of your mouth begins to twitch."

"Never mind what you think is my twitching. There's nothing going on here. A new security chief came in, that's all. You want an explanation all of a sudden for *every* crazy thing the Army does?"

"All right," she said. "There are things going on around here that I'm entitled to know. Maybe not as a captain, but as an American citizen. And as the woman you share that bed with." She pointed to it.

"What's that supposed to mean?"

"You're in Intelligence, mister. See if you can figure it out."

"You know I couldn't tell you even if I *did* know. I've taken an oath not to tell a thing to anybody who's not cleared for security. How many times do I have to go through that?"

But as he spoke he moved to the table again and wrote rapidly on the yellow pad: *I'll tell you. Keep yelling at me while I write.*

Then, as she proceeded to tell him all the horrors she was going to visit on him for withholding the facts, he wrote out for her, as she stood nearby, the barest outline of what he had learned from Colonel Kilburn. Somewhere on the premises there was a spy, a man who was doing to the United States government what the government had been —and perhaps still was—doing to the two of them.

Later, in the bed, she said nothing, as if having built up so much of a momentum of silence in the horizontal past that now her mind was locked into a pattern of soundless discretion.

"Do that again," he said to her. His voice shattered the black silence that enclosed them.

"Sure," she said.

In the darkness they began to laugh, neither of them caring that with the laughter the rhythm of their love had been permitted to escape. One victory at a time was enough.

● ATTACK

For Kilburn it had been a long day, made longer by his having slept very little the first night. He had stayed up to read again through the mound of papers on the case. Now, after the talks of the day, each on a carefully scaled level of secrecy, the groundwork was laid. The fire pattern plotted. He was ready for rest. But questions remained to disturb him, as if lumped under the thin mattress on which, still dressed, he lay.

The purpose of the intruder in the hive was not yet clear; so, then, how much time was there, exactly, to play around with? Could it be that it was already too late? If it was a suicide mission, the whole place might blow that very night. In fact, whatever his goal, the man might be achieving it that very minute, while Kilburn was easing himself toward sleep.

One more chorus of the old tune. He would try not to think of it any more, or his mind just might kick back on him, from all the pressure. The brain was like a horse, a soldier, a muscle. You had to let up on it every once in a while, let it stand at ease. He barely thought, this time, of the brigadier's star that had been hinted at, when—if?— he reported in, soon, with "Mission accomplished."

It was a nice little spread he had here. The three neat rooms were more than enough space for him. The furniture, almost new, was a bit more showy than he liked. But he was used, by now, to making do with the gentler standards of those on the heights above him.

In the middle of his second cigarette, lying back on the

soothing hardness—he had had two of the Wranglers re-move the oversized and oversoft bed of the previous tenant—he reflected on the comfort that had afflicted the modern Army. The modern soldier, too. Because it had afflicted the modern man. But not all modern men, soldiers, or armies. *They* were able to march, fight, endure without bitching to their officers, their congressmen, and their women. They had the kind of spirit that this country had been able to take for granted in so many of its earlier everything-on-the-table wars. Now, for what we lacked in the human scale we had to make up in the inhuman one. Technology. Supplies had to be overwhelming. Output of everything that could be counted with a dollar was all boxcarred up. And only be-cause it was getting harder and harder to find men who would put out, extend themselves, give everything they had in the name of something worth believing in: their country. But then, as long as there were such as himself, and a few others he could think of, to cheer and scourge the other bastards on, the country would still float.

He took an extra-long puff of the cigarette. Saw by his watch that it was late. Felt the ease of the end of a good day's work and the receptive serenity of his own quarters. He got off the bed, picked a copy of the *Infantry Journal* from the little stack of unread issues he had set on the lower shelf of the night table, and went into the john. He closed the door and turned the latch. He was not being absent-minded in doing that. The fact that he was now in his own quarters did not make a difference exceptional enough to alter the habit of many years.

Seated. Relaxed. Not so much the touch of nature that makes the whole world kin as a kind of ritual, marginal, and defensible joy. He noticed in the table of contents that the article titled "Overdependence on Reserves: Thoughts on a Common Command Failing" had been written by a captain who had the same second name as his ex-wife. Well, if the man was anything like that Wanda, then the article was probably full of big words that didn't add up to a hell of a lot. Plenty of potatoes but not a sign of meat. When you run your life according to rules you read in books, then watch out, everybody. He wondered for the briefest instant what she was up to now. Were those big blue eyes looking at some other man the way they used to look at him? Did *she* ever wonder what *he* might be up to sometime, when she dragged not a magazine, of course, but some goddamned book into the john? He turned the page as a relieving interior spasm permitted a throb of grudging sensuality to balance the memory of the one that got away.

The lights overhead went out. Dead.

He tensed in the darkness, and without his even thinking about it, the machinery of reflexes in which he lived, complex and acute, flashed a signal that threw him off the seat and flat to the floor. It never occurred to him, not till later, anyway, to think that the reason he must have jumped like that was the obvious one. The electrical system at the Ranch was covered by a back-up unit that went on automatically in exactly this kind of situation. And if it did not, in such a moment, it could only mean that it had been prevented from doing so by human design. And because part of that human design might just have depended on his being a sitting duck, so to speak, he leaped from the expectations of the (guess) enemy pattern.

In the same instant that his body flattened out on the cool tiles, the door came slamming open with sudden and brutal force. Tapes whirred in his mind: whoever it was that had crashed at the wood, breaking the door loose from its lock, obviously had no worry about making all that noise, because the rooms were completely soundproofed. No noise in. No noise out. And then, in a barely functional sliver of moonbeam, he caught the dull gray glint of something in what could only have been a man's hand. All reflexes humming at once, messages flying around inside him like battle signals in a beautifully greased command post, he flung himself forward and upward, before that killing weapon could fire for the first time at where he was supposed to be seated. Yes, say it again, a sitting duck. In the gun's flash from only that first shot, he would have been revealed on the floor, and the second shot, with something true to aim at, would get him for sure. His hand was on the wrist that held the gun, slamming the man's gloved fist (lean, steely fingers, no rings) against the doorjamb, hearing only a grunt of air rather than the more articulated pain he would have expected and wanted. A well-drilled son of a bitch, no stranger to this kind of situation, one who would not give an inch. They trained them like homicidal seals over there. And meanwhile Kilburn's other hand was forced to reach at his pants, because the goddamned things were loose, the belt unbuckled, hampering him about the knees. (For want of a nail, a kingdom was lost.) As one hand fumbled down there desperately, trying to achieve a measure of security that would permit him to act more freely, the other hand slammed the man's fist one more excruciating time against the solid wood corner of the jamb. He heard the gun drop to the floor. Just then he felt a knee come up out of nowhere and catch him under the jaw. His head was jolted up and back. Off balance, he let go of the enemy wrist and his own pants, knowing that he was going to fall to the floor. He did not even have to plan it, think about it, to fall exactly where he guessed the gun to be, covering it with his body. The man might try to kick him senseless as he lay there, might try something else to fulfill his mission. But no, he turned with a kind of trained suddenness and silence, slipped through the dark of the living room, and away. Out there the door opened and shut.

The harsh metal object pressed against Colonel Kilburn's ribs as he lay on the floor for a moment of breathing time. Then he pulled himself slowly to his feet. As he came erect, the lights once more went on.

He recognized the make of the gun and it surprised him. A cunning little item. But why would they use it, so obviously one of theirs? Everyone knew that they, at the end of World War II, had dismantled brick by brick, machine by machine, the factory that made them in Leipzig. They had moved it over into the Ukraine. Was this just some form of professional contempt for American assumptions, American methods, American utensils? Were they really that sure of themselves? Or was it only that the killer felt more at home with precisely this weapon? Anyway, it was no anonymous local piece. A small, sleek, and expensive import. The bullets were small too, and honest. No cyanide pellets, and no brucine or rotenone, either. As he flushed the toilet, adjusted his pants, washed up, he wondered if the man would come at him with a pistol—another pistol—next time. Because there was of course going to be a next time. Or did the son of a bitch have other equipment lying around in odd places to draw from? The colonel did not feel any sense of fear. He felt, rather, almost a kind of satisfaction at the audacity—and, for the time being, the elusiveness and ingenuity, too—of his opponent. The one they had sent on this man's errand was a man.

And incidentally, of course, the bathroom door would have to be fixed.

There was little point in sending the gun off to Washington, to scrounge for clues. Not worth the trouble. Besides, they might get too excited back there. Some dumb young hustler of a major, with a college degree and the ear of a general whose daughter he was shacked up with, just might blow the whistle with some brilliant idea about sending in reinforcements.

No. Kilburn felt sure that he could deal with the enemy alone. Besides, it might be a nice touch to poke a hole in the guy with his own weapon. Not kill him, of course. Just kind of wing him, to let him know who was chief.

He set a chair against the front door, a small table lamp poised on its rim, just in case.

In bed, he went on thinking as he put out the last cigarette, and a kind of stowaway thought sneaked in among the official others. He wondered how it would be to have Wanda beside him right that minute. Just once, anyway. She sure as hell seemed to know a lot about the kind of thing you couldn't really get the hang of just from books.

● COMMUNICATION

Twenty miles outside of Billings, Montana, a select group of communications experts were at their code machines and transmitters on a round-the-clock basis. The international air was deluged with messages, many of them long, all of them in yet uncracked codes. And even if penetrated by the devious machineries of *them*, what would be discovered? Passages from the *Iliad*, Herodotus, and Pindar. (One of the officers was a classics major from Swarthmore.) Passages from the nursery: "Mary had a little lamb." Passages from the sporting pages of old newspapers: "The strong right arm of Slingin' Sammy Baugh did it again, this afternoon, when—" The enemy machines would have to be set to whirring once more to discover what these Delphic findings were all about. Those clever Americans were still one crucial step ahead of other countries with the mechanical ingenuities that would inevitably assist all to an even earlier oblivion.

Camp Blue Boy 4, with its narrow, sentried access road, its mined lawns (DANGER: DO NOT STEP ON GRASS), its troop of communications experts, its handsome grounds, building, and budget, was an elaborate false trail. It functioned as a decoy. Since all radio traffic was automatically policed by alien powers, it had been decided to flood the air with fake messages that would originate in bulk from some area not too near the Ranch, and yet not so far from it, either. And so, should the enemy ever turn its lethal attentions to that most secret of caches of national military treasure, the focus of those attentions would fall several hundred miles, at least, off the bull's-eye. And forcing the enemy's hand in the wrong direction, toward the dummy setup, would gain precious time in which to maneuver for tactical advantage. The lieutenant colonel who wrote the memorandum for the lieutenant general who submitted it was very persuasive about the need for the project. Caesar's work in Gaul was reflected on for profit and example.

One of the more compelling points in the memorandum was Item 5: Since the project would necessarily be in the Top-Secret category, no details, no itemized breakdown of expense, no formalized result sheet would have to be supplied to groups or individuals normally licensed to pry and complain.

It was equal to the most sophisticated message center ever contrived. But because of the fear that *any* message that might be clarified into usable sense might expose to alien parties the nature of the necessary American duplicity, there was the strictest operational taboo on easy comprehension. For this reason, on the rare occasions when contact had to be made directly with Washington, the general in charge (Signal Corps, one year from retirement) would have himself driven into Billings, where he would use a public pay phone, never the same one. Even *he* did not know about the Ranch. He knew only that this was a far far better thing he did than he had ever done before in his career. He was personally responsible for covering a national action of supreme importance.

But three months after the camp had been set up, there was a shock.

The camp dentist, a scholar of cryptography, horoscopy, and the double-crostic, in routine examination came upon two stainless-steel teeth far back in the mouth of a blond and amiable corporal. Cover facts: the corporal could recite professional baseball's reserve clause from memory, word for word; he knew the lyrics of every Rudolf Friml number; he hated liberals; he was the second-best crapshooter in the camp. But molars like that told the dentist a less American story. He saw in them another breakthrough in the Eureka! dentistry of the steppes.

The corporal denied everything. (Brilliant display of grins, wisecracks, and patriotic affirmations bordering on the religious.) He was shipped off to Bethesda, where a special Truth Squad broke him down. A product of the American Academy outside Taganrog, of course. But he knew only his own assignment: infiltrate; memorize all details; await contact. Someone over there had not trusted this agent with vital information, perhaps because—one of ours pointed out—he had had an American grandmother.

Message unit quotas per diem were increased for each man.

This event, as well as the attack on himself, was very much on Colonel Kilburn's mind the next morning. He thought again of his decision of the night before. Washington should really be told something of what had happened. Even if it was only the briefest progress report (STRANGER HERE AND HEARD FROM). But then he thought once more of what that would almost surely bring: a deluge of queries and orders, with much stirring up of the hothouse brain power of soft-bottomed men in command of desks. Panic disguised as efficiency.

No. At least for a while, he would not reveal the attack to Washington. He would stamp the event with the highest security classification he knew: MY SECRET.

● TEST

Sergeant Yost came into the office at exactly one minute before eight. Sign of an old Army man, one who gives no more and no less than the contract with the uniform calls for. The colonel beckoned him over to the other desk.

"I wonder if you'd help me with this thing." He pushed a piece of paper toward the sergeant. On it was a single sentence of penciled writing. "Look at that."

It was the first sentence of the Gettysburg Address.

Yost nodded.

"You didn't spell that word right—'Fourscore' has a *u* in it."

"Exactly. So what I'd like you to do, Yost, is take this eraser here, and rub out that whole word for me."

"Sure." He made a special effort to keep a straight face. After all his years in the Army, it would have been naïve to express wonder at yet another example of some officer's quirk or folly. In a moment he had erased the word.

"I see you're left-handed, Sergeant."

"Yes, sir. Always have been."

"Here." Handing over a pencil. "Let me see you write 'fourscore' in there. Spell it the way it ought to be."

Yost accepted the pencil with his left hand and quickly wrote in the word. He lifted his eyes to look directly into those of the examining colonel. He knew it was a test of some kind. When you ran into a man like that, all kinds of tests might come shooting at you from out of the woodwork. The Army was like a vast compound in which many buildings shared the same area, and a lot of those buildings were staffed by mental cases. He hoped this wasn't one of them. Because then, just maybe, he would have to tell Susan she was right, and try to figure some way for the two of them to get out of there. Taking orders for another year and a half from a psycho commander was too hard a way to earn a base for even a law degree.

"Is that all, Colonel?"

"Almost all. You must have had training in firing a forty-five, Sergeant. That right?"

"Yes, sir."

"When you had that training, did you use your left hand?"

"No, sir. The time I did it, they made me use my right."

"Were you any good that way?"

"Only fair. If I wanted to kill some guy with it, I'd probably hold it this way."

He made a symbolic pistol of his left fist, thumb and first finger extended. He could see that the colonel's gray eyes, very clear, were tracking everything he said and did. He wondered what this was all about.

"If you wanted to kill somebody like me, Sergeant—in a place like this—how would you go about it?"

"I hadn't thought about it much—a thing like that."

"Think about it."

"You mean now? This minute?"

"That's right. I just want to hear the way your wheels sound on it."

"Well, just off the top, not thinking about it too hard, I'd probably try to brain you, sir. Right here in the office. With something hard enough, something we always have lying around in here."

"What would you do with the body? Mail it to Arlington?"

"Nothing. I'd just leave it right here. I'd get the pistol from the drawer in the file over there, and stick it in your hand. Then I'd holler for everybody to come running. I'd tell them you'd gone crazy in here, I thought. But all I knew, you'd pulled the gun on me and were going to shoot me. You were raving something about how I didn't deserve to live, things like that, and I couldn't figure it out. All I know is, I was lucky to put you away before you got me. I was only trying to defend myself, to knock you out, that's all. I was sorry about the whole thing. Sir."

"Why should anyone believe a dumbbell story like that? If that's all there was to it, you might have sergeants in this man's Army running around and killing officers all day long."

"You just got here and I never met you before. They'd check out my record. They'd look me up black and blue. They'd ask me all kinds of questions. You couldn't say anything to contradict me because you'd be dead. They wouldn't be able to find a single reason why I'd want to kill you. No intent. No motive. They'd have to believe me."

The colonel kept looking at him, giving him the cool weight of those eyes. Then he almost smiled.

"O.K., Sergeant," he said. "You haven't finished that course yet, but you're beginning to think like a lawyer. I guess I can trust you."

"You could have trusted me without going through all that, Colonel."

"In a case like this, I wouldn't trust the Secretary of Defense without going through something like that. Someone tried to kill me last night. He brought a gun. And he was right-handed. I couldn't see him. It was too dark. But I judge him to be about five-eleven, about a hundred and seventy-five pounds. That description wouldn't be too far off for you, would it?"

"No, sir. But it wouldn't be too far off a lot of people around here. You thinking of moving in on all the ones who're right-handed?"

"It might come to that."

"What do we do before then?"

"He tried once and he missed. He's got some reason for thinking I have to be knocked off. So he has to try again. All we have to do is get him first. But I don't have to tell you, Sergeant, that we've got to be more polite than he is. We have to get him alive."

"You got any ideas, Colonel? For a starter, I mean?"

"Yes. Is there something around here that makes coffee?"

On the way to the closet where the electric percolator was kept, Yost felt pretty good. The colonel now seemed not only tough, but sensible. The kind of officer a man could feel pretty much at ease working for. It was only a few moments later, putting the coffee into the cups, that he began to feel a bit less pleased by the situation. He was a staff sergeant in Intelligence, a noncommissioned officer in a unit designed by decree and function to be above and beyond the sound and fact of battle. And here he was, nearing the end of a long-term workout for a law degree, while a killer was arranging murder under the same roof. Sometimes it hardly seemed to make sense for a man to make plans.

● EXPERTS

At the blackboard, Dr. Bosca was at last able to finish what he had started. The chalk squeaked as he wrote out the ground plan for the morning lesson. He paid no heed to the sounds of obligatory inattention among the students. They were firing only with blanks. He knew that the reflexes of appropriate discipline were now more firmly installed, even perhaps for General St. John.

When the general had burst snarling from the room some moments before, the two Wranglers outside the door had brought him back immediately. In front of the class, excessive force was once again used to restrain the free will of a four-star general. The Wranglers were earnest, quiet, almost scholarly, as they went about their attentions. They ignored his cries of rage and threat, as well as the demands of eminence. They neither kicked nor punched but only pressed, yanked, and shook him with insistent though well-meaning harassment. As if they were training a large, unruly dog to obedience. They did almost everything but slap a newspaper at his nose. The doctor had instructed them well. The general made dark promises for the future, but he took his seat at last. Now there was a relative stillness among the club chairs that was more than serviceable. It spelled out a distinct change in normal patterns of behavior.

It would be some time, the doctor could tell, before one of the students would dare to walk out of class without permission. Whatever else they might choose to do, they would remain fixed in their chairs, feet firm to the carpeted floor.

That was good. Even the best of works are accomplished one step at a time.

It was only when Dr. Bosca reached the bottom of the list and chalked in the words *Pearl Harbor* that there was a cry from among the civil murmurings behind him. Admiral Byngham, in his best on-the-battle-bridge tone: "What the hell is *that* for?"

All murmuring ceased. All eyes turned to the front of the room. At the top of the blackboard the usual capital letters indicated the theme: EXPERTS. Under that, there was a list.

> Public-opinion polls   (1948)
> The Maginot line
> The Titanic
> Britain loses the war   (1940)
> Russia loses the war   (1941)
> North Vietnam loses the war   (1961 to 1972)
> Pearl Harbor

Dr. Bosca turned to face the class, looked around the room slowly, and then tapped his pointer against the desk top.

"All right, gentlemen. Today's lesson is on a subject that should appeal to all of us. The expert. The man who has reached that point in his profession at which he doesn't have to give the kind of reasons we expect from other men when they throw out a conclusion. And if he *should* give a reason, nobody is expected to look at it too closely, because he's an expert."

"What is Pearl Harbor doing on that list?"

"We've got time to get to that, Admiral. And when we

do, you will instruct the class in the vast amounts of time, planning, money, and energy that went into making it an impregnable fortress."

"What's that supposed to mean?" General Winkler's tone quavered with disbelief. "Everybody knows that air power put it out of commission in less than an hour."

"Wait a *minute!*" Byngham half rose from his chair, but in mid-flight there was a *swack! swack!* of Dr. Bosca's pointer. The admiral sank back, his face rumpled in anger.

A resentful quiet filled the sun-splattered room, and above the Guests the cigar and cigarette smoke billowed in more restless clouds.

"All right, then." Bosca's face broadened with good cheer. "We shall address our combined mental forces first to a nonmilitary area: the public-opinion polls for the national election of 1948. Some of you will recall that they elected Mr. Dewey president of the United States by a comfortable margin."

"Why do we have to bother with that civilian junk?" St. John called out. "We're mostly men in uniform here. I can see a reason for Mr. Wadlow, but I don't know why we have to have this fellow Cadetti around. Can't—"

The pointer whipped almost casually at the desk and the general went suddenly to rest.

"Everybody in this room knows the meaning of real power from personal experience." Long draft on the dark-brown cigarette. "In the past, some of you have had more power than others. But here you are all equal. Here, because of unusual circumstances, a man like me, one who has spent a lifetime contriving an international reputation for unimportance, is in charge. So please, gentlemen, do not interrupt me again, or I may have to cancel for a time one or more of your more indispensable forms of self-indulgence."

Varieties of dismay struck among the faces. They now looked to him with deep concentration.

"Excellent." Smoke cloud. "So, then—why don't we, for a change, see what contribution we can get from our Mr. Cadetti."

But before he could say more, a lean hand went languidly up.

"Doctor Bosca, is this trip through a stale and tiresome period really necessary? Can't we—"

"No, General Daniell, we can't." The doctor's interruption was brisk. "We are going to fertilize our capacity for judgment by studying a little of the debris left in the highway of history by the thoroughbred soothsayer. Here, where we are consecrated only to reality, it will help to examine the ways and artifacts of the only too thriving opposition. We will learn that the hand of the potter may slip, and instead of a Greek vase he produces a broken spittoon. And that the higher up the potter, the more people down below to get hit with the pieces."

"But why—"

"Because I say so. Because at this moment I am in charge. In the present situation, modest as it is, my power is total. So, General Daniell, with or without your permission, but with your unmistakable silence, we will proceed. Now, every man in this room has in some way made a big mistake—"

"Just a minute!"

"That will be enough, Admiral." The doctor's large

brown head leaned forward, the gray brows raised in a semaphore of warning. "If cutting out tobacco does not encourage reasonable restraint, perhaps a week or so without sauna, liquor, and films?"

"Shut up, for God's sake, Byngham," St. John said.

The admiral grumbled into silence.

"All right, then." Dr. Bosca nodded. "Just a few more facts to help Mr. Cadetti and the rest of you through the darkness. In all these unfortunate memories, a treasure. I shall supply the historic background and ask the rest of you to extract the moral."

"Do we get anything for that?" The mind of General Winkler was often at work among the permutations of accidental and fractional reward.

"Well, if the class produces what is in my judgment an appropriate degree of comprehension—if you can convince me within the next two hours that the lesson has been learned—an extra movie will be included in this week's program. A musical."

A satisfied "Ah" ran among the seats.

"I wouldn't mind hearing about 1948," Winkler said. "I was still in England then."

"I was in Washington," St. John said. "Working."

"You guys, you still don't know how to hold a meeting." In Mr. Cadetti's tone a patient contempt. "Somebody with a baseball bat—that's what you need in here."

Dr. Bosca, pointer in hand, seemed to have his mind elsewhere for the moment. Then he rapped lightly for their attention.

"Gentlemen, let us proceed with the lesson. In that year of 1948, all the experts at appraising public opinion assured decent and kindly Americans that Mr. Truman was going to be thrown bodily out of the White House. For a variety of reasons, it was clear to them that the President had outlived his usefulness to the country. So, with the experts' opinion in hand, great plans were made, farseeing dreams put to the drawing board. Men sat about in high places planning the How, What, and Why of a beautiful and efficient new America to come. So then, perhaps Mr. Cadetti can give us the lesson in all this."

"Dewey lost. Truman won," he said. "You don't have to make a big thing out of it. You got a result, you got to ride with it for a while."

"A sound conclusion, as far as it goes. What else?" The pointer was raised like a baton, as if it might draw exactly the correct note from the student.

Mr. Cadetti tried again.

"You had all this talk, talk, talk. Nobody was getting his ass off the ground to find out what was really going on. You know what I mean? I know you don't like me to say those things around here, but it's like a time once in Kansas City. We sent some guys in, to just stand around in certain places—not just to hear the mouth but to watch, to see what happens when they got their hands on their money. So then, after a while we got an idea what was really doing. We got what we call *direction*."

"That's a very good point too, Mr. Cadetti." Dr. Bosca nodded. "Not quite the one I had in mind, but an excellent observation nevertheless. Now, does that exhaust your capacity to draw a moral from this situation?"

"It all happened. What's the use even talking about it? Whatever problems anybody's got, they got them *now*. Like that liver thing of mine—that pain—like it's a golf ball—"

Down went the pointer. "Thank you. That will be all."
Teacher looked among the students.

"I know you are all as grateful as I am for what Mr. Cadetti has afforded us," he said. "Unfortunately, it is not quite enough. Also, it lacks a certain precision of observation that I think you might all be able to profit from even more."

A hand went up.

"I have to use the latrine," General St. John said.

"You know that no one is permitted to leave the class." Dr. Bosca's look was not even reproving. "Especially while I am the one who is talking. You have all been briefed on the wisdom of occasional control—the need to contain—"

The general rose from his chair, the dead cigar tilted in anger. Even in the mandatory chinos, artfully frayed, he sizzled with the habit of command.

"I have to *piss!*" he said. "And nothing and no one is going to stop me."

Dr. Bosca put his hand casually to the underside of the desk top. It was a clear signal of oncoming action.

"All right, General," he said. "If you insist that you must, I can have one of the men bring a specimen bottle from the Dispensary. You can use it right here, while you're listening. Shall we do it that way?"

For a few seconds he waited. No answer. Then General St. John sat down slowly, muttering a barely heard "Never mind."

"In the old days," Mr. Cadetti said (tone of instruction), "we'd just handcuff some bigmouth to a radiator. Get his girl to come over and watch, and then we'd all piss on him. People got to learn."

"Thank you again, Mr. Cadetti." The doctor cast a look

around the class. "Once more, immediate experience has fleshed out something we have all been at pains to learn here in dry, skeleton form. The importance of compromise. General St. John wished to urinate in seclusion, a situation that would provide a sense of his own power to control the secrecy of his most private acts. We could not spare him this courtesy, since it is a rule of our group that the obligations of the curriculum must supersede all other considerations. The general, in the course of his career, has known great power. That is a fact. But all that former power now comes into collision with the meaning and function of the Ranch—with present power. Another fact. One of these two facts must give way. So then, the lesson once more: when a fact of the past collides head on with an organized fact of the present, and one of them must yield, it is usually the fact of yesterday that winds up in the emergency ward."

"Do your pissing before class. That's the lesson," the admiral said.

"Not entirely." The doctor shook his head. "But let us continue with our original lesson—it proves that even an expert can make a mistake. And what is an expert? On the simplest level he may be someone like me—one who knows just a little more than those he is talking with, about whatever they're talking about. Sometimes he doesn't have to know more—but he has a larger office, more money, or a loaded revolver. Anyway, in 1948, practically every one of them made a mistake. Such things are possible, gentlemen. Increasing the number of experts does not make their consensus a fact. For most of history our planet was fixed at the center of the universe because the experts put it there. Each of you can think of other examples. So the wisest and firmest minds, we see, are again making a mistake. The first duty of such minds—minds not too different from our own, gentlemen—is to see things as they really are."

"I need air." General St. John put a hand to his collar. "I think I'm going to faint."

All eyes turned to him.

"Faint, by all means, General," Dr. Bosca said. "But please do so here. There is no better place for it than a nice soft chair of the kind you are in right now. I prescribe this as a man of medicine."

The general groaned softly, slumped noticeably, and the angle of his cigar seemed to decline.

"And now once again the lesson," Teacher said. "Mr. Truman, as the records will show, won that election. And some of you still, perhaps, after all these months, permit your minds to be troubled by a question: why is that man Bosca bringing *that* up at a time like this?"

"I don't believe that any of us, Doctor, are likely to ask that one any more." General Daniell sounded, as so often, far too patient. "I remember once in Biarritz, an ambassador's lady—"

"Thank you, General. One lesson at a time. At the moment, mine will serve." The doctor continued. "I bring it up once more because it is the most important lesson we can learn. I am not saying that power is no better than the person using it—that fact is so well known, they are even teaching it in some colleges by now. What I offer here is a much more useful lesson. One that each of you will have to learn if you are to graduate from our class: reality means what *is*. You must learn to see things as they are—not as you think they are, and not as you would like them to be. Out of that may come judgment. And only then can you hope to guess with accuracy."

"We know all that," Winkler said. "How many different ways are we supposed to learn it?"

"As many as necessary, General," the doctor said. "You are all experts here. In one way or another, you are—or certainly have been—experts in the use of power. But I am an expert, we might say, in the mistakes made by men of power. If you wish, we will try a little experiment. I will not ask if any of you has ever made a mistake. But I will go around the room and ask each of you in turn if you think the man alongside you has ever made a mistake. I will encourage the presentation of specifics."

"Shut up, Winkler," Byngham called out. And then to the doctor, "Don't listen to him. Just get on with the lesson."

"Excellent, Admiral." Bosca nodded. "Already you are one of our better students." His look examined the others. "But I believe the theme of today's lesson has made some impact. So we will now address ourselves to some of the supporting material. General Daniell."

"Yes, Teacher?" In the voice a built-in yawn.

"You have had considerable experience as a specialist in mass misconceptions. You were a professional interpreter of the community dream, I believe. You also know the Continent well. Why don't you, then, spell out for us a few of the interesting points that made France invulnerable to enemy attack on the eve of World War Two. Review for us the firmly held conviction about that great chastity belt of national defense, the Maginot line. And please do not spare the class any of the official language: 'impenetrable,' 'impassable,' 'no enemy will touch France for centuries.' That kind of thing. Commence firing, General."

● SLEEPER

When he was a boy, his family, well endowed with private keys to every public possibility, was mystified by him. They thought it odd that a son of theirs would turn his back so steadfastly to the heights of industry or diplomacy, and even to the prospect of some decent eminence in law or Wall Street. The boy, so precociously elegant in so many ways, wanted only to be a soldier.

After West Point, and special courses at the Army's expense at Harvard, there were additional courses at the Sorbonne. Along the way he discovered a ripening passion for secrets. He came to love other men's facts the way more obvious men love money or women. In an Army of specialists, his own special faculties were noted and approved. He was placed in a discreet position with an important polling organization until he had mastered question-loading techniques, evaluation, the mystic power of the slide rule, the methodology of the How. Then he was sent off to London, where he set up his own polling organization (Know-Power, Inc.).

In England, the publicly admired function of a national opinion checker and question asker served as an excellent cover for a man whose real profession was to get answers not readily available.

Afterward, there were branch offices in Berlin and Copenhagen, Vienna and Rome, and of course Paris. The elegant and successful Mr. Daniell was invited everywhere, went everywhere, asked intelligent questions everywhere. Always, while his employees knocked on doors, stopped people on streets, asked, pressed and probed for answers, he was drinking, dancing, chatting, asking questions of his own. And why not? It was his profession. It never occurred to any of his hosts, any of his clients, to anyone at all, in fact, that he was anything but what he pretended to be: a scholar of the more sociable sciences, deeply immersed in the scholar's dream of learning everything, and of performing an honorable and rewarding public service while going about it. That was believed by everyone, of course, except *them*.

It had been thought wise, for some years past, to include among the Know-Power employees, on a free-lance basis, a number of ladies whose services were usually purveyed in a professional atmosphere of intimacy and confidence. Much was discovered in this way, most of it useless. But the reports of one of these ladies (London—Maida Vale) were written with a special vivacity. They indicated a sense of intelligent and ardent purpose well beyond the normal call of such duty. She seemed to have an unusual aptitude for providing ingenious tranquillities. And besides, her photo, attached to the official personnel sheet, was so immediately fetching that General Daniell decided to test her qualifications personally and in the field.

He had always been careful about sex, recognizing it as the most casual and destructive of traps. With him it was always less an engagement than a lightning raid into the territory of a dangerous enemy. It was his custom to spend as short a time as possible in the necessary embrace. He carried discretion to the borders of the furtive. He liked sex, but his work was his life.

Under another name, he made a professional appointment, and enjoyed himself so thoroughly that, the evening having worn on, he decided to spend the night with her. It was then that his own secret made sudden, startling, and public confession of itself.

He talked in his sleep.

Not only that, but he answered every question put to him while in that condition.

The next morning the lady was rewarded handsomely, just as she had hoped, when she made her report to *them*.

In time, of course, even our own side knew that too much was becoming known to too many. And when it was discovered that General Daniell's almost banal human frailty of talking in his sleep could blow all, the man whose business was the asking of questions was himself asked one: How could he not know about this, after so many years on this earth, so many separate nights of sleeping? Had his wife—now unfortunately deceased—never told him? No. She had not. Prim, virtuous, aristocratic, she had been, before their marriage, untouched by nonmedical hands. She must have reasoned, he explained, thus: having known no other man in sleep but her husband, she could not fairly assume anything unusual in his babbling. To her, all men were no doubt this way at night.

General Daniell was flown home immediately. But there were many nights left in his life, and many of the secrets he knew were not only embarrassing, but devastatingly so. And since there could be no way to prevent his seeking solace from other women, or spending a night in a vulnerable enclosure (hotel, railway car, home of obliging friend or stranger), in any casual accommodation, in fact, almost sure to be bugged for the occasion, he had been sent out to the Ranch. There something would perhaps be done to resolve the situation. And even if it was not resolved, then with every moment of his stay his fund of secrets was being kept secure, off the international market. No way had ever been found to keep a man permanently awake.

● FIRST INCITEMENT

In the softly lighted, lushly carpeted Playroom, the group was alone, at rest, unsupervised. Two of the men were reading (one medical encyclopedia, one magazine). Two were playing billiards at the table at the far end of the room.

He turned to the man in the chair beside his own, put a warning finger to his lips and, in a very soft voice he said, "I think we ought to hold a meeting—a staff meeting."

When he saw that the man was going to exclaim, to make in some way a hinting noise, he leaned over and put a hand across the offending mouth. He kept his back to the others nearby as he did so.

"Sorry." He whispered the word, his mouth close to the man's ear. "The bugs are there, and there." He pointed to the separate innocent air-conditioning vents in the ceiling. "If we keep our voices very low, we can talk without their knowing what we're saying."

"Why in hell do we have to keep our voices down? If we have anything to say to each other, let's goddamn well say it." The eyes shot out a cold blue fire.

"Because," whisper, "the things we're going to say now may mean the difference between life and death."

He arranged his face in an expression that would convey a sense of revelation both ominous and authentic.

"O.K. What's it all about?" The voice was now appreciably lower.

"I've decided to talk to you because the others, most of them, look up to you. They haven't said so, but one can see such things. You are the acknowledged leader, even if they don't admit it out loud."

"Keep talking."

"Have you ever thought about this place much? What's actually going on here? And please, let's not use names or rank. No point in giving them any clues, if they do manage to pick up our voices."

"This place is just one more big mistake, if you really want to know what I think of it. And the only reason I'm here is the same reason you are. Because they put a cannon to my head. We've all talked about that often enough. Is that what you want to hear?"

"No. I want to talk about the real reason."

The other man, though seated, brought his chinoed body into a state very much like attention.

"You've got the bugle," he said. "Start blowing."

"Thank you. I wonder if you have ever looked at our situation as I have. Consider this: suppose you wanted to strike an ultimate blow at some enemy. You wanted to render him powerless. Or at least as powerless as you possibly could, without making it seem like an act of war. You wanted to make it impossible for him to move against you, at least with any likelihood of success, and yet you wanted to do it in such a way that the enemy wouldn't know what you were up to. The worst that would happen is that he would eventually see it as one of his own mistakes. Bad judgment. Meanwhile you would have achieved supremacy, close to total supremacy, at very little cost and with total immunity to yourself."

"Are you talking about this place? This place here?"

He nodded and then continued.

"Look around you. Don't look at the faces. Just add up the power. A deputy chief of staff with one of the best records in American battle history. An Air Corps leader of unique gifts. An admiral whose record, despite a single tactical error, is an ornament to our armed forces. A general of Intelligence who performed marvels in snatching out the secrets of the enemy. The toughest and most effective secretary of State we ever had, a born fighter against those men over there. Every one of these represents a form of major fire power in confrontation with the enemy."

In the sudden stillness, the click of a billiard ball.

"Keep talking," the other man said. But for some moments he had neglected to chew at his dead cigar.

"I don't want to say much more. There's enough for both of us to think about in what I've said so far."

"Think about? There's been too goddamn much thinking around here as it is. What we need is some action. How sure are you about this—what you're telling me?"

"Put some of the pieces together by yourself. Let's say *you* were in charge of organizing the kind of operation we've been told this is. For our own good—for the country's good—security. Would you put a man like Doctor Bosca in charge of it?"

"That know-it-all son of a bitch—"

"Not because he's a son of a bitch—but because *he's a Bulgarian.*"

"You're right. He is. But he's been checked out, swarmed over. Got a top clearance."

"Of course. If they have managed to do what I think they have, then they've arranged that too. In a really crucial operation, why shouldn't they do everything necessary to make their man look good?"

Over the unfired cigar, the pale-blue eyes appeared to tremble in their sockets. Unspoken questions radiated from them. Life itself, perhaps, was being subjected to an intense third degree. After a moment there were words.

"You've given me a few things to think about, haven't you?"

"I hope so."

"Well, let me march it back and forth a few times. When I've done that, then you and I are going to have another meeting."

"And I would suggest that you don't discuss it with any of the others. Not just yet. There's plenty of time to do that when you've made up your mind."

" 'When'? You're that sure of me?"

"I'm sure of the conclusions that are bound to be arrived at by one of the most acute military minds this country has ever produced."

Behind the pale-blue eyes that mind was already at work.

● FLIGHTS

"Look, Doctor, I never told you this before, but actually, when I was younger, I mean a kid, practically, I always wanted to be a poet."

"I knew we would get to the root of it, General Winkler, if only we persisted. Now I want you to tell me about it. Everything. Here, in this office, while you are on that couch, there need be no secrets between us. There need be no shame and no apology. All that you have been and felt and done before can be understood. In here we know only one law, borrowed from a great Roman: 'I am a human being, and nothing human is alien to me.' Please speak about it freely."

"I never got a chance to stick with it. My father couldn't see things my way. He wanted me to work in his bank."

"You might have pointed out to him, General, that when Robert W. Service, the poet of the Yukon, died in his château on the French Riviera, he left an estate of two million dollars. Not counting the subsidiary rights."

"It wouldn't have made any difference. My father was in World War One. He didn't like the French."

"All right, then. There you are, wasting your fragrance

on the desert air of Lansing, Michigan. Your rose, you discover, has a big thorn in it. So then what did you do?"

"After college I just ran away, practically. Had a big fight with my father because of it. So, in New York, a fraternity brother got me a job with the phone company. The customer relations department. Then the war came, and I jumped right in. They needed people who could handle facts, words—make the images that could help us win the war. A man flying a plane, running a ship, a tank, or even a rifle, he's only a technician, a kind of glorified mechanic. He makes a thing do what the factory says it should. But someone who can make that technician perform his job at peak efficiency, that's the man who really makes the difference in a war. In anything, if you ask me."

"I shall certainly ask you a great deal, General. Now, as I understand it, you were retooling the visible facts to function more in accord with the emotional and spiritual needs of the situation. Is that correct?"

"You could put it that way."

"Another way we could put it, I suppose, is to say that you were still writing poetry."

"Well, I wouldn't actually go that far."

"But whatever we choose to call it, the Air Corps must have put an exceptionally high value on your services."

"Yes. I was one of the youngest men to make general in the history of the Corps. And I didn't have the benefit of all those headlines they wrap around an officer who flies. I had to do it with both feet on the ground. I was the man who had to create those headlines."

"And the suggestion that perhaps things were not as they should be—were you aware of this before or after you reached the command level?"

"Well, Doctor, that's where you and I are going to have a difference of opinion. I didn't see anything wrong in it then, and I still don't. If they want to send me out here, drop me in a slot like this for a while, because they think I need a little retooling myself, then all right. I'm a good officer. I know how to give orders and I can take them. I'll do what they want. But don't expect me to buy the package, just because I'm willing to carry it for a while."

"Dear General Winkler, please understand that what I am about to say is not my own verdict. I will only repeat what others who examined you, before you arrived here, have made a part of the record. Important people were worried about you. You had reached a point where you could no longer describe a pencil, a propeller, a lamb chop, a discarded newspaper, or a trip to the barber in terms that were less than noble, extravagant, and even grandiose. In the judgment of formal psychiatry, too much verbal campaigning had brought you down with a form of rhetorical dysentery. You and I, of course, might prefer a different image. Icarus flies too close to the sun; the wax melts and his wings drop off; Icarus falls into the sea. But in any case, in the critical areas in which you traveled, you had become a menace to public navigation."

"Well, suppose that's true. Not that I say it is, mind you. But just suppose they couldn't see things my way. Is that a reason for pointing a finger at a man, a general, and telling him to drop out of sight for a while? Get his brain deloused?"

"Not in my judgment, no," the doctor said. "But then I am not yet in a position to impose my own standards on society. Those in charge of quality control for products like you have sent you back to the factory. You now clank when you ought to purr. Or perhaps you purr too loud, and in too many unpredictable situations."

"Doctor, I'm not going to fight you on a thing like this. I tried that for a while on Guam. You know, they picked that place to examine me because they were afraid of my condition leaking into some Commie crap-sheet. They worked through my speech and thought patterns with computers. I had electrodes coming out of the strangest places. I left my arguments all over the floor with those people. I don't think they even listen. I like you, Doctor Bosca, because at least you give a man the feeling he's talking to somebody who's really there."

"I'm glad you feel that way. But I can understand the interest of the men who examined you. Every human being, General, is like an ancient pyramid. Secret treasures may lie within, undiscovered. There you were, a very important repository of public faith, and they could tell that something inside you was sending out some very queer vibrations. You had ceased to see people and things as they really are. Destruction was victory. Misery was hope. Mass resentment was peace. In many events the human element was ingeniously deleted. In fact, lyrical readjustments of reality were everywhere. You know, when Aristotle, Bacon, and Freud clambered about in the machinery of man, they had the use of only a primitive tool—each had only his own unaided brain power to work with. But those lucky fellows on Guam could explore the essential you with superior modern technologies."

"Right."

"And their report is no secret to you, General. According to them, you are a person of superior creativity—I use their language. You have an extraordinary imagination.

They saw that you had managed to achieve an enviable stage—perhaps too soon—of human development: you had abolished any capacity for comprehending the idea of nightmare. This is a thing that even the three giants I just mentioned were never able to achieve. It is my own judgment, for what it is worth, that your wife must have found you an extremely unusual fellow in times of stress."

"And not just my wife, Doctor."

"Well, anyway, we know why you are here. You violated some official law of selective excess. It is our job, now, to bring you back within the boundaries imposed by that law. Then you will be returned to your post."

"I've been here three months now. How much longer do I have to wait?"

"Always that question, General. My answer will have to be as before. You are definitely improving. There are now more frequent evidences of comprehended reality. But we need just a little more time before the appropriate miracle is passed here. Soon, we can hope, we shall achieve that delicate balance between things as they are and things as your peers wish you to see them."

"Well, a lot of those men never could see things my way."

"Of course, General. And now, if you please, tell me something about your wife— Does she drink?"

● MEDICINE

In line with the suggestions of the panel that had considered it, the Dispensary was white, functional, yet touched with grace. It was a small sanctuary to which a man might take his aches, visible outer and unseen inner, and have them ministered to in an atmosphere of wholesome sensuality. On the floor, a carpet, dark green and giving to the foot. On the walls, framed prints (Post-Impressionist), the colors warm, the subjects tranquil. In one corner a grandfather clock (ticking and on time). Many shelves lined with bottles, tins, boxes in many colors, some labeled in English, some in Latin, all at attention, ready to serve. At the dark-wood desk, each of the two chairs had soft green cushions to soothe the moment's unease. Near the head of the room a small leather couch served as a waiting area. To the rear, another door opened into a smaller room that contained shelves with the more serious drugs (DANGER: To be administered only under doctor's supervision) and a small cot, suitable for naps and, in a number of surprised-by-joy situations, connubial quickies. It was one of the few enclosures at the Ranch, Norm said, that was not bugged.

It was an emergency, of sorts. General Daniell had notified her by calling her room just before dinner. Could he see her at the Dispensary perhaps an hour after the meal? He had a pain. A condition, rather, that caused him some distress. He did not care to go into details at that moment. It was too embarrassing, he said. And he was sure their conversation was being overheard or at the very least recorded on some official tape. He did not wish his most intimate ailments to be considered so indispensable a part of the national history. And so on. It was an unusual request.

Sick call was once a day, shortly after breakfast, and there were now no exceptions. There had been some in the first weeks, but Dr. Bosca had put a stop to them very quickly. Sickness was only a form of self-indulgence, he said. You got sick only if you really wanted to, and he was going to discourage that kind of thing. Crassus, Hadrian, Admiral Nimitz, and other such had been able to live and serve without irrelevant ailment. It was enough that the coughers and snifflers would be accommodated each morning. A military man should not expect special attention for anything short of an open wound.

She had reminded General Daniell of that. He had confided that once she understood the nature of his problem, she would accept the need to make special allowance for him. She could have refused, carried the issue to Dr. Bosca, but chose not to. Unlike some of the others, General Daniell was not cranky. He was a gentleman. He would not make a Major Medical out of this unless there was some reason for it. Besides, Norm was going to be in his own room for an extra hour or so, working on the new assignment the school had mailed him: Evidence.

He was barely seated when she asked, "What is it, General?"

"Shouldn't we talk for a moment or so? I've always felt it somewhat mechanical to be attacked immediately with a stethoscope, or whatever you may have to use on me."

"There's nothing much we need to talk about," she said. "I checked your medical record before you got here. I could ask you again how old you are, how much you weigh, what diseases you've had in the past. But it would be unnecessary. So you might as well tell me what it is. Besides, I have things to do back at my room. You said this was an emergency, General."

"Yes. And I hope you can understand it as one, not only as a woman but as a nurse."

She sensed a red flare shooting up over the room, spelling out some pattern of oncoming danger. A warning alertness began to form in her mind.

"You're a handsome woman, Captain Thors. But then it's rather silly to call you Captain. Do you mind if I just call you Nurse?"

"That will be all right. What seems to be the problem, General?"

"I have developed a form of severe strain. Localized."

"Where is it localized?" But she could see by the way he looked at her that her question was almost unnecessary. Under the cool defiance of the eyes there was a giveaway tinge of disquiet, the look of a small boy reaching for something he feels may cause him to be spanked. She had seen it often enough before. But *never* here.

"I don't know if I ought to say, right out." His eyes lowered to the desk. "I ought to talk more about the symptoms first, so you'll understand."

"What will I understand?"

"About a thing like this, that seems so ordinary. The sort of thing that can be lived with, I suppose, by any prisoner, any soldier—priests do it all the time. But to the man accustomed to a more worldly life—part of the duty assigned to him, actually, as a man in uniform—the problem becomes inverted. He becomes a kind of priest, too, even though it may not seem so. His is the priest's vocation turned inside out. Such a life becomes in its own way a kind of commitment, of dedication, even. For the sake of the national interest he turns his back on the things he might really prefer—the life of books, quiet, contemplation— and devotes himself to the frets and passions of the bed-chamber. Patriotism and duty make it necessary for such a man to deny himself the kind of life he might wish to live, the kinds of things he might want to do. It forces him, very often, into paths he might choose to avoid. And all this in the interests of the larger goal. There is the achievement of ends which, in the judgment of those from whom he accepts his orders, are important, if not indispensable, to the country's security."

"Let me see—you did some things you might not have wanted to do. But you did them because you were under orders. Is that it?"

"In a way."

"I'm under orders too. And I'm doing something right this minute that I'd probably rather not do. I've already told you that this appointment is keeping me from something else I have to do."

"I'm only trying to give you the background."

"Of course. But I'm only a nurse. Perhaps you should be telling this to Doctor Bosca."

"I don't think I need a psychiatrist."

"All right, then. What is the problem, General?"

He stood up from the chair, and she realized in the instant that while sitting there he had kept his legs crossed. It had not occurred to her to draw the obvious conclusion from that. But there was a mitigating fact: she had not had to face this kind of thing for a long time. None of the Wranglers, younger, fitter, had ever presented this kind of problem. It was as if sex, by special Washington order, had been canceled from their lives.

He rose from the chair. Standing at the side of the desk, he unzipped.

She remained seated, not showing by any signal of eye, voice, or motion that there was anything urgently medical in the condition he was thrusting toward her.

"I see nothing particularly unusual about that," she said.

"I don't wish to waste your time by congratulating you, Susan."

"I'm a commissioned officer in the United States Army," she said. "You can call me Captain or you can call me Nurse."

"I need to address you now as a woman."

"Is that what this is all about? Why you called me?"

She felt glad to be married. It was a kind of insurance (in addition to everything else that was good about it, of course) against being overrun. Because, surrounded as she was by all these men, the lone woman in this remote place, being faced (if you could call it that) with a thing like this, just might have made trouble for her. Because for a man who was supposed to be sixty-one, General Daniell was, to use a phrase her mother had always been fond of, a fine figure of a man.

He was telling her about the sacrifices he had been forced to make at a recent combat station, Paris. All those women he had been obliged to dance with, talk to, support through every social extremity, and all in the name of duty. He had carried the flag into the bedroom for his country.

"Your country, too, my dear."

"There are some sacrifices at which I draw the line," she said. "There are some things I don't believe in doing for my country. Because if it gets to the point where it asks me to do certain unpleasant things, then it's not the kind of country I want to be a part of. Do you intend to rape me? Try to, I mean?"

"I don't believe in rape," he said. "I thought we could come to an understanding."

"We have. You had better leave now."

"Not yet. Please. Even if you saw it only as a medical problem. If you could do something, almost anything, to 'conjure it down.' That's from Shakespeare. I am 'keen,' Susan. That's one of his too. He understood such matters. He would tell you that I'm set on 'groping for trouts in a peculiar river.' "

She rose from her chair.

"You'd better leave, General," she said. "I don't seem to know Shakespeare as well as you do, but I know my job. And your problem is one that's outside the scope of Army medicine. Take that thing out of here."

But in the briefest movement he had come around the desk—she almost found herself admiring the quickness with which he moved, a man of that age—and he was upon her. She felt the insistent thing pressing or rather prodding at her belly, and she pushed at him, trying in the crushing tightness of his embrace to strike at him. Could not. She tried, too, to raise her knee and crash a shot into the control room, but he was too foxy for her. He was placing the greatest weight on her shoulders, so that she could not brace herself for a lifting of the knee. For God's sake, she caught herself thinking, has he done this kind of thing before? What kind of a general is he, anyway? And if it was true, and she *was* only one of a crowd, then maybe the thing was a medical problem after all. But she would be damned if he was going to use her as a tranquilizer. She put up a more savage, less thinking fight now, but it was no use. As he pressed her toward the door that led to the inner room and the cot, she did not bother to scream.

She knew that no one would hear her. And even if the event was being recorded—unlikely—the tape would only inform someone later, in the morning, probably, that an emergency had been in being. But the *Andrea Doria* was sinking tonight.

"All right," she said. "I'm not going to fight you. I had to go through the motions of just being a nurse, General. That's part of my orders. But there's such a thing as carrying one's sense of duty too far. Especially with such an attractive man."

His lean face, a cool toughness under those elegant features, appraised her for a few seconds. Then he released his grip on her arms. But still he stood between her and the exit. Obviously he was not yet taking any chances.

"Come on." She turned briskly through the doorway, into the room that held the cot. Flicked on the wall switch. "Let's see to that problem of yours," she said. There was a great rage inside her at the injustice of it. Easily, quickly, trying to make it seem casual and innocent, she half turned and grabbed at a large blue bottle on the nearest shelf. She was going to slam it at some vital area. But her hand, quick as it was, could not outrace his own. His fingers on her wrist were like iron, and his smile was not much softer.

"Please," he said, "I wouldn't want either of us to feel too personal about this."

"You may have to feel personal about it," she said. "I intend to tell Doctor Bosca. That should mean the end of all your privileges for a long time."

His smile now was a kind of shrug.

"Even Doctor Bosca," he said, "cannot take from me the memories that I will treasure of *this* privilege."

In his grip, breathing harder than she would have wished, she said, "Well, then, if we must, we must."

He had not even bothered to zip up, do the decent thing, at least for the look of it, as they came to what he would call their "understanding."

He did not move from his position between her and the door. There was a bathroom she could excuse herself to, lock herself into, but what was the point? It had no window she could climb through, and he could easily break down the door.

She took off her dark-brown suède jacket, the one Norm had bought for her birthday, before they were married. She reached for the button at the collar of her dress, then stilled her hand there, as if holding back in the act of unbuttoning.

"Don't you think we ought to be a little more informal about this?" she said. "How about taking your pants off? Then we can both be sure it isn't just rape."

His gaze fixed on her, eyes unblinking, he reached for his belt and began to unbuckle it.

At her collar, her hand loosened the button, and then, as a casual afterthought, she walked past him easily into the main room of the Dispensary. He followed her, his hands holding to his pants.

"Where are you going?"

"Look, General," she said, reaching for one of the drawers of the desk, "a lot of women might consider it an honor to have a child by you. Here it would only be a nuisance."

She turned her eyes from him, pulled the drawer open, and began to rummage in it.

She thought he would ask her how she could happen to have security measures in a place like that. She had an answer ready, but he did not ask the question. She made a cool but showy business of looking for something in the crammed drawer. Would he just stand near her like that, staring? Because if he did, what could she do? She could not really hope to hit out at him, down there, smashing her fist at a man that age, or, anyway, that prominent. Because by now she knew his quickness and his strength.

Surprisingly, without a word, he suddenly turned and walked back into the inner room. He acted as if he was sure, now, that she had signed on for the party. She could have said something, something nice and graceful to speed him on his way, to give him a sense of repose about the few moments he would have to wait for her. But the hell with that. Before he could even bring himself back to the doorway there was the sound of her flurried footsteps, and she was out the front door and running down the narrow corridor to the other wing, where her husband should be sitting, bent over Evidence.

She didn't care if she was seen hurrying into Norm's room. She didn't give a damn, at the moment. She thought only that it took a man to protect her from a man, and this was the one she depended on. But even so, when she let herself in his door, she felt a touch of relief at the thought that no one had seen her.

● JUSTICE

Behind him, the table was piled with papers. Law.

Her voice and thoughts in disarray, she told him what had

happened. Attempted invasion by superior forces of her—and in a way, his—most intimate privacies.

"O.K., O.K.," he said. "Sit down for a minute. We don't have to talk about this while we're standing up."

"Why do we have to talk about it at all? I've told you what happened."

He was now back in his working chair, but she remained standing.

"Because we don't want to go off somewhere and explode," he said, "without even thinking in advance about all the pieces we might leave lying around."

"You want us to just lie low like this, talking and thinking, while the man who tried to rape your wife is sitting behind a cigarette and some brandy, telling his friends about it? Is that the kind of thing you want us to be thinking about?"

"Take it easy, Susan." He raised a propitiating hand, the kind intended to stop riots, insurrections, wars. "In the first place, under the Law of Parsimony—that's part of what I'm working on right now, at the table here—you can't prove he was trying to rape you—"

"Now, Norm, just watch it!"

"I'm not talking about you and me—what *we* think. It's what other people might think—a judge or a jury."

"I wasn't taking this into court."

"So then it's your word against his—without any real evidence, I mean. And he's a lieutenant general. Three stars. You know what we'd be up against? We'd be fighting the one big thing that keeps this Army in business—the chain of command."

"Are you trying to tell me that because he's got three stars and I've only got two bars, that lets him operate under laws that are different from mine?"

"Absolutely not. Not in a democracy like this one. It just makes it come down to that, though, if we try to lock horns with him."

"And suppose you got up from that chair right now, went to wherever he is, and punched him in the nose? You don't think he would get a special message out of that?"

He shook his head.

"I'd be the one," he said. "For taking the law into my own hands. They'd ship me to a hard-shell stockade somewhere. Maybe in fifteen years they'd let me out of there. On crutches. Then I'd really need a nurse in my life. Is that what you want?"

"Norman—don't make me mad. A man tried to rape me just a while ago. He's wandering loose around here now, enjoying himself. And you're telling me there's nothing we can do about it?"

"I'm not saying that. There are things we can do about it. I can go out there and sock him, like I just said. I can go get a forty-five and shoot a hole in him. We can bring charges against him and he can deny everything. But any way you look at it, it's us—me and probably you—that'll have to pay the freight on it."

"I see. In other words, just sit tight. Say nothing. And then, if we're lucky, he'll try it again. And the next time I should let him go all the way. And meanwhile we'll rig up some kind of camera in the back room so we can make movies out of it. So if I can ever get my lawyer husband to bring it into court, we'll stand a better chance of winning our case. Is that what you're saying?"

"No. In the first place, he tried it once and he goofed. He's not likely to try it again."

"But he did try it once, Mr. Husband. Are you going to

let every man I meet try it once on your wife, and you're just going to sit there like some damn Supreme Court justice working out a traffic case in New Jersey?"

"No. You're thinking about it like the victim. The one it happened to—"

"This is your wife talking, Mr. Lawyer—remember me?"

"Let me finish what I was saying, Susie—"

He didn't even sound angry, and that was the part that bothered her most.

"Go ahead. Why not? Somebody just tried to rape your wife, so we might as well just sit here and talk it over and wait for something else to happen. Maybe when that general gets through telling the others, they'll all want to try it. Maybe we can have a gang-bang every Friday night—"

"No," he said, still not angry at all. "They wouldn't want to do that. That's one of the nights when they have a movie."

Joke. He was trying to calm her that way.

"Well, then maybe Doctor Bosca will let them do it during one of his classes. Maybe it's one of the things they can all learn something about."

"Look, Susie, why don't you listen to me for a minute, instead of enjoying all this top-blowing you're doing? Running off somewhere and throwing rocks is only going to make you feel good for a few minutes, that's all. I'm not talking about justice, getting justice. There are some situations in which you just *can't* put in for something like that. That's for people who have houses with thick rugs on the floor. They have charge accounts, and a big piano in the living room. For you and me, we'd be finished if we ever tried to get General Daniell. We're aiming at retiring some day. Not too long from now, either."

"And is this the price you want to pay for retirement?

Turning your wife into a mechanical doll that just smiles when somebody steps on it?"

"Susie, I'm telling you there's nothing we can do about it. Nothing that makes any sense. We're aiming at security. When we get that—"

"How secure do you think I'm going to be, remembering that I had to sit still for a thing like this? If I can't feel like a human being in this place, then I want to get out of here right now."

"Look, it's happened and it won't happen again. He did something he ought to get his balls kicked in for, but if we do that, even though he deserves it, the system is rigged in his favor. They would probably fix it so we could kiss my pension good-by. You want to give up everything we've worked for so far? Everything we're in sight of from here? Just for the satisfaction of playing Sacco and Vanzetti all by yourself?"

She looked at him for a long time with a kind of stillness in her large green eyes.

"Norm," she said at last, "of all the men I ever met, you're the one I picked to spend the rest of my life with. I guess I love you, or I wouldn't have done that—cut you out of the crowd and put a rope around you. And everything you say about this makes a kind of sense. I won't argue with you about that. But it's only one kind of sense. There has to be another kind of sense that will make me feel just a little better about what happened to me in that Dispensary. And I'm going to find it."

Before he could holler *Stop!* or call out to ask what she meant to do, she had ducked through the door. A check mark went up somewhere in her brain, to let her know that this was the second time that evening she had run out on a man.

● THE PHILOSOPHY OF RAPE

"Ah, Miss Thors. Please." He pulled the door wide to let her in. He was the only man in the place, aside from Norm, who never called her Captain, and she appreciated that. She walked past him, wondering what that oddly pleasant music was that came softly from his phonograph. Melancholy but soothing. The room was thick with his cigarette smoke, just as she remembered it from a visit of months before. He closed the door and looked calmly at her.

"You have the look of emergency in the eyes, the chin," he said. "Something has happened in the last few minutes."

"Something has happened, all right. Someone tried to rape me. One of the Guests."

He motioned her to sit on the sofa, and she began to tell him about it. He took a chair nearby.

He listened and yet he seemed also to be listening to something else, perhaps a concurrent story being unreeled in his own head. She would have wanted a more severe expression in that calm old face, at least a hint of outrage, but she saw only a slight frown. She hurried to a finish.

"So then," he said, throwing off a broad plume of cigarette smoke, "our General Daniell is causing problems."

"Is that all you see in it, Doctor?"

"What I see is not important, Miss Thors. The law sees, perhaps—if you have enough money, influence, that kind of thing—an attempt at rape. A social worker, if she thinks hard, could see a personal problem that got out of hand. A man lonely and proud up there, where everybody thinks he's got all a man could want, but he doesn't have real love in his life, so this is his dramatic way to announce it. Like Jack the Ripper. An event like this, not everybody sees it from the same seat in the balcony."

"General Daniell tried to rape me. You have authority around here, Doctor. What are you going to do about it?"

"The first thing we ought to do about it, Miss Thors, is relax for a few moments. That never hurt anyone in a crisis where there isn't anything you can do until the morning. So why shouldn't we take a few moments to deal with the larger perspectives?"

"There aren't any. A man tried to rape me."

"Not just a man, Miss Thors. A general. A symbol of national power, prestige, and security. And that word *rape* becomes harder and harder to apply the higher up one gets in the scale of history." Smoke cloud. "If the man is important enough, it becomes a minor impulse of love, or power, or biology. Napoleon used to walk up to women at parties, married women too, and nod them into the nearest bedroom. Was that rape? Did the woman protest? No. It was usually considered an honor to be selected by such a great man to soothe the fevers that were perhaps preventing him from achieving even greater glories for his country."

The music had died out as he talked, and he went now to turn off the phonograph.

"A man came into the Dispensary for medical attention. He tried to rape me. I had to fight my way out of there. Is that what democracy is all about?"

"No, Miss Thors, certainly not on paper. But the wise person must live his life off the paper, otherwise there is much trouble."

"What just happened to me wasn't on paper. General Daniell tried to rape me."

"And many people would see it that way, Miss Thors, many of those who heard the story from you. But even so, think of all the extenuating circumstances. In this period of history, when our country is in torment, almost ready to make its will, General Daniell is like a specialist—one of them, anyway—who just might save the patient. For reasons that may not be revealed, but are of the utmost military importance, he is at present stationed in a sealed and sexless compound in the middle of some backwoods mountain nowhere. Consider the facts as many will perceive them: you are the nurse here. This very important general comes to you for a sleeping pill, or whatever, to bring himself back to physical par. The strain of manning the battlements for the rest of us has temporarily laid him low. In the course of this consultation, you, as the only woman here, younger than he, and no doubt feeling an acute sense of your own hormonal deprivation, began to squeeze a little too hard, crooned your diagnosis too seductively, perhaps, did something, anything, bound to arouse in the mind of the national jury the image of the eternal Eve. An attractive woman like yourself, Miss Thors, then becomes in the average mind a danger to the *status quo*. You may have your nursing license taken away, not to mention being discharged from the Army, and, for all I know, deprived of your right to vote."

"You mean to say that if I complained to Washington about this, nothing would happen?"

"Let me put it this way— By the way, do you drink? I have some excellent brandy—"

She shook her head. He continued talking between puffs at the cigarette.

"You would *hope* after a while, that nothing would happen. Do you think the laws of this Army—or any other, for that matter—are designed to facilitate the downfall of a general? Of course not. Generals usually write the Army code, and are careful to include enough cracks in it— empty spaces—to permit a thing like this to fall through with a minimum of noise. Shoulders will be joined, all with stars on them, to protect one of their own. One thousand generals don't represent a caste, a rank, or even a professional trade group. They represent a conspiracy against everybody who is *not* a general. If they didn't protect each other, then how could they ever trust each other? They're like kings, doctors, even senators. They know how nice it feels up there, on top, where a few men can make a tornado just by blowing together in the right direction. They have no intention of encouraging disaster by taking seriously any of that barking they hear from down below."

"And you think that's all right? You don't see anything wrong in a situation like that? Even if it's the way you say it is?"

"Of course it's wrong—at least it's not good. But it's like a lot of other things you and I cannot control, Miss Thors. It may rain all day tomorrow. I had a cousin once who was a hunchback. A dear friend may get killed in a motor accident. A statistical law may catch up with us, and we come down with one of those diseases our country is always running long television shows about. None of these things is 'all right.' I see a great deal wrong with them. But we must have our priorities, Miss Thors. We have to address our moral energies in directions where the investment will show signs of producing dividends. In most of the world, sex is only a commodity, very common. It has its uses, like aspirin. History understands such matters. It gave to powerful men the right to make love to the new bride even before her husband. *Droit du seigneur*. Was that rape? Or was it only a recognition of an important fact of life? The samurai of Japan, professional warriors, they had the right to do as much with the average woman they ran into. Was that rape? Or was it just an interesting and exotic tradition? Of course, many of those fellows were homosexuals anyway, and nice people don't talk about what was really going on out in those rice fields."

"In other words, Doctor, you're telling me to forget what happened? Pretend it never took place?"

"Certainly not. I'm telling you to remember well what happened. To think about it, not the way an injured party might, in a courtroom—because this isn't anything like that. You have to think about it so you learn from it. You keep learning from things, from people, from situations, Miss Thors. So then, when you get to be about as old as I am, you know how important it is to stay away from psychotics, from generals, from Ministers of the Interior, from the only sons of very rich men—in a word, from all those who live by their own laws, and act on whim."

"Yes, but I don't see you staying away from types like that. You're swimming in them here."

"Of course, Miss Thors. Because this is my trade. The proctologist, for instance, does honest and necessary work in places that others choose to avoid. A certain irregularity of the intellect permits me to profit in many ways from immersing myself in such men. I learn. I work on a book here. Perhaps I may even someday make a contribution, as they say. But there is no excuse for a fine, healthy woman like yourself."

"Yes, there is." Her tone was firm.

He nodded the large browned head very gently. The almost-black eyes eased into a smile.

"Naturally," he said. "Always there is a reason. And for your sake, Miss Thors, I hope it has been a good one."

"There's nothing *you* can do about it?"

He shook his head slowly.

"I will certainly discuss this event with him. But nothing you or I can do will remove him from here. He is fixed in our world for some time to come."

"What if he tries it again?"

"A good question. The answers would run something like this: He may never try it again, because you presented too many difficulties. Or because he assumes that your reporting him may produce consequences that are at least embarrassing. Or it may be that his *amour-propre* has been bruised by your refusal. After all, he is a star, and you are only a bit player."

"And suppose he does try it again?"

"I was getting to that. A scalpel prominently displayed on your desk could be a help. You have only to grasp it the next time he enters for any reason."

"He's very strong."

The doctor shrugged, nodded, and smiled gently.

"Not only that, but other generals do not like the idea of one of their own being killed indiscriminately."

"That's what they'd call it?"

"No. But that's what they would think, which would carry much more weight in their judgment of what to do about it."

"So if I don't use that scalpel, what then?"

"When Hiroshima is inevitable—" He shrugged.

"I'm just supposed to lie down and take it?"

"Your turn can come later. Tell him to his face that you

find him an unsatisfying sexual partner. A boy. What is known in this country as 'a lousy lay.' Go into detail about his deficiencies. After that, he will probably stay away from you."

"But you're telling me to let him try it at least once more." She could not keep her voice from rising as she said it.

"Dear Miss Thors," he said, "please believe that I have your problem clearly in focus. It may not seem that way when I talk like this, but we are addressing ourselves to a very special situation. Someone with as little power as you have is facing someone with as much power as he has. That leaves you with minimum satisfactory options."

"Suppose I told you I have a boy friend? Suppose I had one right here, in this place? You still think I ought to go right ahead and let another man use me like that?"

"Miss Thors, the whole point of the sexual revolution, as I understand that strange development in this country, is that one time more or less, with the odd man in, as it were, is inconsequential. The stodgy qualitative is being super-seded by the chic quantitative."

"I'm not interested in that, Doctor. I'm a one-man girl."

"A woman. Remember that, Miss Thors. As a woman, in an all-male environment here, you stand alone."

"I'm not going to complain as a woman, Doctor." She rose and began to walk slowly to the door. "You've con-vinced me that wouldn't get me very far. But I also happen to be a captain in the United States Army. I'm not going to rest until that man gets punished for what he did. What he did to a commissioned officer of the armed forces."

"Good luck, Miss Thors." An almost-sad smile fell into the furrows of the old face.

"I'm going to tell the story to Colonel Kilburn."

"You may not have to." Dr. Bosca shrugged. "It will soon, in a manner of speaking, be a matter of record. You are no doubt aware that this room, like most of the others, is bugged."

On the way up the corridor she thought about the colonel. If she went to his room right now, and told him everything, he would probably not yet have heard it from the tape. This way was more direct, and he just might rouse himself to do something about it.

● BRASS

When Colonel Kilburn opened at her knock, she had the odd feeling that he was observing her entry through the crack in the hinge side of the door.

"Colonel," she said, "something has happened that I think you ought to know about."

He did not ask her to sit down, and as she talked his face remained without expression.

"All right," he said when she had finished. "General Daniell made a pass at you. What would you like to happen now?"

"It wasn't a pass. He tried to rape me. There's a difference."

"O.K. He tried to rape you. What would you like to happen now?"

"Isn't rape a crime, even in the Army?"

"Lots of times. But you've been around this man's Army

ten years, according to your sheet. That's long enough to know that with a general everything is different."

"Does it make it different for you? Do *you* think he has a right to do a thing like that? In a place like this? I'm telling *you* the story, Colonel, because you're in charge of law and order here. You're wearing the badge."

"I'm wearing the badge, all right. But what you're talking about isn't exactly covered by my orders."

"You mean there's nothing you can do about it? If he decides to come at me again, that's just fine with you? That's Army justice?"

"Captain, don't get carried away with yourself. Take a good hard look at the situation and you'll see there isn't a hell of a lot anybody can do about it. You want me to take away his privileges for a while? You want me to have a talk with him? He'd give me his version of what happened. You're an American. You think it would be fair if I just listen to your side of it? There were no witnesses. So unless you can get a little more evidence than your say-so, he's going to be in the clear. There's only so much you can do about a three-star general, anyway, when he goes berserk. He's not somebody like you and me. He's got friends all over the jury."

"A crime has been committed, but the Army isn't going to see it as a crime. You're asking me to wait till next time and then cut off a piece of his equipment and bring it in on a platter. Evidence."

The gray eyes were calm and unblinking. He took a deep breath, as if making a great decision.

"All right. You've made your point. Would you like a transfer out of here? It won't be easy—you volunteered for this duty. But I can arrange it. If you leave, though,

Captain, you leave alone. Is that what you want?"

"I want justice."

"Why not? Everybody wants it. But until we get certain things straightened out in this world, we're not going to have time for that. First comes the straightening out, and then we can get around to the kind of thing you're talking about. If General Daniell, with all the expert knowledge he has, could make the difference between our winning and losing against the enemy, would you still want him thrown into the tank for what he did to you? Or would you want to go easy on him, let him get on with helping us win our war?"

"I'm not a lawyer and I'm not an important thinker. I'm just a victim, Colonel. I'm here to ask you to do something about the person who attacked me."

"Do you want that transfer?"

For a moment she did not answer. Then she shook her head. The colonel must certainly have known that she would not want to be separated from Norm for more than a year.

"It's settled, then," he said. "I'll talk to General Daniell. That's the best I can promise. Maybe, at least, he won't bother you again."

It wasn't much, but it was something.

She said no more, no thanks or good-by as he showed her out.

Within minutes, she was again at Norm's door. His face filled with surprise, but she had expected that. This was the second time in one evening that they had run the risk of having someone see her entering his room.

"What happened?" he asked.

On his table, still, that pile of papers that were going to

make him an expert at helping people find their way through the ins and outs of the law.

"I'll tell you later." She went over to the bed and began to remove her clothes, dropping them onto the chair nearby.

"What did you have in mind, Susie?"

She noticed that he had not removed the cigarette from his mouth.

"I'm getting into this bed, and I expect you to get into it too. Right beside me. And then I want you to hold me."

"What's this all about? You run out of here after a big fight, and then you come running back in here after a while, all on a night when I'm catching up on homework, and I'm supposed to lie down and hold you?"

He seemed honestly puzzled, and that made her a bit angry too.

"Yes, Norm. That's exactly right. And if you don't get your ass into this bed in exactly one minute, then you're going to have a real wild woman standing in the hall, outside your door there, yelling her brains out."

Without a word, he stubbed out the cigarette and began to remove his pants.

● THREAT

General Daniell did not seem at all surprised that Colonel Kilburn should suggest a chat. A moment after entering the colonel's quarters he accepted a cigarette, a comfortable chair, and an inch of bourbon. Then, with no noticeable concern, he raised his eyebrows to the now seated Kilburn and asked casually what the chat was to be about.

"Rape."

"Are you talking about our Susan?"

"Captain Thors. She's a commissioned officer."

"Yes. Of course." He sent a lazy scud of blue smoke spinning toward the colonel.

"What do you think we ought to do about it, General?"

"Ignore it, of course."

"You don't think rape is covered in the Articles of War? You don't think a captain in the United States Army is entitled to all the protection we can give her?"

"Yes to both questions, Colonel. But a limited yes." More smoke. Much calm. "In normal times, under normal conditions, I would join you in wanting to see the culprit in such a case pinned immediately to the national bulletin board. There should be no place for imprudent depravity in the Army. But then, these are not normal times. And you would hardly describe as normal the conditions under which we live here. Now could you?"

The son of a bitch wasn't even smiling when he said it. As if what he was pointing out at the moment was so sensible, so obvious to the naked eye, that you would have a hard time finding any joke in it.

"I don't think the whole point of what went on between you and the captain is going to depend on my powers of description, General."

"Well, then, what will it depend on, Colonel? One learns so much in a place like this—Doctor Bosca has been so very instructive about so many things—perhaps even you have a lesson for me. Go ahead. Move to the blackboard and teach away. The cigarette is pleasing, the bourbon excellent, and time hangs heavy. The battlefield conditions are, as they say, superior."

"Captain Thors claims you attempted to rape her. I haven't heard you deny it."

"Of course I don't deny it. The captain is a well-formed woman, with a kind of antiseptic sexuality about her. And here we are, in this monastic environment, military Trappists all, dedicated to chastity and obedience, if not to poverty. Given such conditions, and comparing them with the conditions under which—in the professional life that preceded my arrival here—I was encouraged to live, it would be a form of insanity, would it not, to expect me *not* to attempt to remedy a basically antihuman situation?"

"I can't go into the logic of it with you, General. We've both been in the service too long to worry about logic. The Army has its own way of doing things. We both know that, too. And a wrong has been committed. A complaint has been made—a charge—and you haven't denied it. What would you say to having to do without alcohol, smokes, all privileges, for two weeks or so? Maybe for a month? Would that affect your thinking any?"

"Without question, Colonel. But it would have very little effect on my actions."

"Could you spell that out for me?"

"Why, all I'm saying is that, given the nature of my original conditioning, and then given the thoroughly different conditions under which I'm forced to live here for the moment—although I must say it has been one of the longer moments in my life—you could hardly expect me to pervert the habits of a professional lifetime merely to conform to the moral requirements of, say, Muncie, Indiana, around 1910."

"Are you saying you might try it again?"

"I'm sure that's one of the things I'm saying."

"Suppose you were confined to quarters? Or suppose a couple of Wranglers were assigned to watch over you, keep you company wherever you went? That's two of the things *I'm* saying."

"May I remind you, Colonel, of the penalty for the injudicious act, in the Army? Rank has its privileges, and it also has its responsibilities. Your responsibility, right now, is to beware of melodrama in the face of the frivolous incident. The three stars on the uniform hanging in my closet will weigh far more in the balance than the eagle on your own uniform."

"I'm on special orders here. In this place, right now, nobody outranks me."

"You may very well be right, Colonel. And if this is the only assignment you will ever have in this Army, then anyone with your best interests at heart would encourage you to fire away. But is this the be-all and end-all of your career as an officer? What happens when this situation is wrapped up and tucked into the files? When you're reassigned somewhere? When I'm finished here, presumably cleansed of my inner wound? Remember, once I leave here I'll be passing around my own side of this little story. It will be heavily slanted in my favor, of course, as such things almost always are. And I'll be telling it to men of my own rank and station, men with the power to determine your fate in uniform with the wave of a pen. Consider this, Colonel—I am at the blackboard now—if people like you are to be permitted to trample at will on people like me, then what would be the point in anyone becoming a general?"

He puffed through a circled mouth, as if trying to blow a smoke ring. No ring.

"Are you threatening me?"

"I certainly hope you will see it that way. Otherwise this discussion is going to be a complete waste of time for both of us."

"I don't want to buck you, General, but I'm an old-fashioned soldier. I believe that what's right is right."

"And I don't want to destroy you, Colonel, but you might say I'm a new-fashioned one. I believe that nothing, no single individual's whim, for instance, should be permitted to impair the fierce and necessary rhythm of national security."

"You try to rape a nurse and you call that national security?"

"Unquestionably. I am a lieutenant general in the United States Army. I hold an extremely important position in the security apparatus that guards the thin and invisible outer perimeter of the American way of life. It is absolutely essential to the national welfare that I never for a moment waver in the expression of my most vigilant and alert capacities. Should I falter even for an instant, I don't have to tell you what disasters might ensue. Please remember, officially I'm still a general on active duty here. And if, in the course of that duty, a momentary release of nervous tension is required, and it happens to make some nearby woman squeal peevishly, just how seriously must we regard that squeal? Remember also, she is herself a soldier, sworn to give her own life, if necessary, that our country may be adequately protected. Are you going to say, Colonel, that her life is less valuable than her virtue? If it *is* virtue, in this day and age."

"Then you're going to do whatever you feel like doing, and you're going to tell me to go to hell?"

"I certainly wouldn't put it in quite those words, but I

think you have gathered my essential meaning. Do we understand each other?"

"I don't think so."

"What do you intend to do about this defect in our signal system? If I dare to ask?"

"I'll think of something."

"Good. I'm always charmed by a soldier who tries to resist the irresistible. That, too, is very old-fashioned of you, you know. Good luck, Colonel."

He rose, flicking a half-inch of cigarette ash into the saucer.

"It's been nice talking to you," the colonel said. He got out of his chair.

At the door, before opening it, General Daniell turned.

"Tell me, Colonel," he said, "as one Intelligence man to another—and after all, we are, still, in the same army— what *was* the hurry-up nature of your assignment here? It's obvious to anyone that you're a quite different type from the man you replaced. You're not a desk man. You're a field man. It's written in your face, your bones, the way you move."

"You really think that?"

"Yes, I do. So my question is, Colonel, to repeat, What are you doing here? What special event caused Washington to rush you out here, to this military catacomb, this retreat for the shriving of elite souls?"

For a moment Kilburn looked quietly at him, the gray eyes bearing down.

"I won't tell you," he said. "See if you can find your way through that one."

General Daniell nodded approvingly and left.

● PROVOCATIONS

ITEM:

Next evening, as the men filed into the lounge (Play-room) that served them as a center for casual and after-dinner repose, Admiral Byngham, first as usual to the billiard table, let out a warning cry. General Winkler, alongside, stared down unbelieving.

"What's been going on here?"

The admiral's fiercely furrowed brow reinforced the tone of alarm, of the enemy looming out of the mists ahead.

Mr. Cadetti, the H–L volume of the medical encyclopedia snug under one arm, hurried over, looked down and offered a professional comment.

"Someone's been working it over with a knife. And he's knocked a few holes in that slate under there too. We used to do that, when I was just a kid—whenever we ran into a no-pay."

General Winkler's frown was grim. "Who would do a thing like that? It must be some kind of accident."

The other men left their chairs and came alongside the table to shake their heads at the scarred and crumpled green baize.

"If that's an accident," General St. John said, "then so was the Civil War."

"Quite right," Daniell said. "It shows intent, thoroughness, and efficiency. If Bosca cared to teach us the best way to destroy a billiard table, he might well use this as his example. You'll never play on this one again, I'm afraid, Admiral."

"Well who in hell would want to do a thing like that?" The grooves of time and weather in the admiral's face were knotted in torment.

"Someone who very much wanted to, I'm sure." Daniell nodded wisely.

"But why *would* anyone want to do a thing like that?" Winkler presented the question in a tone that Zola himself might have been proud to use, at the Trial. "Here? To this table—our table? To us?"

Mr. Wadlow, his lap hidden under a half-pound of readings from a United Nations report on trans-nationalism, had not bothered to rise from his chair. "Gentlemen," he said, "have you considered the possibility that it may be one of *them?*"

There were no billiards played that evening, but the game was well lost. There was enough material in the event to provide hours of speculation, and to stimulate much remembrance of billiards past.

Because it was an emergency, a radio requisition was dispatched that night (Secret and Urgent), and a new table was immediately on the way.

ITEM:

Next morning, Colonel Kilburn was called from his office by Ramrod, who walked with him to the locked closet in which the more valuable stores were kept. On the floor were nine boxes of expensive cigars, opened, the contents in disorganized piles on the wood-tiled floor. They were crumpled, damp, beyond use. Garbage. Hanging in the still air of the closet was the unmistakable scent of what had been used to render the cigars unsmokable.

"What do you think?" Ramrod poked carefully at the debris with the toe of his boot.

"I think that whoever did this picked on the one way to get this crowd around here really steamed—pissing on their cigars."

"And you figure it must be some guy with a reason?"

"A *real* reason."

"I know my boys. I know each one cold. I can't believe it was one of them."

"Well, there's a hell of a lot goes on in a place like this that's pretty unbelievable." Kilburn almost smiled.

"Any ideas?"

"Yes. Two. Intensify normal guard duty. And see that these cigars are replaced within twenty-four hours."

ITEM:

General St. John, returning from the sauna, let himself into his quarters to a surprise. An eleven-inch span of his medals was missing from the top of the dresser, where he kept it at parade rest. These medals were not the conventional knee-jerk allocations of his own government for career services rendered. They were formal presentations of other governments that had reason to reward, soothe, honor, and otherwise express gratitude for services rendered or hoped for. Missing, among others, were: one Order of the Redeemer (Greece); one Order of the Thistle (Great Britain); one Order of the Seraphim (Sweden); one Order of Alexander Nevski (U.S.S.R.).

Despite the absence of the visible authority that would flow from a uniform, the general never questioned that even in his chinos the real godhead of a deputy chief of the Joint Chiefs was visible and all-commanding. He demanded of Colonel Kilburn that immediate action be taken.

"Any recommendations, General?"

"I'll leave the matter entirely in your hands, Colonel. But I expect results. And soon."

"I'll do everything I can, sir."

"I'm not interested in your methods, Kilburn. Just find me those medals and find me the son of a bitch who took them."

"General, if he's smart enough to get through your door by picking the lock, he's smart enough not to get caught in a hurry."

"Colonel, are you giving me an advance briefing on your excuses? Do you want me to take over the investigation personally?"

"No, sir. Washington sent me out here to handle things like this."

"Well, then, handle them."

"I'll do my best, sir."

"That had better be good enough, Colonel, or I'll have your ass."

"Yes, sir."

● DISCOVERERS

At General Daniell's next regular appointment, he ignored, as always, the richly brown, coolly expensive leather couch. He sat himself down, as always, in the wooden chair near the small table that served as a bar.

"This afternoon, just for once, General, I would like to try you on a needle—if you would not mind?"

The doctor raised his thick eyebrows high, as if reaching for the impossible psychotherapeutic dream. Of all the patients, Daniell was the one who had never permitted, during these sessions, the use of a drug. The casual shake of the general's head gave the expected answer. This time would be no different.

"Dear Doctor—I would like so much to please you—our Father Damien—but no."

"I think, in this one case, it may permit us to get past a

certain residue of psychic blockage, General. Once we out-flank this inner enemy, as it were, then who knows what wonders we might not be able to flush out, to subdue, even, beyond that final pale?"

"No." Again that slow shake of the head. "I don't really care to know everything about myself, Doctor. That would be a very depressing situation, from my point of view. I don't wish to live in a world deprived completely of mystery. If I were to become an open book to myself, how could I ever do anything that would provide me with the thrill of surprise? The unexpected, the unforeseen, these are the grace notes that touch with a little excitement the straight and narrow progress of the predictable. They add some necessary ornament to the obvious, don't you think?"

"It's not a question of what I think, General. You and I are in separate professions. You talk now very unlike a soldier. But I suppose it may have been all your years on the Continent that corrupted what must once have been a fine military mind. Now, apparently, you are reduced to thinking like a mere human being."

"In some ways I'm sure that's true." Daniell rose and began to pour himself a drink. "In others, of course, you and I are pretty much in the same business. Each of us tries to discover the things that someone else is trying desperately to hide. And even a modest success at that is likely to bring to either of us—as it certainly has, I would say—somewhat extravagant rewards. The world often tends to overvalue, I suppose, the thing it has the least of. Secrets, for one instance. Virtue, for another." He sat down again, sipping at his tumbler of brandy.

"Virtue?" Behind the dark-brown cigarette, Dr. Bosca's face crinkled into a wry expression. "An odd word to crop up in the conversation of a man with as much European experience as your own, General."

"I wasn't considering my European experience. I was thinking of something that happened right here."

"Oh?"

Only ever so slightly, the general's eyelids rose.

"Yes," he said. "The little scene with our nurse. Rampant vice and triumphant virtue. The Rape of the Nightingale. Florence, that is. Isn't that the main topic on this afternoon's agenda?"

"Just so, my dear General. But please, as a personal favor to me, if not to my profession, I would like you, in your own mind, to separate my interest in this matter from perhaps anyone else's."

"Certainly. Fire away."

"I'm not concerned with the morality of it, or trying to discover why a man of your obvious intelligence and achievement would trifle with the possibility of official rebuke in this way."

"Good."

"What I was hoping you might be able to afford me, General—and I feel a good deal easier asking this, since you agree that we are both, basically, in the same profession—Exactly what were your feelings when you decided to approach Miss Thors?"

"Lust."

"Well, of course. That is certainly one of the better headlines to describe what you felt. But visible somewhere on the brow of this raging Minotaur, this unthinking monster of a passion, there must have been a glint, a ray, of some other, more congenial feeling. A rose clutched in the teeth. A dandelion fixed in the hair. No?"

"No. My vital organs had been kept in chains for an extremely long time. Even for a man of my age, that can be cruel and unusual punishment."

"Of course. But wasn't there some feeling other than the very obvious desire merely to pour oil over a grinding of the biological gears? Something you could identify for me? It's a professional refinement of distinction I'm making here—the law or the armed forces would have no interest in making it. But I appeal to you as one whose life, like my own, is devoted to the idea of discovery. We who are in lifelong pursuit of the elusive final secret, the fundamentally unattainable, we are the only ones who really know what true joy and excitement can be. Is that correct, General, or do I misread your earlier remarks?"

"It sounds like a fair enough reading, I suppose. But I said, earlier, that I preferred to leave some things intact, untouched inside me. I wouldn't want to disturb their capacity to astound me someday."

"Naturally. A worthy ambition in these brutally predictable times. But I wasn't thinking of anything unconscious. I address myself now only to those thoughts and feelings inside yourself which can no longer be a surprise to you. They are so close to the surface that they have been identified—friend or enemy is not important—but you know exactly what to expect from them. You understand me, I'm sure?"

"Yes, Doctor." He nodded over his glass. "You may ask any question you wish. I place my mind, shamelessly naked, on the altar of your science—if it is a science."

"Perhaps not yet." Large bald head to one side, the doctor shrugged. "But if it serves a useful purpose to throw a cloak of such respectability over the pryings of someone like myself, then why shouldn't we use the best available cover story?" Another shrug. "So then—when you reached for Miss Thors, put out your hand and touched her for the first time, what was the feeling that you noticed in yourself?"

"I just told you, Doctor. Lust."

"There were not other feelings as well, perhaps not as noticeable as the main theme? There was not some obbligato, tender or sinister, in the background?"

"None whatsoever. My passion—if, for the purposes of this discussion, we may call it that—was untarnished by any modifying feeling or motive. My lust was simple, unadulterated and pure."

"I see. I admire your candor, General, although I find the precision of your judgment a bit unsettling."

"Why so? I see it as being honest and unaffected."

"A little too honest, perhaps."

"You interest me, Doctor. In what way too honest?"

"Because an act which, as you describe it, might be completely understandable in a barnyard may, when engaged in by someone of your sophistication, experience, and training in varieties of motive, be a masterpiece of duplicity—I speak now of unconscious duplicity, of course."

"I thought we were going to conduct this meeting without demanding answers of my unconscious."

"I do not ask for answers from it. But there is nothing in our rules of order that prevents me from offering a few suggestions about it."

"Ah, Doctor." The general's hand shook in gentle reproof. "I thought you and I had come to an agreement of sorts. And here you are, peeking down into my innermost being with that inverted periscope of yours. You are trying to take advantage of me." The smile he presented was too casual, too sure of itself to support any claim to unease.

"Well, General Daniell, an instructive parable occurs to me: Suppose you were to capture an enemy agent, and suppose you asked him why he had chosen this extremely dangerous profession. He answers immediately, so: 'For the best reason in the world, General. It pays more money than the other job I was offered—being conductor on a streetcar in Budapest.' Would you be inclined to accept this as the only explanation?"

"I think it might depend on some of the other things I knew about this man, this agent."

"Exactly. And I hesitate to make you sound like a specimen in a medical jar, General, but you must give me some credit for observation, in the month or so you have been with us here. You are hardly the kind of man to commit an act of rape. And even if you did, you would not be likely to do so for the reason you present here today."

"You accused me, earlier, of thinking like a human being. Are you now denying my right to act like one?"

"On the contrary. I'm assuming that you acted very much like a human being. You perhaps are familiar with the observation of De Maistre: 'I do not know what is in the heart of a scoundrel, but I know what is in the heart of an honest man—and it is horrifying.' For that reason alone your motives must have been far more complicated, more subtle, more devious, for all either of us know, than you may be willing or even able to admit. Not what may be admissible only to me, but also to yourself."

"Well, Doctor, it seems to me you are exploring philosophy. Fantasy, perhaps. In any case, you travel now to that undiscovered country from whose bourn no traveler returns unchallenged—at least by me. I might ask, even, if your mental passport is in order."

"You deny the possibility that there may have been other motives?"

"No, I don't. I deny only that I am aware of them. You see, Doctor, you are now choosing to compete with me in the one subject on which I happen to be, without fear of contradiction, the leading expert in the entire world—"

"And that is?"

"The subject of what General Darwin M. Daniell happens to be thinking or feeling at any given moment."

"Of course."

"And in that connection, addressing ourselves to the topic of this discussion, I think you ought to know something important. In terms of my own thinking and feeling, I could not promise that an attempt would not be made again."

"You mean Miss Thors? Rape?"

"Yes. The mind is so often the slave of the passions, Doctor, as we know. I foresee a strong possibility that you and I may very well have this kind of conversation again—for the same immediate reason, and perhaps with the same immediate result."

"Well, General," Dr. Bosca said, "you are depriving me of the joy of being surprised. And perhaps you are depriving yourself as well." He rose from his chair. The meeting was over.

"Perhaps," the general said, as he went to the door.

The doctor felt a rush of liveliness tingling at the channels of the mind. That man was dangerous.

● ADVERSARY RELATIONSHIP

"This is from Phoenix—an exam they sent me in the mail. It's not just a love letter from some old flame in San Francisco. I'm supposed to be sitting here and thinking about the questions. Trying to figure out the answers. I'd like to be a lawyer someday. Unless you think we'll both be just as happy selling bait off a pier somewhere, in one of those dried-up towns in Florida."

"All I want is five minutes. Then you can get back to the law. A man tried to rape me. Colonel Kilburn, who's in charge of justice around here, can't help me. The man who did it is too important. Doctor Bosca is supposed to know everything about human behavior, but he can't see anything he can do with what he knows. And you just sit there and don't move a muscle."

"Look, Susie, you're getting into one of your things again. Like the time with that bank in Washington—when you thought the teller was deliberately giving you all those dirty bills—"

"This is different, and you know it."

"And that time at that dance—you wanted me to stuff my fist down that lieutenant's throat because you thought he got his knee into you somewhere—"

"That was all you saw in it? No wonder you won't do anything now. No wonder it's just fine with you for General Daniell to do his thing with me—"

"Susie—I don't think it's so fine. There are a lot of things I'd like to do, but I'd only wind up with a court-martial.

And a three-star general always knows the head of the court-martial by his first name. Why in hell do you make me spell it out for you? You know it as well as I do. Now, can I get back to those questions on Evidence?"

"In a minute. What if I told you this just about wraps it up for me? I'd rather spend twice as long in uniform in some place where I didn't feel like one of the prisoners."

"Susie—we agreed to put on a hair shirt for two years. So we could get security handed to us in a hurry. Is that bad?"

"Norm—right now I need another kind of security. I'm a woman. The only one here. If I stay, I'll scream loud enough and long enough so they'll *have* to do something about it."

"Sure. They'll drop a net over you and fly you to some clinic out in the middle of the Grand Canyon. You think they want *anyone* making trouble in a place like this? Or talking about it later? You'll get so filled with needles you won't even remember your own name. And while that's going on, what am I supposed to be doing back here? Writing myself notes about the wonderful woman I used to be married to?"

"They'd let you out of here, with me, if you really wanted to go. Colonel Kilburn *must* know we're married."

"Maybe he does and maybe he doesn't. But he also knows that in some things the Army doesn't like to bend. Especially for two like us. You think, with the investment, all the important security they've got wrapped in this place, they're going to let a couple of volunteer nobodies like you and me ram a hole in it? Just because one of them got excited over a general making a pass at her in an idle moment? Don't look at me like that—I'm only saying it the way *they* will.

And when they finish checking us out, and know a lot of the things Kilburn may or may not know, we'll be lucky not to wind up in Leavenworth."

"So we're back where we started. Sit tight, do our jobs, and act like nothing has happened. Just let them get away with whatever they want."

"Not they. It's only a 'him.' "

"When a 'him' is protected by everybody, then it's a 'they.' "

"Have it that way. But look, every day brings us closer to being on our own. Then we can sit on our porch, with our feet on the rail, the pension coming in, and we can tell the whole world, if we want to, to go to hell."

"All right, Norm. You study your law. But I'm going to get some justice out of this if I have to get into a pair of platform shoes and kick your General Daniell where he'll feel it most."

● ANOTHER NIGHT ATTACK

There was no moon on this particular night, as the corporal performed the two-to-four guard patrol around the innermost fence (Shield 1). There were several reasons why he felt no need for special vigilance:

This was America.

There were no enemies nearby—at least he had not heard of any.

In over a month there had been no sign of a backpacker, and these came only during daylight, anyway.

He therefore felt the knife go through his thigh before he was even aware that someone had sprung out from behind one of the evergreens, someone who had obviously been waiting for him. He turned instantly, his arm striking out and down. It was a flashing, smashing response that had leveled in its time many slopes, gooks, creeps, and others whose alertnesses were not up to the demands of modern necessity.

When he almost fell off balance, he felt surprise. No contact. The ambusher was gone. Quiet, quick, and sure, he had escaped. He must have expected exactly that kind of return chop. A real pro. As the corporal reached for the wound, and felt the blood on his hand, it seemed to him strange that the attacker, who could so easily have struck higher, who could have killed, had not done so.

He wondered what that new colonel, Kilburn—the sheriff —would have to say about a thing like that.

● WAR PLANS

The meeting lacked the brisk and reassuring drive of a staff conference. For one thing, it did not have a guiding hand. With so many born—or at least officially certified—leaders present, it was understood, perhaps, that no single one could be permitted to take charge. Also, the nature of the problem, unlike that in which the enemy is plainly seen under a foreign and challenging flag, could not be clearly discerned. In General Winkler's words, they were simply "doing a little brainstorming."

Seated in one of the Playroom's few wooden chairs, General St. John spoke softly, the words barely audible as they struck past the sentrylike cigar.

"First the billiard table and then the smokes. And then my medals. They haven't even found them yet, much less the son of a bitch who ran off with them." His face was cramped with rage and disgust.

"It might be only unenlightened mischief, of course," General Daniell said. He spoke with even more than his usual softness.

Each of them understood the importance of not being overheard.

"It could be many things," Wadlow said, the bleak eyes narrowed down to more exacting intensity, "but it's hardly likely to be merely mischief. And certainly not unenlightened. Consider, genetlemen, what this particular enemy has accomplished so far. He has caused the men here, in meeting assembled, some of the finest thinking and fighting minds in the free world, to consider the possibility that they must deal with him. We are being forced into a species of détente with a powerful unknown. Whatever we are facing, gentlemen, it is of an order considerably more critical, more vital, than mischief."

"I agree with the secretary," Byngham said. "And now maybe some of you will see the point of what I've been trying to explain. When that ship was pushing through that mist, the largest goddamn tanker in the world, and no way for me to tell—for anyone to tell, for sure, anyway— that it wasn't an aircraft carrier out to sink everything we had— Well, can any of you here tell me I should have waited with our planes? Should have taken that chance? Let the whole American world go under? Just so I could be polite in the face of a crisis like that?"

"I'll tell you men what it is." The dead cigar stuck straight out, at attention, in the St. John mouth. "It's one more example of what's wrong with the country today. Nobody wanting to put up a fight any more for the things he believes in. Everybody trying to slob their way to overweight. Even right here at the Ranch, there's no one willing to do his job right."

"My point, gentlemen, is that it might even be someone in this very room," Wadlow said. "One of us. Who else would have the capacity for bringing men of our standing to such a crisis of confrontation?"

"Well, we certainly cannot exclude that possibility." Daniell's frown was judicious.

But Winkler seemed puzzled. "What would anyone hope to gain from that? It's not as if we're out there in command, somewhere. None of us, right now, is in a position to make anything important happen."

"The minute we find the little bastard, we should kill him," St. John said. "Someone who would do a thing like that just doesn't deserve to live."

"Do we really have that right?" Wadlow's hands made a kind of cage, the spread fingers pressed together at their tips. "Do we know everything there is to know about his reasons? What explanation he could give us for the Why of all this? Isn't it possible he serves a master that we have an obligation to know more about?"

"We'll get all those answers if you want, Mr. Secretary," St. John said. "But we'll kill him anyway."

Mr. Wadlow sighed.

And so they talked. No conclusions were arrived at. But there was general agreement that Colonel Kilburn might not have quite the ability to do the job. They would put him, in effect, on notice. If he proved delinquent, then they might have to take over. St. John and Daniell did not wish to wait. They wanted to move immediately. (Where? How? —Unstipulated.) But the others, more cautious, prevailed.

● POSSIBILITIES

Colonel Kilburn offered the courtesies of his bar table, and his guest nodded at the brandy.

"If I was as sure about everyone else as I am about you, Doctor, then we wouldn't be having this problem."

"Thank you. I accept the endorsement."

"This isn't only my opinion. I'm leaning on the wagon-load of clearance material I've read on you. If you're one of theirs, then we might as well all pack in over here. Give up while we still have the strength."

"An extremely provocative idea. We must pursue that one day. The ethologists are doing work in this area all the time. Of course, I don't happen to agree with them, but I would be the first to admit that their judgments are provocative."

"We've got a higher-priority topic, Doctor. And not enough time."

"When you say not enough time, you imply a conclusion. Something is going to happen, or something must be prevented from happening, soon. Is that so?"

Kilburn nodded.

"You have at least some idea of what we can expect?"

"Too many ideas," Kilburn said. "This guy wasn't sent here just to kill me—he couldn't have known I was coming. He's some kind of guerrilla—a raider. The billiard table, the cigars, those medals of St. John's—then the surgery on the Wrangler. All that in addition to trying to deck me. We're covering too wide a range of fire. We've got someone in here who knows exactly what he wants to do, and he's figured out the most complicated way to do it. To confuse us."

"Surely, with the most elaborate and expensive Intelligence apparatus in the West, you can make some inspired guess. What is this agent up to?"

"He's up to doing his part in knocking over this country. It's not just somebody out to get Cadetti. This one's out for more than a lousy million dollars."

"Have you extracted all you could from that defector? Could he not be withholding something? Could he not be, even, a decoy, sent deliberately to mislead you?"

"No. We got him a new name, a new background, and a head start out in the Midwest. He's already bought himself a color TV set and an air conditioner, joined a bowling team, and, for all I know, is about to get someone pregnant. This one's come to stay. He's real."

"What will you do, then?"

"Doctor, you're a man who keeps his eyes open. Since our last talk, have you picked up any clues?"

"Anyone here could be guilty, Colonel."

"You're not exactly making my job any easier."

"I talk only of the Guests. Each of them has known power. Real power. And now each one is in a position where that most important muscle is temporarily dead. Worse, he is made to spend his time with men who have memories exactly like his own. Every man a toppled Bismarck. There is nobody to sit still, in exile here, and listen to long stories of the glory days, when a word, a gesture, a memo, could send masses of men jumping into their pants, to march. Because the worst possible audience for the nostalgia of power is someone who happens to be bursting with that kind of material himself. In such a case the house rule is always: Why should I listen to him, when it's much more important that he should listen to me? And so, no man gets to feel his own strength. A bad situation. For each Guest it is like being Mozart in a world that is deaf. Such a man is capable of any enormity, and in good conscience, of course."

"You really think it could be one of them?"

"Why not? Each of us has the most glorious possibilities inside him. In wartime the nicest boy in town, the one who sings in the glee club, helps out with the charity drive, and gives the course in junior theology at the Y, he's the first one to volunteer. They plug a special coded signal into his brain, and he goes off and wants to bomb, blast, shoot, and bayonet everything in sight. You must know that, Colonel. It is only a matter of pressing the right button with any man. I include you and me, of course."

"But it isn't *likely* to be one of them."

"No. But it *could* be. And it would be unwise to overlook any possibilities."

"Take Wadlow. You think a man like that would be capable of it?"

The doctor shrugged. He drew deeply on his dark cigarette.

"He as much as anyone. Consider his view of what is wrong with the world—everywhere people are being annihilated without intelligent discrimination. Too much tyranny by *them*. He makes unseemly noises about this view, at least in public, and is sent here to have his voice pattern readjusted. And who surrounds him here, during this retuning process? Men whose professional concerns can only stimulate the fevers that got him here in the first place. His mission, then, destructive as it may appear to others, could have something to do with public service, as he sees it."

"You think a man of that age could almost put *me* away?"

"Colonel, do not underestimate the powers that can be drawn on by a man who is positive that he is right."

"You think, then, that anybody here can talk himself into it?" It was a finding rather than a question.

"We are all members of the human race, Colonel, and, as a wise man once put it, 'less than that can be said about nobody.' "

"Would it help to check the backgrounds again?"

The bald brown head shook slowly in a No.

"Put not thy faith in paper, Colonel. Just as *good* has its moments of greatness, so *evil* has them, too. Good is always celebrating itself—trumpets and billboards all the way. But evil is usually very discreet, even bashful—it tries to disguise its triumphs. So you are unlikely to find real clues, in official writing, to the man we are looking for. Consider, Colonel, what he has achieved. Can you imagine the skill and experience of their man, to have come so far? This is not the work of the fellow who handles the Idaho territory for them. This is one that the movies would call a superstar.

And let us suppose, just for the pleasure the fancy gives me, that he is attached to no modern government—in our world, in their world, or in any other that currently claims our attention. Let us consider the possibility that he is self-employed—free enterprise is an old American custom. What can he be up to, then, I wonder?"

The almost-black eyes twinkled as the gaze traveled upward to a corner of the room. Dr. Bosca seemed to be relishing the thought, trembling at the marvels that might be found if he could only poke about among the motivations of a mind and will capable of something like that. "Soon he will extend himself, probably. He will give you a clue."

"Sure. A clue. After they bombed Pearl Harbor, we knew the Japanese were mad at us."

"Time, Colonel, contains all events, all clues, all signs and fingerprints. Wait. He will show himself, one way or another. I am almost positive. The criminal loves to be acknowledged as the creator of the crime. It is part of his reward. Our job is only to hope that the moment of revelation does not make everything else an anticlimax. This country, remember, recovered even from Pearl Harbor."

The lids hung low over the gray eyes as the colonel listened. Then:

"Suppose you were on the other side. And suppose you needed a man for dirty work—a job like this—and you had to move with someone we've got here. Who would you pick, Doctor?"

"You, without question." Bosca did not even smile.

"And in case I got sick—who would you have on the bench?"

"As an alternate I would pick General Daniell."

"So would I. Except, if you knew his record all the way, you'd forget about him."

"Colonel, in my business we are permitted to forget nothing."

● SUMMIT MEETING

When the mind has been trained to operate in a certain way, it becomes in time a mechanical instrument. It then produces with minimum deliberate effort what had formerly been produced only by crudely conscious design. Like many keen-minded men he not only knew that but depended on it. And now, as he lay back in bed, the darkness of the room throwing over his thoughts a more formal blanket, he proceeded to review the events of the past, address himself to the needs of the future. A one-man summit meeting, as it were—always the best kind. And come to that, would it not be a world much better run, certainly a less disorderly world, if everything could be directed by a single intelligence? Of course. Most men and women were already, in fact, presold on the principle. Wasn't that, basically, what believing in God was all about? A more tidy arrangement for the spirit. But on the realistic, more earthbound level, too, it would be more practical. Everything would be so much neater and more pleasant all around—so it could be proved, probably, by computer, think tank, position paper. But such thoughts were only frivolous. Because when they did get around—if they did—to seeing the wisdom of such a resolution of the general sloppiness of *things as they are,* would they be likely to assign Desk Number 1 to himself? Or to anyone remotely like him? Hardly. It would go to some street-corner Svengali, a trench-coated dazzler with the usual crass essentials of the crowd pleaser. Or some especially slick timeserver in that one field that repelled him more than any other—politics. But even without that, there would be victories enough.

Review: Allowing Kilburn to slip away like that was bad. Guilty, but with an explanation: practice is indispensable if one is to perform certain manual functions with efficiency, and it had been years since he had done anything like that. But there were aspects of the operation that pleased him. Certain skills had come into admirable play, even if the ultimate prize had dropped from his fingers. And then, Kilburn dead would have brought in a replacement. Would the new man have been more, or less, or exactly as much of a problem? Not known. But Kilburn was a known. In this case, the devil we know is worse than the devil we don't. Then again, suppose, with Kilburn dead on the floor, Washington had panicked? Had rushed in troops of men to suffocate the Ranch with security? Fine. There was always more safety for him in an excess of numbers. The more men, the more human fallibilities. The incident of the cigars, the stealing of the medals, the attack on the billiard table, these were minor but useful triumphs. The ambush of that young sentry was also sound. Bound to draw Kilburn's nose away from the main spoor. But perhaps there was no point in eliminating Kilburn. If Plan B proceeded as it just might, as it could, as he hoped, then with or without Kilburn's dead body, the outside would be achieved. After all, only an hour out there might be enough. He would be able to make his way to Contact 1, to release, to glory (muted, of course, but nonetheless gratifying), and to some place that was not America, and most certainly not Idaho. But until that happy time, there was work to be done. His mind continued to review, to assess, and to create.

● TARGETS

It was in the midst of Bosca's talk on the belief in miracles (fundamentally unreliable, but essential to any modern democracy) that he became aware of it. A ripple of unease, more insistent, more rebellious than any he had noticed in a long time, was running through the class.

"Something is troubling you, gentlemen?"

General St. John apparently accepted the words as a signal to open fire. He was on his feet immediately.

"Something sure as hell is troubling us, Doctor. And we might as well talk about it right now."

"Absolutely."

"It's about time."

"Get it to the mast."

"Everybody talks. Nobody is doing anything."

Teacher rapped at the desk with his wand.

"All right, students. General St. John, could you outline the problem for us?"

"Doctor, if you don't know that something goddamn funny is going on around here lately, then you can't be as bright as some of us have been led to believe."

"What I know and what I do not know is not the subject

of this discussion, General. Or have I been misled? I was under the impression that you were going to tell me something that *you* know."

"All right. If that's the way you want it. There's something going on around here that none of us like."

"An excellent definition of the known world at almost any period in history, General."

"I'm not talking history, Doctor. On this one, you can shove diplomas up the national ass. I'm talking about now —a tactical problem."

"Let us hear it, by all means, General."

"You know about someone wrecking the billiard table? And about the cigars?"

"Yes."

"And running off with my medals?"

"Yes."

"There are no surprises in this world." Mr. Wadlow's voice was firm but quiet. "Those people are everywhere."

"Well, you must know that on top of all that, one of the Wranglers was stabbed in the leg while out on guard duty the other night."

"Correct. A minor wound, the intent more interesting than the result."

"A jab like that, you hardly need a doctor for it," Cadetti said. "It's the things inside—they're the ones that get you."

"All right, then"—St. John's mouth took a firmer purchase on the cigar—"so we agree on the combat conditions. Now, you were shoved down all our throats because you're supposed to have one of those outsize imported brains. We'd like to hear your thinking on this."

"You mean on the possibility that someone is at work

among us, trying to do something not approved by officers and gentlemen?"

"That's one way to put it."

"It seems to me," General Daniell said, not rising, "that the situation is quite serious, even if the government does not appear to think so. We are the most secure, the most impenetrable sanctuary against prying or invasion that the military power of this country—perhaps even of the world—has ever been able to devise. A United States senator could not penetrate here—even should he know about it, which he undoubtedly does not. And yet, we have to consider that some alien agent has, free as you please, gained access here."

"You want to get in someplace, you just lean on the door," Mr. Cadetti said. "Sometimes you push a little harder, that's all."

The general was not interrupted, and continued to talk.

"The man has done a number of things to demonstrate his resourcefulness, but by sending a Wrangler to the hospital, he has shown us that he is not above killing."

"Well," Bosca said, "looking at it as a problem in logic, don't you think that if he was not above killing, then the Wrangler would now be on his way, rather, to a cemetery?"

"The son of a bitch may have been fought off," St. John said.

"Exactly," said Daniell.

"Or maybe he didn't want to kill the boy," said General Winkler.

"Why would he be so sparing?" Daniell asked.

"I think he might be some kind of a nut," Admiral Byngham said. "Some pacifist who just goes after members of the armed forces."

The pointer whipped the desk. Bosca dressed his face in a deliberately calm expression.

"Remember the advice of a famous American worker of miracles," he said. "We have nothing to fear but fear itself."

"What in hell is that supposed to mean?" St. John sounded almost personally affronted.

"It means that those in charge know exactly what they are doing. That all events—at least the ones under discussion here—are under command control." His smile was now especially cool.

"Doctor Bosca," Daniell said, "is there a subtitle you can provide, in English, or some other language we're likely to understand, to help us decode this message you're trying to send us?"

"Of course. I'm simply trying to tell you gentlemen that everything is known."

"Everything? Are you saying that the man responsible for what's going on is known?" General Daniell, like the others, seemed suddenly calmed, fascinated.

"That could well be one of the things I am saying."

General St. John's voice shot out the obvious question:

"Then why in hell don't you shove a rocket up his ass? Why are you letting the little bastard run around loose in here?"

"Because, gentlemen, there is more at stake here than the apprehending of a single individual. You are all—almost all—leaders of men. You know that sometimes in war, as in chess or even in love, we are forced to do things that call for sacrifice. To give a little in order that we may gain substantially more."

"What kind of a sacrifice?" Daniell asked. "We're dealing with someone who has already attacked a Wrangler. Next time he might just decide to kill."

"I'm afraid that's true, gentlemen," Bosca said. "But try to remember that you are soldiers."

"Baloney!" Winkler called out. "You're saying we have to sit here like this, and let the enemy just drop a bomb on one of us any time he likes?"

"I've got four stars." Byngham rose to his feet. "I don't play bull's-eye for anybody. I didn't get to be a top dog in the greatest fleet in the history of the world just so I could sit around in chinos and let some sneaky son of a bitch take pot shots at me any time he felt like it."

Hullabaloo.

With the exception of Mr. Cadetti, all were on their feet, shouting their minds together. In one form or another, brassy echoes of the admiral's position plowed the air. Tradition, history, the prerogatives of an ancient calling were cried out. The training and experience of a dedicated lifetime had not been designed to make such men expendable. The national welfare dictated that no single one of them—with a few exceptions—could be allowed to serve as a target.

"Who is he?" Through the chaos, General Daniell's voice came knifing at the doctor. "If one of us is going to be killed by a known assassin, I should think that common courtesy would persuade you to tell us who the killer is. That way it won't be the work of a complete stranger."

"I'm sorry," Bosca said, barely heard above the din. "I owe to all of you an apology. This portion of our lesson plan was meant to be presented to you somewhat later. Class is dismissed."

They were still on their feet, shouting, as he left.

● DIAGNOSIS

As a first reaction, Colonel Kilburn blew up.

"You come here and tell me that? Don't you realize you've probably gone and knocked the whole thing sky-high? Do you mind telling me what in hell you had to go and do it for? What do you think we gain when we take out a full-page ad on a thing like this?" And so on for several minutes more.

Dr. Bosca, seated on the end of the green leather sofa, gazed with interest at the stack of periodicals on the nearby table. It was clear that the colonel had little interest in any subject matter unrelated to the Army and its affairs.

Full stop at last.

"I had a very good reason, Colonel. More than one, actually. This is not entirely an Army problem, as I see it. I ignore for the purposes of this talk the fact that I may be a possible victim—we have no evidence to the contrary—and therefore I permit myself certain defensive liberties. Mr. Cadetti and Mr. Wadlow are not in uniform either, and this widens the area of civilian concern."

"O.K. So you're scared. But just tell me what you think you accomplished by spelling it out on the blackboard for everybody to see. And what—"

"I'm coming to that, Colonel. Whoever the enemy is, he must know that we are aware of certain peculiar events having taken place. These could have been performed only by someone who chooses deliberately to annoy us. And since you believe that defector, then the man we seek is not merely someone with enlargement of the behavior problems."

"Keep talking."

"If I may make a professional suggestion, Colonel, why don't you sit down? It becomes much harder to display tension from a sitting position."

"Right now, I just want to know what you think you were getting at, hollering that we know who he is."

"Of course. You know, Colonel, a useful lie is not unknown in warfare."

"Tell me why laying this one on to that roomful of blabbermouths is such a great idea."

"Because, given the human situation here, the closed environment, the limited number of people, the word is going to be out within a few hours. The criminal will then be forced to consider the possibility that we know who he is. He will have to assume that we are not taking him into immediate custody because we are watching him, observing. In the same way that a scientist permits cancerous mice to live out their lives in his laboratory, we hope to achieve some larger goal. That he will lead us to some person, some facts, more important than himself."

"Doctor, you're now talking like an educated civilian. If this mystery man of ours is here all by himself—he'll know *that*, too—then he knows goddamn well there's nothing we can learn from what he does until after he's done it. Until we catch him. So what does he lose in a case like that?"

"Nothing—if it were only a case like that. But since he cannot read our minds any more than we can read his, the important weapon we have is his imagination. He asks himself a question: Why don't we pick him up instantly, when we know who he is? Therefore—"

"Therefore he knows we don't know a damn thing, that we're bluffing, that he's got us backed into a corner. And meanwhile, you've got all the brass in this place jumping out of their jocks because we're supposed to be letting some guy with a knife trot around loose in here, hacking out thrills."

"That too is part of the risk. Calculated. It has to be weighed against what we may gain—"

"Which is what, Doctor? Lay that diagnosis on the table for me. I can't see it from where I'm standing."

"Like all of us, this man is a human being. He is for that reason at the mercy, to some extent, of the irrational. It is on that that you must depend, if he is to be caught."

"This is no psycho, Doctor, if that's what you're counting on. This guy is trained. He doesn't make mistakes. He's a professional."

"Please, Colonel. You and I must not debate a matter like that. You must believe me when I tell you, as a doctor, that even doctors—also professionals—occasionally make mistakes."

"Like the one I'm listening to, you mean?"

"I ignore that. The point is, if the criminal hears that we claim to know who he is, then, logically, he may think one of two things: either we are bluffing, or we actually do know, and for some reason choose to do nothing. He cannot know which of these is true. His imagination then proceeds to light a fuse under proposition two—that we do know. It presents many new opportunities for his consideration and anxiety. A germ—tension—could begin to grow in the formerly pure vessel of his calculations. There is nothing like an irrational human thought, a seepage of the imagination, to glue up the most coldly efficient machinery of the brain."

"Do I hear you promising me something?"

"Yes. Hope."

"What are you doing now, Doctor? Holding my hand and telling me the operation is going to turn out all right? Even if they take out my kidneys, an eye, and half of one lung, I'll still be a wonderful human being? Is that what you're giving me?"

"No. You are prejudging the results of this hope."

"Aren't you?"

"My hope, unlike yours, is based on the realistic expectation that the enemy's plan will have to be altered to meet the needs of a new situation. The new situation may result from certain assumptions thrust upon him by his power to imagine. After all, you and I have no evidence that we are dealing with some new kind of mechanical intelligence they've developed over there—something that operates from a printed tape, unaffected by such bourgeois disabilities as the human imagination."

"O.K. So he changes his plans. Is that going to make catching him a lot easier for us?"

"In my judgment, it might. He could very well be forced to do things, or do them in some way that he had not considered in the time when he was completely unknown to us."

"Sure. And then again, Doctor, if I can hit you with a little irrational reasoning of my own, he might not. And all I'm going to say is this: you had better be guessing right. Then we'll all call you a genius. But if you're guessing wrong, then when I get to make my full report, you will be playing a star part in it. And I might as well tell you that under the McCarran Act, you, as a naturalized citizen, could be deported back to your native country. I don't know what things are like over there these days, but I have a feeling that if you really enjoyed it in Long Island City, then you're not going to enjoy it in Bulgaria."

The doctor did not seem angry at all. He smiled almost gently.

"If you choose, Colonel," he said, nodding approvingly. "But that is for the future. Why even think of such a thing at this moment? Our problem is not in the future. It is here, in the present. In the now."

"For your sake, I'm hoping," Kilburn said. For the first time, drink in hand, he sat down.

● ARTIST

He did his best thinking on his back, with his clothes on. After flicking off the reading lamp alongside the bed, he lit a cigarette. Only then did he proceed to the real luxury, feeling the joy of what he had created. Michelangelo, he thought, might have felt just this way the first time Pope Julius looked at that ceiling (Work In Progress) and said, "Not bad so far—not bad at all."

Either they really did know, or they did not. The second possibility came to brief attention in his mind and then departed. The first, he decided, could only be a bluff. They did not know. But suppose they really did? He wished for an instant that it was so. Then he would achieve, very shortly, what he must—escape from this hermetic chamber to some outside point where he could pass along what he had learned. Perhaps he might even present himself next morning, if not right now— No, that would be discourteous; let the man have a good night's sleep—and identify himself as the culprit.

Imaginary speech: "I believe you have been looking for me, Colonel. I have been informed that you know who I am, and it seems crude that two grown men should continue with this tiresome masquerade. After all, we are not characters in a comic book. This is life. I therefore present myself to you, with my compliments."

Much excitement. The plane out of here to somewhere. But then everything under another seal of maximum guard, maximum security. That would make it just as difficult to communicate with Contact 1 as it was from here, from this crater on the moon. And then an even bigger, a mind-crushing objection: exposure would no doubt bring permanent isolation from that faraway continent that was for him all lotus. He had missed it so much from the moment he had comprehended the Why and Wherefore of the Ranch. After all, he was not so young. His remaining years were taking on separate and outsize value with each new stroke of the calendar. Unlike a younger man on such a mission, he could not face with calm the prospect of some long skein of time being chopped from what life and joy still owed to him.

But why, if they knew, did they not pick him up? Was it because they suspected that:

1. He was not alone? Perhaps.
2. His confederates were right there, at the Ranch? Perhaps.
3. Allowed his head, he might somehow blow the apparatus? Perhaps.

He reached for another cigarette, another match. And now his mind thrilled to the pursuit of the problem: how to achieve what he must achieve, with minimum risk and maximum gain, given the new possibility that they might know.

He felt it as a triumph of the spirit, as well as of the brain. Chess was a middle-class diversion compared with this. Here there was a secret trafficking with noble inner demons, and if all went as it should, there would be an earth-shattering effect. But it was an act that in a way would not exist, would have no written history. He thought of Van Gogh painting through a lifetime of anonymity. Great works. But were they great when none knew of them but Vincent?

Of course.

The real artist pressed on. His work was enough. The masterpiece existed and it was a success, even if the world —so often a failure—could not see it.

● PROVOCATIONS (2)

ITEM:

In the afternoon, returning from his regular hour at the sauna, General St. John discovered that someone had once more invaded his room. On the floor near the closet were his four pairs of shoes, but each right shoe had been sliced with a knife—or was it a hatchet?—into three separate pieces. Useless. Unwearable. The general, enraged, rushed off to see Colonel Kilburn. What in hell was going on? If the colonel was not capable of maintaining a proper pattern of security, then perhaps he should be relieved. Perhaps a more efficient sheriff should be sent in. Perhaps the general would inform Washington of this personally.

"And how would you go about informing them, sir?"

Firing persisted, but the battle was over. Before the general left, the colonel assured him that new footgear would be ordered by radio. His shoe size was on record. Meanwhile, he could wear sneakers. The general saw no point in explaining to the colonel that it was difficult enough to maintain one's sense of command while walking about, tieless, in chinos. In sneakers, it would be almost impossible.

ITEM:

The following afternoon there was no hot water in the sauna. A crucial valve had been carefully damaged. In addition, the saboteur had gone to exceptional pains to insure his handiwork. The Wrangler who normally mended the plumbing discovered that the wrench necessary for this particular repair had been stolen from the tool closet.

ITEM:

When it was discovered that the liquor stores had been broken into, and all but one of the bottles emptied into the closet sink, there was a seething among the Guests.

The almost-full bottle of vodka gave emphasis to the waste. Admiral Byngham, especially incensed, demanded to know why, in view of the pattern of unusual events, no special precautions had been taken to protect the liquor. It would be almost twenty-four hours before a new supply could be brought in.

Secretary Wadlow, who did not drink, was entrusted with the responsibility of portioning out the last of the vodka to those who desired it. It soon became evident that the liquor had been powerfully doctored with a laxative stolen from the Dispensary.

"For such men," Dr. Bosca said to the colonel, "these are not pranks. They are acts of war."

● CANDIDATES

He knew that what he had done so far was not enough. The series of incidents had aroused in the Guests an anger that was only bad temper, a muscle spasm of self-indulgence. There was insufficient steam to produce an event likely to blast him from the place. What was needed was an act that would strike every one of those men right down to what was left of his roots.

A death.

Of course. To each of them, through example, a whiff of his own vulnerability. Death was the one piece of gossip about himself that every man had to take seriously. To know that someone might be coming to flip the switch on the body electric, that was the most personal insult of all. It was bound to bring each of them charging into action.

Who?

He reviewed the possibilities. The death of a Wrangler was not close enough to the bone. It would not give to the members of the group that intimation of mortality so necessary to the working out of his plan. Dr. Bosca? No. A harmless though not uninteresting crank. His demise would serve only to make them feel even more removed from the situation. He was not one of them; he was, indeed, a foreigner. Another try at Kilburn was not worth the risk. Too tough. Of course, for that reason the challenge of it had a special appeal. But this was no time to take unnecessary chances. And then again, did they really feel that close to him? Did they consider him one of their own? After all, to them he was only a colonel.

It would have to be one of the Guests. Good. "Death loves a shining mark."

At this moment his thoughts registered a message from a far corner of his mind. It was a kind of last-minute request for commutation of sentence for three of the men under review. An ancient loyalty was calling out to him, an overwhelming "Please!" It was a threat to calculation, and yet how could he deny the absurd appeal, the soap-opera power of a demand like that? He could not. He knew then that the example would have to be someone who was not of his own kind. There was a fraternity of the uniform that transcended the parochial boundaries of nation, anthem, and idea. It was a call from on high. He would have to let the air out of one of the civilians.

Mr. Cadetti? In every normal way he was an obvious candidate for extinction. There were some who were willing to pay a million dollars for just that result. The country abounded with opportunities that no Chamber of Commerce had yet considered. But Mr. Cadetti was very much of a zero among the guests, presenting no visible contact with their reality. The whole point of such a death might escape them.

Even before he began to consider the possibilities of Secretary Wadlow, he felt a prickling of the soul. There was a logic here so manifest that it made further thinking a clumsy pursuit of the inevitable. A civilian and yet not a civilian. Was he not the prince of warriors in a struggle that each of them could see immediately as his own? And his continual crackpot prating about *them,* about the need to maintain sleepless watch along the walls, and the other conventional formulations of a traditional paranoia with redeeming social value. Was not this an extension of their own fight, their own holy war against a Hydra that never seemed to run out of heads? Wadlow, despite his lack of a uniform, wore a general's stars on his spirit. A Trojan horse's ass. They would recognize him as one of their own. Wadlow's death they would surely feel.

He felt marvelous. He was within a few brush strokes of the end. In a little while, everything would be neatly in place and his handiwork could be a milestone in the history of an art. *It is finished.*

That deserved a drink. He went to the bathroom and emptied from the after-shave bottle what was left of the Scotch he had poured into it during the assault on the liquor closet. Then he rinsed out the bottle. After a few gargles with mouthwash, he was ready for work.

● STATESMAN

As a young man hurrying through the obligatory process of growing up, Mr. Wadlow had found no difficulty understanding the ways of the world. The understanding of the ways of people came somewhat harder. It simplified matters, he learned, to resolve with cool reasonableness those human situations normally disarranged by warmer modes of consideration. Even in his marriage, *eros* was persuaded to defer to a more reasonable *agape*.

He made himself a priest of the law.

An uncle of his wife had at one time been vice-president of the United States. It therefore did not seem unnatural that Mr. Wadlow should contrive an interest in modern American history, and the company of the men who shaped it.

Few were surprised when he was appointed Secretary of State. He was a man of known and formidable skills. The celebrated aptitude of a mind accustomed to move with iron logic through every merely human situation seemed ideal for deploying our diplomatic energies over an intractable world. For every situation and every country, just as for every man, there was an argument that could surely persuade.

He liked his new job even more than he liked the uses of the law. He worked long and arduous hours, happy to assign his energies to the solution of problems much larger than his own. And then, hardly noticed at first, a kind of ball bearing came loose in the precise engineering of his brain, causing it to throw off unusual and even startling sounds. He became obsessed with the unnamed *them*.

At first it was only a private horror. His valet and his secretary, his deputies and the servants—all who were closest to him for the longest periods—tried to misconstrue the visible fact. They assured themselves and each other that it was only temporary, the predictable "fate of place." He was not the first important public servant to be afflicted for his patriotic pains. (Washington and his teeth; Lincoln and his melancholia; Wilson and his stroke; Harding and his women—these and more were invoked for example and consolation.) But so clear a mind could not remain fogged for long, they agreed.

When he refused, at a dinner party, to sit next to the Romanian ambassador, it was seen as an undiplomatic act, but with a certain logic to it. The man was a known dumbbell. When the Polish envoy suffered the same treatment, new excuses were found. But when, a week later, he refused to see the Yugoslav minister, a born charmer, the professional explainers were given true pause.

The first time he said a flat No to the Russian ambassador, it was not so bad. A rather gay fellow, the darling of the TV interviewers, he made appropriately jesting remarks about why many a busy person might want to avoid him at the present time. But when, a few weeks later, the man was again refused an audience, he turned away with the most metallic of smiles, frozen in a film of silence.

There were many more such incidents before a special meeting of the Cabinet was called. Mr. Wadlow by then had lost almost all control of his public warning system. Too often and too embarrassingly he went about alerting the companions of the Siege Perilous to the fact that *they* were everywhere.

The secretary knew too much. He could not be permitted to wander about freely after having been deprived of his official station. His condition was too evangelical by far. For his case, orthodox psychiatry was not even considered. He was flown immediately to the Ranch, and a cover story was released along with the surprise appointment of a new secretary of State. Mr. Wadlow, a deeply religious man who had given much to his country and to the world, had embarked on a period of stern contemplation. He was now, the announcement stated, in residence at a religious retreat somewhere in the West. There, under the fraternal name of Brother John, he would make a separate peace with forces not included in the covenant of the United Nations.

Many were puzzled by the news. Was it not odd that so celebrated and discriminating a churchman should choose even briefly so foreign a mode of devotion? The official reply was silence, mystery, and "No comment."

● SECURITY

"I don't know how you can even *think* about being a lawyer, after what's happened."

"Can't we drop it for a while, Susie?"

"Someone tried to rape your wife—remember? And nothing's going to happen to him."

"Come on—the guy is sixty-one years old. That wasn't rape. That was probably something like nostalgia."

"Are you trying to tell me that when *you* get to be sixty-one, all we'll have to work on is nostalgia?"

"Put the meat ax down. You know what I'm saying. This guy lived in Paris, places like that. He misses all those boulevard things he was used to. And remember, he's a general, so he was used to a lot. And then, you're the only woman in the place. In a way he was giving you a compliment—"

"You see that as a compliment, Mr. Husband?"

"You know what I mean—and do you have to yell like that? They might still have a bug around here somewhere. You want Colonel Kilburn to hear you?"

"Absolutely. And never mind what *you* mean. I want you to know what *I* mean. This man committed a crime. This is a government installation. I give the facts of the crime to the people in charge, and they're not even interested. I'm not a captain to them. I'm only a woman—"

"Susie, how much time do I have to put in listening to this one? You get onto one of those hobbyhorses of yours and you keep rocking till the roof almost comes down. That time—"

"Forget about 'that time'—stick to *this* time. Right now my own husband, who's making such a big study out of law and order, who's going to bring a little public decency into Arizona life, isn't interested in bringing a little of it into his own family life."

"You want me to go to his room right now and sock the guy? Is that what you want?"

"I just want you to do *some*thing. I want to hear you

sound like an outraged husband. I want to feel that you really care, that's what."

"We've been all through that territory, Susie. You know what would happen if I hit him."

"You could tell me all about it, and then I'd know I've got a husband. A man who's going to love, honor, and respect me. Even though I'm not a client."

"I see. You won't believe I really feel that way about you until I do the one thing that'll put me out of your life for about fifteen years."

"If there's nothing we can do, then what's the good of our staying here? What's the good of your memorizing those lawbooks, as if they're really going to mean something?"

"They *are* going to mean something. I keep spelling it out for you. S-E-C-U-R-I-T-Y. We're not going to be cooped up in here that much longer. We're not far from the homestretch by now."

"Yes. And suppose, some afternoon, while you're out helping a client through a misdemeanor, the mayor flies in the window. And suppose he tries to rape me in our own bed. How do I know you won't try to talk me into seeing that as nothing wrong, too?"

"You're so steamed up you're beginning to sound like an Italian movie."

"I am like hell. You're so worried about losing your ticket to the moon you're letting everybody step all over you. All over me, your wife, anyway. And you're making excuses for it. That's what's really got me mad."

"Look, Susie, what happened with Daniell, that was bad. And nothing happening *to* him, some people would think that part is even worse. Because when you live in a country like this, the least you can expect, when someone gets caught committing a crime, he'll get punished. The minute you start making exceptions for special guys, then you tear out a few of the wires that keep the whole machine humming along. You know what I mean?"

"If I said yes, would it get something done about him?"

"All I'm trying to say is that if you look through history you'll find lots of guys like Daniell getting away with murder. Allowed to, sometimes. Even today. But the law goes on—"

"The law? Stalin had laws. Hitler had laws. I don't want to hear about law for a while, Norm. I want to hear about justice. A crime was committed. Everybody knows the criminal, but what is anybody doing about him?"

"I'm trying to tell you, Susie. Guys like that—something always catches up with them in the end."

"Don't say always, Mr. Husband, unless you can prove it to me. Are you going to catch up with Daniell in the end? Is that what you're saying right now?"

"Look—"

"I don't want to look. I want to see. I want to know that Daniell is going to pay—something, I don't give a damn what—for what he tried to do."

"What do you want me to do around here? Change the world all by myself?"

"If it's going to be this kind of a world, then what good is all your security—and for whom? For you and me it's not real."

"Calm down—you're all excited. And I'm not getting this assignment finished, either. Why don't—"

"All right. I'll calm down. I'm not going to talk about it any more. I'm the only woman in here. Maybe I'll just have to do something all by myself."

"Remember, Susie, even in that nothing outfit, you're still in uniform. You took an oath to the United States Army. We've got an awful lot riding on this. The average person can't fight City Hall."

"I'm not an *average* average person," she said.

● A NECESSARY DEATH

He was not like Schubert, Rossini, or one of those other born geniuses who simply turned a faucet and let the art gush out. His natural talent had had to be elaborated by character, training, experience, and a number of other homely modifications. It was spurred also by the sense of challenge. A multiplicity of talents, excited into action by the contingencies of the moment, might produce art. Or something very close to that, he thought. It was very artful to intimate so slyly to Mr. Wadlow that a matter of crucial importance, one that could be coped with only by two such minds as their own, should be addressed that very evening. The secretary's quarters would serve. And it was imperative, of course, that their exchange take place in an atmosphere of confessional privacy. It would therefore be wise to remove institutional intruders. He had persuaded Mr. Wadlow to lend him the key, and preceded the man into the rooms by fifteen minutes. It took him less than ten to discover the bugs. One was pinned to the back of the

Millet *Angelus* over the bed, the other taped to the bottom of the coffee table.

On his way to the bathroom with the two pieces, he felt a twinge of professional disdain at their awkward shape and dimension. Surely it was not common practice to use these old models in important domestic surveillance? Did they represent the hint of a budget problem in the Department, so long immune to fiscal neurosis? As the two metallic objects dropped into the water and began their noisy journey into the earth, he wondered what special music they would report back to headquarters via the receiving tape. The thought warmed him, an incidental pleasure of the work.

Smoking a cigarette, he sat in the soft leather chair in the far corner, to wait.

At exactly the fifteenth minute there was a turn of the knob, and Mr. Wadlow let himself in. The moment of entry was predictable with such a man. Punctuality was bound to take the place of larger but less orderly virtues. He motioned to Mr. Wadlow to lock the door.

"We can speak freely now, Mr. Secretary," he said. "I have taken the liberty of discharging the transmitters from active duty."

"What did you do with them, General? Won't they be missed? Won't Colonel Kilburn have things to say about this?"

"To answer you serially, Mr. Secretary: I threw them down the toilet. They will be missed, but only sometime tomorrow, when the tapes are normally checked. And finally, yes, Colonel Kilburn may very well choose to say something about this. Should he do so, you have only to remind him of his rank. Please sit down, Mr. Secretary— I will feel graceless if I remain seated here while you stand before me like that. That's better. Anyway, a number of replies would appear to be useful: Kilburn is only a colonel, a spear carrier, while yours is a stage-center role in the epic in which we serve. You cannot permit yourself to be troubled by his routine cant. Or you can simply deny everything, placing the burden of proof on him. Just keep saying no, or it's a damned lie, to any charge he makes that you feel to be counterproductive to your own well-being. Or you can tell him that you are glad to have his thoughts on this matter, and will certainly take them under consideration—"

"You are going to unusual lengths, General, to formulate my position for me. Is this—"

"Or if you do not choose to play games with him, you can simply tell him to go to hell."

Mr. Wadlow almost smiled. At least there was an elusive glint in the steely gray of his expression.

"Well, General," he said, "I'm not sure your suggestions are well thought out. What if he answers any one of these statements by presenting me with a major diplomatic incident—he withdraws all my privileges and reduces me to the status of a glorified vegetable? What then?"

"I can assure you, Mr. Secretary, that he is unlikely to do such a thing. It would be very unrealistic of him."

"It has been my experience, General, that once we think of people, we have to think in terms of unrealistic possibilities. History will bear me out on that, I believe."

"My point wasn't meant to be quite so ambitious, Mr. Secretary. It was a far more immediate and practical one."

"All right. But I suggest that we can get into the plotting of Colonel Kilburn's mind a little later. At the moment

I'm more interested in the primary reason for our holding this discussion."

"As I am, Mr. Secretary. But in a not unusual way, the two topics are intertwined." He took from the pocket of his brown leather windbreaker the small Beretta. It felt almost lost, a kind of metal foundling in his long fingers. He saw the eyes going wide behind the rimless glasses.

"That's a gun!" The words, fighting their way past the barriers of glottal constriction and alarm, had some difficulty presenting themselves in order.

"Mr. Wadlow," he said, "I am truly sorry about this, but it has become necessary for me, for reasons that might be at least objectively convincing to you—if I had the time to make a formal presentation of them—to kill you."

"Kill me? Why? Why are you going to kill me?" The lean jaw trembled, seeming to stab at the air as he rose to his feet, only a short distance away. "I—I—" He could not seem to find the correct words.

"You may say anything you like," the general said. "I will have no objection should you wish, in the next few moments, to denounce me, to rehearse the major triumphs of a constructive lifetime, to ask, Why you?, to make your peace, if possible, with whatever God you may believe in. Other options will be condoned as well. You have only ten seconds, but you may speak as loudly as you care to. We are completely soundproofed, as you must know."

Mr. Wadlow turned suddenly, awkwardly, and, almost falling as he moved, ran for the door.

"Please," the general said, without rising. "You are violating my rules." He raised the weapon, arm extended, and fired three rapid shots. He rose and went over to the body. Face down on the carpet, it was curled into the self-containment of the primary fetal position. The general could read that telltale sign, but he leaned over to feel the carotid artery anyway. Dead.

"Thank you, Mr. Secretary," he said.

There was no one in the corridor when he peeked.

● CLASSIFIED MATERIAL

Mr. Wadlow did not appear in the Dining Room for his customary breakfast of oatmeal, warm milk, and a slice of unbuttered rye toast. Because he had left no evening request to have breakfast served in his room, Colonel Kilburn was notified as a matter of routine. He went around to the secretary's rooms to speak to him personally.

The body, he could tell, had been dead for hours.

He fetched Bosca immediately and watched in silence as the doctor went through the assorted medical motions necessary to establish the approximate time of death.

"Sometime last evening, I would judge, Colonel. Three bullet wounds. Someone has expressed the ultimate form of disagreement with this world-famous diplomat. It should make some handsome headlines for a while."

"Yes. Your class begin at its regular time this morning?"

The doctor looked at his watch.

"In a little less than an hour," he said. "We are going to study the critical importance of belief, even when it has no basis in fact. How a belief in even the wrong thing can have an important effect on history. I have a feeling that the secretary's life might provide us with some useful illustrations."

"Forget it. I don't want anything leaked on this. It hasn't happened yet. You get your class going and keep it that way. Don't let anybody leave the room. When you finish with them, you come around to my office. We're going to have a conference."

"Of course. But, you know, I do my best work among the living—"

"You just might be a help anyway."

The doctor shrugged.

"I will be more than honored, Colonel—I will be interested."

At his office, the colonel worked for exactly one hour. Then he called out to Yost, writing at the other desk.

"Sergeant—go over to Supply and draw out a sleeping bag. Then meet me at Secretary Wadlow's quarters. Fast."

"Yes, sir."

Shortly after, the sleeping bag under his arm, the sergeant was staring down at the blood-stained body on the carpet. He looked questioningly to the colonel.

Kilburn nodded. "Shot. Three in the back. And whoever did it, he found the bugs and put them out of the way first. Now open that."

Before they stuffed the body into the bag, the colonel removed the eyeglasses and instructed the sergeant to put them in an envelope, at the office. They carried the bag outside the building and around to the rear of the kitchen and then through the door. They asked for no help from the four incurious men who were busy at the chores for the midday meal. They set the body down in front of the great door to the meat compartment of the walk-in refrigerator.

The colonel then removed from his back pocket a large red label, gummed, which he pasted to the center of the bag:

DO NOT TOUCH

CLASSIFIED MATERIAL

EYES ONLY

The colonel opened the door and led the way as they carried their burden between the lines of hanging beef that glimmered with an arctic mist. In a far corner, he arranged the bagged body neatly on the stone floor, the warning label in bold display.

"There," he said. "That should hold him for a while."

● PERCENTAGES

"Before we start this meeting," the colonel said, "I think we ought to know what we're up against. Just in case."

"Just in case?" Dr. Bosca was already thickening the office air with smoke.

"If we don't catch our rat in thirty-six hours or so. Because that's about all the time I can keep a blanket over this."

Sergeant Yost looked surprised.

"You're not going to let Washington know immediately? A thing like this? That's a violation of the manual, Colonel."

"It sure is. And for that, I could leave egg all over my record. I could even be cashiered."

"Surely you exaggerate, Colonel."

"Not a chance, Doctor. But if we let them know right now, according to the book, give them the big news about one of *them* firing at will around here, what do you think they'd do? They've spent millions on spyproofing this place, and somebody goofed. They don't design men like Secretary Wadlow to get killed. Men like us, we get trained, fed, and paid to see that things like that don't happen."

"I can assume, Colonel," the doctor said, "that you use the military 'us'?"

"I do like hell. It's your ass too, whether I tell them now or tell them later."

"Even though I could not possibly have prevented this? Even though it is very remote from my own professional sphere of action?"

"Doctor, you're making me waste some of our time just teaching you something you're supposed to already know. Do you think when this thing hits the sidewalk anybody is going to worry about details like that? We're all handcuffed together on this. Important people are going to feel important heat. Bodies will have to be thrown over the wall so those wolves can calm down, get the feeling something positive has been done. The only way to shut them up is to give them people like us to chew on."

"I'm sorry I brought it up." The doctor shrugged. "I've been in this place so long I've almost forgotten how human beings can act. It will be disappointing to have to leave here. I enjoy this place, this work. A personal project of mine will suffer. I will be sorry to be discharged."

"Firing you would only be step number one, Doctor. You got any proof you didn't do this?"

"I have all the proof any reasonable man would care to hear."

"That's a start. Now that we've taken care of that reasonable man, how are you going to handle the rest of the country? You're a foreigner, remember."

"I am a naturalized citizen of the United States. You accept this country by the accident of birth, Colonel. I can claim that of all the nations in the world, I *chose* this one to come to. I elected it above all others."

"Sure you could claim that. Until somebody points out that the son of a bitch who put Wadlow on the floor last night, he also elected this country to come to."

The doctor sighed.

"Colonel, you have convinced me," he said. "You must call upon any and all of my resources."

"Good. I'm depending on you too, Sergeant. Just from a few of the things you've done, we could have you doing a solo in a penal barracks for ten or twelve years."

Deadpan, the sergeant nodded slightly.

"O.K., then. Let's start the meeting. Now, as far as we can tell, aside from the guy we're after, nobody but us knows what happened. We have to keep it that way. Otherwise we'll have a bunch of screwballs around here, climbing in and out of our hair. And we've got enough to do without that."

"What exactly are we supposed to do?" The doctor looked concerned.

"You're blueprinted as a genius at figuring people out," the colonel said. "I've decided you're probably right about the Wranglers. One of them might have had the bright idea to kill Wadlow, but none of them could have thought up some of the other things. So—"

While the colonel continued his blunt review of the situation, the sergeant said nothing. But there was a cloud of sadness hanging over his thoughts. The precise calculations of an honest and well-meaning mind were about to be overthrown, trampled on, buried under the debris of accident and the unpredictable. Or, rather, someone else's precise calculations, those of a dishonest and far from well-meaning mind, had overrun his own. This was much worse than the trouble he was having with his wife. Perhaps it was true that a nation's troubles were merely a fact of history, and only one man's troubles might be a tragedy. But now the national ache was becoming inseparable from his own. He saw a thrilling headline run around the electric signboard on that building in New York's Times Square:

SGT. YOST, SCAPEGOAT IN WADLOW KILLING,
IS CONVICTED. DENIED LAW DEGREE.

It occurred to him that the last three words were only marginally pertinent to the major charge against him. But he did not choose to object, at the moment, to the irrelevant and immaterial obiter dicta of his own mind.

"What about Ramrod?" the doctor said. "Shouldn't he be here with us? Surely you trust him. I understand you have served with him in the past."

"That's right. I served with him, and he's a fine soldier. I'd trust him right to the wall. That's why I don't want him to know a goddamn thing about this—at least not yet. He'd turn in his own mother for waving a Confederate flag at him. He just might insist on getting a message out of here. The guy we're after isn't worrying about any rules, and until around the time tomorrow's plane comes in, that's just the way *we* have to play it."

"Well, then, Colonel, where does that leave us?"

"Doctor, you and I have had this part of the talk before. It's just possible that one of those sheep you're standing guard over is wearing a fake coat."

"I try never to be shocked by anything an event may choose to say to me, Colonel. But assuming it is one of the Guests, then why does he have to be an enemy? These incidents which are causing all our concern may then simply be the natural and even logical actions of a complete maniac. A psychotic in full cry is not ordinarily bound by the conventions of Geneva, the Book of Common Prayer, or those of the Boy Scouts of America. So the question must then be asked, Colonel: What proof do *you* have that this man must be considered one of *them?*"

"First, we know there's one of them around. That's why I was sent in. And second, he tried to kill me." Then he rounded into the moral. "No psycho would have operated that way. This guy has cunning, but not the kind you get from thinking the whole world is out to jump you. He's been trained that way."

The doctor looked almost wistful.

"Have you ever made a mistake, Colonel?" he asked.

"Lots of times. But I guess right too, often enough to put me ahead of the national average. And right now I have to go along with percentages."

"All right. But why a Guest?"

"Because even if we're only guessing, we have to start somewhere. And that's where most of the know-how is."

They began with a discussion of General St. John.

"In a way, a marvelous product," the doctor said. "Man is the only animal known to kill for reasons of the spirit, and here we have one who—"

"Never mind that," the colonel interrupted. "We've got

time right now only for a verdict: is he capable of doing what we've been talking about?"

The doctor shook his head.

"This man is trained to kill only in the plural," he said. "I believe he would have qualms about killing a single individual all by himself. Assault, yes. Homicide, no."

"What about Mr. Cadetti, then?" The sergeant threw the idea quickly, happily, at the colonel. His words, as he heard himself speak them, seemed to form a judicious compromise. Only the week before, he had been reading about the merits of Plea Bargaining. But the colonel did not seem to hear.

"Never mind, Doctor," he was saying. "I just wanted it for the record."

"Then would we not save even more time," the doctor said, "if we assumed incapacity—or at least innocence—for all but the man we spoke of once before?"

In the immediate silence, the gray eyes gave no hint of what the colonel was thinking. He puffed out some smoke and then rose from his chair.

"Thank you, Doctor Bosca," he said. "Our meeting is closed."

Sergeant Yost did not dare to ask what in hell was going on.

● SECOND INCITEMENT

During the day, the absence of Secretary Wadlow from class, from lunch, from the serene forms of self-indulgence that passed for Activities, caused no special comment from his fellows. This was because there were times when each of them, for reasons of indisposition, had chosen to stay in his room. And besides, the secretary had a local as well as a national reputation for remoteness and contemplation, for the solitary thinking of deep thoughts. The fact that he might choose to have some of those thoughts in this place, on this day, and in privacy, struck none of his fellow Guests as being at all unusual.

In the late afternoon, in the lounge, General St. John grumbled to General Daniell a complaint about not having received any mail for two days. Washington normally rerouted to him, daily, the string-tied bundles of mostly handwritten adulation that were addressed to him from places far and near.

"We should be grateful," Daniell said, "if that remains your most serious problem while we are here."

"What do you mean?" The cigar stood almost vertical, as if challenging the idea that anything could be more serious than the nondelivery of personal mail.

"Haven't you noticed a rather odd thing today?" Daniell's voice was calm and low, but his eyebrows hinted at a scream.

"Like what? Intelligence is *your* field. Don't make me guess. Just say it."

"Secretary Wadlow has not been with us all day."

"What of it? He's probably been trying to get deconstipated. If he doesn't make it, we'll all know about it. He'll have some brand-new idea to scare the hell out of us with."

"You won't see him again. He's dead."

"What do you mean, dead?"

"General, even men as important as Wadlow have been

known to die. He was killed last night, in his room." The voice remained low, the tone easy and undramatic. At the moment, he did not wish any of the men nearby to hear. It was important first to make the immediate sale, after which the others would be easier to arrange. "Someone apparently got into his room last night." And then, maneuvering casually through and around the grunted interjections of rage and wonder that St. John seemed impelled to throw off, he told a reasonably coherent, reasonably threatening story of invasion of premises, of murder by pistol. The killer was unknown. The body must still be at the Ranch, because Daniell had observed the brief visit of the afternoon plane, and no large object had been put aboard. In fact, curiously enough, while a number of necessary items had been debarked, absolutely nothing had been put on the plane for the flight out.

"What about the son of a bitch who did it? Do they at least have any clues?"

"If they have any idea who did this, they have not revealed it to my informant."

"What informant? Who told you all this? You can't even get the right time out of the crowd they have running this place."

Daniell arranged his face into one of its more useful smiles. Low candle power, cryptic, meaning all things to all men.

"The ways of Intelligence," he said after a moment, "are not normal ways." And before St. John could pour in answering fire, he added, "But there is no compelling reason for you to believe me. We are all patient men here, because we have to be. Look around you in the days to come, and see if Secretary Wadlow shows up. I would be the happiest man here if the story was untrue. The secretary could be very trying at times, but I often found him, without his meaning to be so, I believe, a rather amusing fellow."

"Look, Daniell, don't play any of those funny little Intelligence games with me. If you have facts on his being dead, killed by an enemy unknown, then tell them to me. What else do you have on it? What about the motive?"

"No motive is known, as far as my informant can guess, but it seems to be assumed that this is only the first of a series."

"Are you saying what I hear you saying?"

Daniell nodded.

"Then the son of a bitch who got Wadlow has a list—"

"Yes. And given what we know, certain assumptions become necessary—that is, if we hope to defend ourselves."

"Well, I don't know about anyone else in this crowd, but if some son of a bitch thinks it's a great idea to knock over a secretary of State, he's sure as hell not going to stop before he packs in a four-star general. Especially one with the kind of campaign ribbons I've been flying. And any scurvy little thumb-sucker who's going to try to take me on is going to get a handful of glass ashtray all over his mouth."

"This man is apparently no fool, and he is armed. He is also completely unknown to us. Do you think a glass ashtray will provide an adequate line of defense?"

The contorted St. John face suddenly relaxed. He sighed.

"All right, Daniell. You're part of this Army too. And you've been thinking about it a little longer than I have. Do you have any bright ideas?"

"Yes," he said. "I try to have at least one of those every week. Today I've had several. Before I begin, however, I think it's important, in view of what and who we may be dealing with, that maximum security be maintained. If you choose to mention this to any of the others, make sure you do so when you are out in the open, not under man-made cover. You must not under any circumstances be overheard. Any talk, ideas, or actions must be kept to ourselves alone."

"What in hell kind of a thing is that to tell me now? Especially after the way we've been talking? What about the bug they're supposed to have around here somewhere?"

"I have already neutralized it, General," he said. "And now, before I tell you of some ideas I have, please believe how important it is that you do not reveal who told any of this to you." His words were barely audible.

General St. John leaned closer, the better to hear.

"All right. Shoot," he said.

● THE THINKING OF SERGEANT YOST

As he walked away from the meeting with the colonel and
Dr. Bosca, a great cube of lead seemed to press on the back
of his mind, the rough edges tearing deep grooves in the
smoothly paneled interior of his spirit. He had not felt
quite this kind of futile rage and dismay for a long time.
Almost two years, in fact. He remembered now how he had
felt when, in hot pursuit of Susan, he learned that she was

simultaneously dating an Air Force major. Well, if not for situations like this, they wouldn't have proverbs like that one about the best-laid plans of mice and men. And here all the calculation that was meant to put a nice gift-wrap ribbon around the shank portion of his life was about to be sabotaged. It was almost a kind of consolation to him to think that the country's crisis in a way paralleled his own. The government too had designed a kind of bulletproof vest for itself, one that was guaranteed to ensure the security of the Ranch. And now look at *that* best-laid plan. An agent had had about as much trouble breaking through it as he would have had buying his way into some neighborhood movie. At the moment, none of the traditional ways and means of the Army survivor would suffice. This was a combat situation, and he could not hold his ground by refusing to volunteer. The facts had volunteered for him. He wished he knew what he could do—without going suicidal—to help bring down whoever was loose around the place. But for that he would need orders from the colonel more useful than his "Keep your nose to the ground." There didn't seem to be a thing about this that could be helped by what he had studied or learned about the law. There you dealt with facts, with the actions of reasonable men. Even when someone ran unreasonably off the Lincoln Highway of the legal norm, he did not become a problem to the law. He wound up then with a specialist like Bosca, just as a spy should be dealt with by another specialist, a counterspy. *This* kind of event, the subject of the talk with the colonel and the doctor, was a menace. Not only was it way out of his prescribed line, but there was no logic to it, no steps in sequence that could be carefully footnoted into an obvious conclusion. And yet he was being held to some degree responsible for a conclusion—and a successful one—nevertheless.

At the end of the meeting, Colonel Kilburn had told him to confide in nobody—"and when I say nobody, I mean not even a woman."

Halfway out the door, the doctor had called back, "I congratulate you, Sergeant."

But given the mood of Susan, the fact that she was now marching through most of their conversations with a grenade in her teeth, he could not decide whether it was such a wise idea to keep the news from her. If he did not tell her, she just might blow a hole in the colonel's plans with some impulsive fool act. And yet if he did tell her, he would be violating security, an act that could very well blast a hole in his own plans.

For the first time since he had joined the Army he wondered why he had not selected a less complicated, less demanding branch of the service. At the moment, there were some pretty good things he was prepared to say about the infantry.

● FEELERS

"Why don't we sit over there." Colonel Kilburn led the way to the sofa.

General Daniell did not reply, but took the only wooden chair in the room, turned it to face the already seated colonel, and then sat down. He sipped at his brandy glass, the eyes looking calmly at Kilburn over the rim.

"I'll get right down to it," the colonel said. "I know

how hard it is to keep a secret, especially a really important one. You're the one man in this place who must know that as well as I do."

The general's eyebrows went through a maneuver that could have been the equivalent of a shrug.

"Maybe even better," the colonel added.

No response.

"But with a man of your background, I see no reason to keep you in the dark about what's going on. Your experience might be a help to us. That's why I asked for this roll call."

"Anything I can do, Colonel. You have only to ask."

"Thanks. I'll get around to that, probably. But first I'd better line you up with what's happened so far. We begin with the campaign against the unit's morale—the brandy, the cigars—"

The general nodded.

"And I know all of you have been talking about the attack on the Wrangler."

"Yes. Of course."

"Now—did you know someone got into my quarters the other night and tried to deck me with a gun?"

The general leaned forward, as if only now awakened to interest.

"I find that fascinating, Colonel," he said. "To declare war on brandy, cigars, or a billiard table is one thing. Even to attack a Wrangler is hardly very important in the total scheme of things. But for our someone to try to put *you* away, the man on top, as it were—that *is* exciting. What happened?"

"He missed," the colonel said. "But so did I—he got away."

" 'The other night,' you said. I take it you did not recognize him, or in any case don't have sufficient leads. Or you would have picked him up by now. Or am I to assume he's escaped somehow?"

"No. He's still with us."

"This gets even more fascinating. Given such facts, one has a great deal of suspense to charge the ongoing story with."

"In a way. Until you figure out who the man happens to be. Then there's less suspense—at least the kind you're talking about."

"And you have come to that conclusion?"

"It's not in full uniform yet—not ready to be shoved into a full-dress court-martial—but it'll do."

"Is it someone I know?" The thin eyebrows, barely touched with gray, went up in a question.

"According to this conclusion of mine, it's someone we all know."

"Please forgive me for prying, Colonel—a professional weakness—but who is it?"

"Well, given the way he operates, it has to be someone very experienced. Good footwork. He knows the way people think and act and he doesn't get nervous about having to kill someone."

"You said he *didn't* kill you. If he's as cunning as you say, isn't it possible he was only trying to give you a scare?"

"Well, let's see—did he give me a scare? Yes. Was he actually trying to kill me? He put a lot into giving me that impression, but maybe I was wrong. Anyway, we have more to go on than that. Would you be surprised to hear that he killed Secretary Wadlow last night?"

"No, I wouldn't, really. I've already heard it."

"Can you remember where?"

"I'm trying to think, as we talk. No—one hears so much around here. You know, Colonel, one of the problems when you sit a group of normally busy and intelligent men down in a do-nothing place like this is that you step up each man's capacity for gossip, reminiscence, and general windiness. In such an atmosphere I must be forgiven for listening at only half-focus. Or even less."

"Sure. Now, about this suspect—maybe you'll agree with me that, given his demonstrated abilities, the degree of his intent, and all that, he has to be the kind of man who would be able to reach the top of his profession."

"I'd certainly like to think so, Colonel. It would be appalling to think they could depend on some run-of-the-mill agent, some peasant in the ranks, to pull the rivets out of a dream machine like this one."

"Exactly."

"And you called me here to discuss who it might be— you have suspects?"

"One, anyway, General."

"Who is he?"

"We've already agreed he can't be any dumbbell. Then we add the fact that even though he came at me in the dark, I got a few leads on what he's like—the physical feel of him—just from shaking myself loose, wrestling with him. So he would be someone built along your own lines. Your hands, for instance, are pretty much like his."

"I'm five-eleven, Colonel, not much above average. Ramrod and Sergeant Yost are also, I would judge, built pretty much to my scale. Are we addressing ourselves to the possibility that either one of them is our man?"

"I doubt it. I've known Ramrod off and on for close to

fifteen years. He's tough enough for something like this, but he doesn't really have the imagination for it. And the sergeant's background checks out too. His idea of success is his pension."

"On the surface, I'm sure both these insights are correct. But if our man is all he seems to be, then shouldn't we assume he's quite capable of throwing you off the scent in just this way? How can you be sure it isn't one of those two? Do you know the story of Gorchak, of the Polish political police? After World War One, using the papers of a dead Bolshevik soldier, he infiltrated the Russian government, married a nice Soviet girl for cover, worked his way up, and eventually became Commissar of Agriculture, I think it was. He sent reports to Warsaw for years. Then one day he woke up to realize that he enjoyed being a commissar more than he enjoyed being a Polish patriot. No more information would be sent along, he decided. His paymasters denounced him to his new national love, and he was executed. There is a lesson in that story, Kilburn."

"Lots of them. But just as a kind of game, let's play it my way for the next few minutes. Suppose we assume it was some man who's not only built pretty much like you, but he also happens to have a background pretty much like yours."

"I happen to enjoy games, Colonel. Why don't we assume for the purposes of this one that he's not 'pretty much' like me but *exactly* like me. That will make the construction much easier for the two of us to deal with."

"Good idea. So he's a three-star general, got all that power, and for some reason, whatever it is we don't know yet, he's got himself into this place, and he's got an assignment to knock it over."

"I can't tell you how exciting it is just to think about it, Colonel."

"Good. The last thing I'd want is to put you to sleep with this theory of mine. Because if it sounds dull to you, I'm not going to have a hell of a lot of luck with it if I pass it along upstairs."

"That's the difficulty you run into, Colonel, when you attack a superior officer."

"You mean even if I had the goods on this guy, and he actually did turn out to be a general of our own—someone exactly like you, for instance, like we've been saying—you mean I couldn't get them to believe it?"

"That, I think, would be a major problem. He would of course deny it and it would come down to your word against his—unless you had some kind of written confession from him, or a color movie of him performing one of the more drastic and obvious misdeeds. Do you have anything like that to support the hypothesis?"

"Not yet."

"Well then, there you are. And look, Colonel, even if you did have it, our man might still deny the visible evidence. And things being what they are, his denial is likely to be more convincing than materials that are only too easily faked. A general of our own hasn't done the kind of thing you suggest since Benedict Arnold, and one such, for a country like ours, is more than enough. What we're facing with this scenario of yours, as much as anything else, is a public-relations problem."

"Suppose I caught him in the act, and there was a witness—what then?"

"Colonel, I'm surprised at you. The very fact that he is in a place like this will give him a certain excusability.

If our man is a general, then he is here, like the other Guests, because he has demonstrated a temporary instability that requires special treatment. That is a 'given,' as we say. And in light of that, any unstable act on his part will be immediately understandable. Besides, a man who has achieved a certain level of power is like a kind of dike. When he springs a leak, fingers rush in from all quarters to hold back the flood—after all, it just might drown them too. Men who have climbed Everest have too much in common to be separated by the drums and bugles, the pieties of the millions who have not. Our Doctor Bosca says things like that all the time."

"What about that commissar you were telling me about? They dumped him, you said."

"A new country, Colonel. Perhaps paranoid. Men not used to power. Perhaps too idealistic. The topmost ranks had not yet learned to close."

"So then, General, what you're saying is that even if he was someone like you, it would take a lot more fire power than a man like me—only a colonel—could bring to bear. Is that it?"

"That's certainly part of it."

"Well, just between the two of us, what do you think will happen next?"

Daniell shrugged.

"Why should we even attempt to find out, Colonel?" he said. "So much in life is so boringly predictable. Let us both be surprised."

● WAR PLANS (2)

As the four men walked and talked through the cool afternoon sunlight, Daniell directed their steps in a slow and
narrow circle. In this way they kept their distance from the
nearest trees. And that, of course, ensured against being
picked up by the nearest possible bug. There was the risk
of a parabolic transmitter focused on them from somewhere nearby, but he was almost certain that nothing like
that was available on the premises. And anyway, part of
the joy of creation came from the sense of What next? The
end product was bound to be aesthetically impaired if it
was only the result of piecing together a heap of stale and
unsurprising knowables. Had not Picasso himself admitted, "I do not search—I discover"?

St. John, good and useful fellow, had already instructed
them to keep their voices low.

"This could be worse than Pearl," Byngham said softly,
famous brow incised with famous frown.

"It could be, but it won't," St. John said. "We've got
the initiative."

"Why do we have to do it that way?" Winkler asked.
"Why can't we just go in a group to his office and demand
an explanation?"

"He's too clever," Daniell said. "He would talk us out
of it, somehow—cast doubt among us. If even one of us
is convinced by him, he'll be able to nail the rest of us to one
of those trees."

"Isn't there some way we can get a message through to
Washington?"

"Winkler—forget about miracles." St. John spat out a fleck of cigar. "This man is sitting on communications. The way he's running things, none of us can give an order to anybody."

"That is the nub of it," Daniell said. "Here we are, three generals and an admiral, acknowledged heroes of our country. We have accumulated many scars and rewards on the front lines that defend America. We deserve better than to be at the mercy, now, of one of them."

"What I can't understand," Byngham said, "is how the son of a bitch made it so far up the mast. Don't they know how to strain out creeps like that?"

"Ours not to reason why," Daniell said. "We are facing not a theory but a situation. We have to deal with it as soon as possible. We cannot expect help from Ramrod, from any of the Wranglers, because it will be his word against ours, and they are sworn to take their orders from him. No one can help us but ourselves. He is only one man, but he is at the national jugular as well as our own. If the country is to be aroused to prevent accomplishment of the enemy design, then it is up to us. It is a responsibility that we four cannot shirk."

"What happens if we don't succeed with this plan of yours, Daniell?" Winkler's tone was not contentious but rather supplicating. As if any answer would do, if only it were plausible.

"What will happen is probably exactly what will happen anyway, if we try nothing. We may, one by one, or more rapidly, go the way of Secretary Wadlow. We have no choice but to put up a fight. And we have to win. For us, and for America, there is no alternative to winning. If we four cannot pin down a single enemy wearing the disguise of an American officer, then it will be a black day not only for our country, but for each one of us as well. What chance do you think we would stand against any *real* enemy if we had to assume that three of our generals and an admiral are no match for a single one of their agents —regardless of his rank?"

"A good point," Winkler said, "but I don't like the idea of having to kill him. He's a colonel."

"We've been all through that, General." The St. John scowl almost swallowed the cigar. "He's not one of ours. And we don't *know* what rank he is. He might be only a civilian, an agent doing this only for money. I say let's kill the son of a bitch and get it over with."

"I'm not so sure that's a good idea." Byngham's crew-cut head shook slowly. "I'm with Winkler. There's a lot I'd like to know about all this. We've got the questions and he's got the answers. We could have a sort of trial—get him to tell us that way."

"Gentlemen," Daniell said, "a trial would be a fine idea if we had the time, the facilities, the other things necessary to take care of this matter in the American way. But I don't have to point out to you again that we are hardly in a position to do everything as we might wish. Remember, he is in charge here, so it is primarily because of him that we are reduced to blunt measures. If he has chosen to deprive us of alternatives, and if the stakes are so high that direct action is the only remedy, then direct action it must be."

Winkler shook his head slowly, and from his lips came the unpersuaded sound of "Well—"

"I don't know what in hell you're getting so damn lady-like about," St. John said. "If it was bombing a city of sixty thousand, you wouldn't even think about it. But because it's this one son of a bitch, and he's carrying a colonel's rank, all of a sudden it makes a difference."

"It's not just that," Winkler said. "Maybe it's because it's *him*—Kilburn—someone we know. Anyway, I think we ought to give him a hearing."

"That's right," Byngham said. "What difference would it make if we held up killing him for a half an hour? If we dragged him to the mast first, for a few questions? I'll feel better too, after that. Besides, it'll give us a lot more to go on when we hand in our report. Up to now, we have only some fancy guessing."

Winkler, sighting the arriving ally, seemed relieved. "Exactly," he said. "Any report we make is going to need real impact."

St. John looked almost disgusted, but Daniell could see it might be a mistake to press the point. He would yield with grace to what it would be unwise or even dangerous to oppose.

"All right—a trial, then," he said. "But tonight."

● THE THINKING OF CAPTAIN THORS

In a way, she was glad that this was one of his really intense working nights. She knew that if they were together, she would spend their time as before, railing against General Daniell, against the Army, against the system that made it possible for a man to attack a woman and get away with it. She would of course throw a few nasty cracks at Norm too, preacher of the Law, and that would really bother her. It was unpleasant to think that her husband was powerless to do anything for her. He was caught like everyone else, trapped in the stripes that made it impossible to raise a hand and call attention to a crime like this. Even Dr. Bosca could think of no way to satisfy her claim to simple justice.

It was not as if this was the first time she had become aware of the Army as a vast assembly line that could produce its best results only when it made the fewest possible allowances for individual need. But this time, now, *she* was the individual. It made a difference.

Around the country, the laws that made for order were being kicked at, trampled on, the criminal often snickering his way to freedom. That was bad enough. But she wore the uniform of a national police force, organized to defend and protect, to see that right was done. And yet, here and now, it would not police its own house. It denied justice to one of its own women.

Because a general had all that power, nothing could be done. He was above her husband's law or anyone else's. Like one of those lord-of-the-manor bastards of a thousand years ago, it was perfectly all right for him to climb down from his horse one afternoon, jump on the passing lady stranger, and push her into the hay. And there was nothing that anybody, anybody at all, could do about it. Or, rather—worse—there was nothing any man seemed to *want* to do about it.

Sitting on the edge of the bed, smoking, unable to sleep, she suddenly thought of how nice it would be to have a drink. She did not enjoy liquor, but now, filled with so many reasons for resentment, she could see a kind of logical necessity about her desire for it. In a case history or a movie, it was right about here—the surrounding world saying a big fat No to one's obvious deep need—that someone would begin to drink. And with the liquor the ungiving facts would somehow dissolve. At least something would happen. Something that would make a change. Anyway, even if the outside world could not be made to give a little, she could certainly depend on the inside world to do that once she dabbed at her blood stream with a bit of alcohol. To take some of the curse out of the wound was not such a bad idea. Even without this searing grievance inside her, it was tough enough to serve out her time in a place like the Ranch. She was willing—half-willing, anyway—to see it to the end with Norm only because of the carrot that dangled there for the two of them.

Once inside the Dispensary she locked the door behind her, opened the prescription closet with her key, and took out the bottle of Irish Whisky. No label was required to warn her that this was meant for medical emergencies only. She had already thought her way around that one. Her agitated condition qualified as a mental state that required immediate professional attention. Army regulations would comprehend that whisky was indicated.

She broke the seal, withdrew the cork, and poured half an inch of the yellowish fluid into a water tumbler. There was no ice, but she felt no need of it. Nor did she care to dilute the whisky with water. She was interested in results, and as soon as possible. After three shots she noticed that she had not bothered to sit down. It was as if she was in a hurry to accomplish something that was a necessary step on the way to a more important something else. Her mind was already warm, clouded, but simmering with so far formless anticipations. When she set the glass down on the desk, after the fourth drink, she could see the wisdom behind these seemingly aimless intentions. The whisky had revealed inside her a magic red button. On it was clearly printed "Ah-*hah!*," the answer at last to so much that was troubling her. She felt something press down firmly on the button.

Striding unsteadily up the corridor, she heard giant choirs rejoicing in her head and knew that the men at Concord Bridge must have felt just this way. In a few moments, when General Daniell opened to her knock, she would herself *do* something to let him know he could not get off so easily. And if he chose to make an Army case out of it, bring charges against her, well, that was fine too. She would have a chance to tell her side of the story in open court. The world would then be forced to listen, to have its eyes and ears rubbed in the kind of dirt shoveled out by a man like that. It would learn exactly how much of a bastard he was, pulling a thing like that on a woman, a wife, a nurse, a captain in the United States Army.

She made a fist and banged three times on the door.

● THE TRIAL OF COLONEL KILBURN

The assembled military brain power, General St. John had pointed out, was more than enough to assure better than a sixty-forty chance of winning any battle short of Armageddon. Therefore the problem of pulling in one chicken colonel by the heels should not strain their reserves. An appropriate plan was soon devised.

Rendezvous time was 10:00 P.M. in Daniell's quarters. All four men arrived early. They smoked and talked, and as the clock moved toward zero hour the room began to thrill with louder and more insistent plans for the future. Speeches would have to be made, position papers written, crisis meetings called and attended. Changes would have to be decreed in matters military, civilian, and political. The word would have to be headlined across the land to all good men that *they* were nearer than you think. Sudden revelation had exposed the Road to Freedom as being potholed, booby-trapped, lined with banana peels.

At eleven, the stillness of the vast Idaho night lay heavily on the Ranch, and at that moment, according to plan, Byngham went around to the colonel's rooms and knocked in agitation.

When Kilburn came to the door, still dressed, the admiral proceeded as briefed.

"Come quickly, Colonel. Something peculiar has happened."

He turned immediately from the door, as Daniell had suggested, and began to hurry away. But Kilburn did not follow. He remained fixed in his doorway.

"*What's* happened?" he asked.

It angered the admiral to see the way the man stood there, asking explanations at a time like this. It was a dumbbell stunt for a man of that rank. That kind of thing, at Midway, could have had the Japs in Seattle in a week. But that General Daniell, smart fellow, had been prepared for this contingency too. The admiral threw out, "It's General St. John. I think he's been shot." He turned his back to the colonel once more and sped away over the carpeted floor.

In an instant he heard the door close. The colonel almost caught up with him, but the admiral stepped up his pace. It was important for him to precede Kilburn around the next corner, and when he did so he turned immediately to wait with the others.

They fell upon the colonel, but despite the surprise, he just might have broken away, knocked one or more of them flying, if Daniell had not pulled a gun from his pocket and whipped it quickly down. It made a dull and ugly sound as it struck the back of Kilburn's head.

"Where did you get that?" St. John asked as they dragged the unconscious man by his arms along the corridor.

"Stole it this morning," Daniell said.

"It doesn't look like one of ours. What in hell is it doing in a place like this?"

"That's one of the things we might ask our sheriff. It's a Beretta." Daniell looked stern.

"I'd rather have a good American gun any time," St. John said.

With two men carrying at each end, they now moved Kilburn more swiftly.

"Why don't we all arm ourselves?" St. John suggested. They were nearing the gun closet. "We could all use weapons for a thing like this."

"Wait a minute," Winkler said. "We don't have to turn this into a rebellion."

"It already *is* that," St. John said. "But we're the ones

putting it down." He made the first move to release Kilburn, permitting his portion of the body to slide more or less gently to the corridor floor. They were standing before the pale-green door that bore the sign SPECIAL SUPPLIES.

"How do we get through that lock?" Winkler asked.

"We can shoot it off." St. John put out a hand for Daniell's gun. "Let me try it. I've never shot out a lock before."

"Look in his pockets first," Daniell said. "He ought to have a key. It's quieter."

Byngham found a ring of keys, one of which opened the door.

They did not have pockets large enough to accommodate so formidable a weapon as a .45, and so, when St. John stuck his in his belt, the others followed the example. Only Daniell was able to keep his weapon, smaller and almost feminine, in a side pocket.

When they got the body through the door of Daniell's quarters and set Kilburn on the carpet, the colonel was beginning to come alive. His head moved from side to side, but his eyes were shut, so they knew he was not yet with them.

"Take his clothes off," Daniell said, nodding to Winkler as he bent over the body himself and began to remove the shoes.

Winkler did not move.

"You mean *all* his clothes?" Puzzled.

"Yes. We want him naked."

"What for?" St. John said.

"Try to remember your own feelings, General," Daniell suggested, "when Dr. Bosca did as much to you."

"Bosca's only a goddamn civilian," Byngham said. "We can't strip this man. He's a colonel in the armed forces of the United States of America."

"Do you still persist in that view, Admiral?" Daniell's tone was cool.

"Daniell's right, Byngham," St. John said. "The whole point of this operation is to get to the bottom of exactly who the hell this man is. We sure don't take it for granted that he's entitled to officer privileges in our Army. Not until he does a lot more proving than he's done so far."

"Well, I'm not going to argue that," Byngham said. "But I'd like to point out something—suppose it was you or me, St. John, who was picked up by one of *their* groups. Would we want to have them coming at us with a lot of questions while we just stood there in the buff? What the hell kind of warfare is that? When you don't even show a minimum respect for the other man's uniform?"

"That's a point," Winkler said. "What's his being undressed got to do with the way he answers our questions?"

"It's an excellent point, as far as it goes." Daniell's nod was encouraging. "But it actually doesn't go far enough. I think I have been involved in more interrogation procedures than any of you—than all of you put together, in fact. It's an important and highly specialized branch of my duties. One thing we have learned about taking from a man every stitch of clothing: it not only removes every visible sign of his authority, his patent from his superiors to demand, to insist, to *re*sist, in fact. It reduces him automatically, visibly, and in his own mind too, most mercilessly, to a nobody. Naked, he becomes anything we want him to be. I need hardly point out, as well, that in such a condition his physical options are reduced. Our guns are only one line of defense. His nakedness will contribute, I assure you, to the general calm and orderliness of this proceeding."

"I don't know that we even have to talk about it," St. John said. "Let's just yank everything off him. He's beginning to come around."

"But at least let him wear *some*thing," Byngham said.

"I kind of go along with that," Winkler said. "Why don't we compromise? It won't hurt to let him wear his shorts."

No sooner said than accepted by all as the sense of the community. Each man leaned down to help with the undressing, as if in this way to offer public assent to the soundness of the enterprise. The colonel's shorts were pale blue, boxer style, unremarkable, but Daniell reached for the belt line, pulled at it, and exposed the label.

"Notice," he said to Byngham. "A standard American brand. Exactly the kind of small detail that one of them, especially a sharp-thinking one of them, would be likely to watch out for."

Kilburn's eyes were coming open for the first time.

St. John pressed a hand to the colonel's shoulder, holding him briefly at rest.

"You can get up," he said, "but don't do anything without consulting us. We've got four pieces trained on you, and we're not going to stand for any crap. You're going to give us some straight answers to some straight questions."

"O.K.," Kilburn said, with a long look at General Daniell. "But do you mind letting me put my clothes on? I don't know what I'm doing here in this condition anyway."

"No, you won't put your clothes on," St. John said. "We're conducting this like a court-martial under field conditions. Next thing, you'll probably want us to wait while you have some high-powered lawyer flown in from New York."

"How about letting me at least put my pants on? What harm would that do?"

"The man is obviously stalling," Daniell said to Byngham.

"Not a chance, Kilburn." The St. John cigar shifted a full inch. "If that's your name. Now you just plan to do things exactly the way we tell you, and maybe you'll get through this thing with something to hang your pants *on*. You give us any trouble, any trouble at all, and we'll put you down so hard your ass will burn for a week."

"General," Kilburn said, encircled by the four men, each with his gun in hand, "if you look through my wallet, in my pants there"—he nodded to where they lay, on the floor—"you'll see my credentials. They should convince you that someone in this crowd may be pointing all of you in the wrong direction."

"What does he mean by *that?*" With a frown, Daniell sought the answer from Winkler.

"Don't waste our time, Kilburn," St. John said. "They may be real—which could mean stolen. Or they may be almost real—which could mean faked."

"Anything we can do, they can do better—they say that every time you turn around," Winkler said.

"All right." Kilburn looked from each to each. "Let's get on with it, then. You wouldn't want to send a message out to check on me, and you wouldn't want to ask Ramrod about me—you want to settle everything right here."

"You're learning, Kilburn." St. John's nod approved. "We don't want to hear what anybody else has to say about you. They've probably bought the official line. If they hadn't, it wouldn't remain for the four of us to get the facts."

"Do we have to stand?" Kilburn said. "We can talk just as well if we all sit down."

"He's right." Byngham turned to look for a chair. "I'm getting tired just standing here like this. This may take a long time."

"We can sit," St. John said. "He's the one on trial, though, so he stands. But keep your pieces out where he can see them."

"There's no harm in letting him sit down," Daniell said. "It may even be a good idea. That way he can't move quickly—take us by surprise."

"He's not going to take anybody by surprise," St. John said. "Not while I'm with the troops."

Daniell placed a chair near the rear of the room for the colonel, and the others arranged four chairs in a small arc facing it, their backs to the door.

"Let's begin this thing," St. John said.

"Just a minute." Kilburn raised a hand. "You said this was going to be like a court-martial. Shouldn't I be entitled to counsel?"

"You won't need one," St. John said. "All you have to give is straight answers. If you don't have anything to hide, you won't need a lawyer to help you hide it."

"If this is just a kangaroo court, that's one thing. But if it's what you said, then I'm asking you to play by the rules. I want a counsel."

"He's got a point," Winkler said. "It's not just what *he* says. It's the way it's going to look when this thing hits the papers, the public. We have to let everybody know this man had his day in an American court. The way *we* do things. Not like what any of us could expect at one of those drumhead jobs they run over there."

"There's no harm in letting him have the benefit of counsel," Daniell said. "But it will have to be one of us, of course."

"Go ahead, Kilburn," St. John said. "Pick one."

"I pick General Daniell, then," Kilburn said. "He can represent me. And does anybody mind if I smoke? A cigarette?"

Daniell went to a drawer and removed a half-gone pack. He threw it, followed by a packet of matches, onto the floor alongside the prisoner.

"All right, Kilburn, question one," St. John said. "Just who the hell are you, exactly?"

In casual tones there came a brief outline of background. Small-town Colorado. Farm. One year of A & M college, and then early enlistment. Infantry. Korea, Vietnam, and other bases touched. Green Beret training. For the past several years, special work in Counterintelligence.

"On behalf of my client," Daniell said, before any of the others could hop onto the final beat, "I think I should point out that whereas any competent enemy agent would be quite capable of memorizing exactly this kind of recital, and conveying it to us with exactly this tone of calm—perhaps we might even say 'studied'—frankness, any jury of American citizens must, under our laws, assume at least the possibility that despite such artful behavior, my client just might be telling the truth."

"Thank you, Counselor," Kilburn said.

St. John banged his .45 against the leg of his chair.

"All right, Kilburn—question number two: why were you assigned here?"

"Because, you might as well know, one of their defectors, in London, knew about this place. And that's known to less than a dozen men beyond the outside fence. He gave our people the message that they had infiltrated here. I happened to be in Washington, and my background was ripe. It was considered smarter, as well as faster, to brief me and send me here, rather than call in the original Sheriff and brief him. They also figured I might do a better job in this kind of a situation."

"I would like to point out," Daniell said to the others, "once more on behalf of my client, that what he says is not entirely beyond the bounds of possibility. We live in a world where anything can happen. It already has, for the most part, or it may, very well, sooner than we may guess—"

"For Christ's sake, get on with it," St. John said.

"—and in this case, for the moment, anyway, we should all give the witness the benefit of reasonable doubt. That is, of course, until and unless he decides it might serve his purpose to point to one of us as the infiltrator." He looked across the room to Kilburn. "I assume we can trust you to spare us that embarrassment?"

"That's hard to say, if we're really living in that anything-can-happen world you're talking about." The colonel puffed out a rolling cloud of smoke. "But am I allowed to ask a question? What do you men expect to do with me if you decide I'm guilty?"

Before any of the others, St. John leaped into an answer.

"If you'd really like to know," he said, "then chew on

this one for a while: We've already got you pegged for guilty. If you want to throw any kind of doubt on that, then you're going to have to be a lot more convincing than you've been so far."

"What about my question? When you all stand up with that verdict, what happens then?"

"Among the four of us," Daniell said to the prisoner, "there are fourteen stars earned in the defense of this country. Given that, do you think we would not know how to deal with a man like you—dangerous as you are? One who has already killed an important figure on our diplomatic front? One who knows what you know? The Ranch may be a small place, but there is room enough here to bury even so important an agent as yourself. If you are convicted, of course."

"Wait a minute," Byngham said. "I think we ought to take him with us, to Washington. Then we'd have him as a witness, and they could work on him there, to get the whole story. Then everybody would know from his own mouth what was going on. Why we had to take over like this."

"Yes," Winkler said. "I don't want to have anything to do with killing him. I've never killed a man this way before, and I don't see any reason to do it now."

"What about it, Daniell?" St. John looked for an answer. "We didn't actually get to agree on killing him here—the four of us. Why can't we pile him into the helicopter tomorrow? If Ramrod doesn't go along with that, we'll just deal with him too. We've got the fire power now."

"I couldn't agree with you more," Daniell said, the underplayed smile hinting at fearful secrets far beyond the knowledge of the others. "With an ordinary criminal, an ordinary troublemaker—absolutely. Put him up there on display, make an object lesson of him to those who might be toying with the idea of following in his footsteps. But this is no ordinary man. Not just that he has killed an American statesman, but, far worse, this is the one man among them who knows everything about the Ranch, about its purposes, its function. And more, he even knows a great deal about each of us. Remember, he sits over those tapes all day long and knows everything each of us has said to the other, knows even what we say in our sleep. Can you imagine the hoard of vital information he's in a position to take back to his commanders over there?"

"Who says he's going to take it back?" Winkler's expression merged curiosity with impatience.

"That's a pretty good question, Daniell," St. John said. "They're going to cement this man into a hole somewhere. Remember, he's not just a killer—he's a spy."

"Precisely," Daniell said, as if he had been waiting for one of them to make that very point. "He knows too much, and therefore it is to the enemy's advantage to see that he is freed and returned to them as soon as possible."

"What in hell do you mean, Daniell?" St. John's face seemed crouched in rage around the cigar. "Why should anyone free a son of a bitch like this? After what he's done?"

"Well, they shouldn't, General—you're right. But they will. *They* will offer us in return one of our own more important agents they happen to have in custody. The secrets that our man—over there—will be able to tell our people will balance out the secrets which this man, over here, will be able to tell his people."

Daniell looked to Kilburn for confirmation.

"Isn't that how things are often done, Colonel?"

"That *must* be how they do it." Kilburn blew a puff from his cigarette. "Because that's exactly the way I saw it once, in a movie."

The admiral seemed bothered. He looked to Daniell. "Well, what's wrong with that?" he said. "If we've got a man lying around over there, and he has as much to tell our side as this man has to tell them, then it's an even swap."

"Yes," Winkler said. "Why is that so bad?"

"Because," Daniell said, "this man has information no other agent in the world can boast of. He knows, because of his listening in on all occasions to each of us, the secrets not only of our country, but of each of us as a man. You, Admiral, may become the victim of a world-wide campaign of mockery and ridicule, initiated by *them,* in connection with the sinking of that tanker. All details will be presented in their most unpleasant form. You may not be able to sleep at night for years to come. And you, General Winkler, you are of course much improved, your symptoms far less obvious than when you first came here, I understand. But how do you think your original stigmata will look in the world press, or sound over the air? We know them, here, as the natural result of having served our country only too well, but how many will have either the knowledge or the patience to make such allowances? The world will be permitted to see only a high-caliber blowhard, a cosmic buffoon. How long will you be able to hold up your head without wanting to run for cover?"

"Well, I don't care what the son of a bitch has on me," St. John said. "I can play it either way. We can drop him here, or we can take him out with us. You three can decide it. Byngham? What do you say?"

"I don't like it at all, but if he's as dangerous as we think, and if he's only going to wind up back with his friends after a while, then maybe we ought to handle the matter here, by ourselves."

"I think Byngham is right," Winkler said. "We have to make a command decision. It's in the larger interests of the nation, probably. And in fact, about our man over there, the one they might exchange for this Kilburn—what proof do we have that he wouldn't be exchanged, sooner or later, for someone we haven't had a thing to do with, someone we don't even know? These things happen all the time, and in our wing of the battle we hardly ever hear of them."

"Well put," Daniell said.

"All right." The cigar shifted slightly. "It's settled, then. We take care of him here."

"What happened to the trial?" Kilburn asked, chain-lighting another cigarette. "Now that you've settled on the verdict, don't you think you ought to ask me some questions anyway? Just for the record?"

"I don't think we have to bother with that," St. John said. "We already know enough to open fire."

"And suppose what you know happens to be wrong? What are you going to do about that when they start shoving evidence at you in Washington?"

"In that highly unlikely situation," Daniell said, "presented with the irremediable fact of your death, I'm sure they will want to help us devise an explanation that will cover all possible contingencies."

"That's right," Winkler said. "I know we have to put this

man away. But even on the far-out hypothesis that we do wrong, the whole public relations of the thing mandates cooling it if it shows any tendency to make a wave."

"All right, then," St. John said. "What in hell are we waiting for? Somebody ask this man a few questions, or let's get it over with."

"I've got a question." Kilburn put up a hand. "Do you mind if I put my clothes on before you shoot me? If I'm going out, I'd like to do it in some kind of a uniform."

"No." Daniell shook his head. "That can come later. We'll see that your uniform is put on you after you're dispatched."

"I'd like to die like a soldier," Kilburn said. "With my buttons on."

"They're not your buttons anyway," Daniell reminded him. "That's the basic point of this proceeding. If you have your original KGB uniform somewhere about here, perhaps we can get it for you. We'll be happy to shoot you while you're wearing that."

"The condemned man usually gets a last wish," Byngham said. "Let him put his clothes on."

"Sure, Daniell," St. John said. "What difference does it make? It's not a real uniform—it's just something to wear. Give the son of a bitch his clothes. The least we can do is let him die like a man."

Before there could be another word, a sharp thump resounded from the door. Through the sudden quiet of the room there was heard, in slow and solid progression, two thumps more. And then silence.

"Who in hell can that be?" St. John's voice was low.

"I don't know," Daniell said. "It might be Ramrod."

"Could he have heard any of this?" The cigar seemed

suddenly infirm. "I thought you wiped out the bugs here."

"I would stake my career on it, General. And you don't have to lower your voice. He can't hear us out there. You know this place is thoroughly soundproofed."

"What do we do now?" Winkler's voice was a whisper.

Again there vibrated through the room a resolute thump as a fist struck at the door. Two more blows followed, the message as before.

"General," Daniell said to St. John, "just put that thing to Kilburn's head. If he makes a move, shoot him. I'll get rid of our visitor." He slipped his own gun into his pocket.

"Good." St. John moved behind Kilburn, put one arm around the colonel's neck, and placed the muzzle of the .45 against his temple.

Daniell flicked the wall switch, and they were all in darkness. As he turned the knob and pulled the door open by a few inches, he said, in a low and tentative tone, the single word "Yes?" But the moment the door came free, it was slammed open, striking fiercely against him, almost knocking him off balance. In the instant, someone came rushing into the room, fell upon him, and began to slap at his face, to punch at his chest and even his jaw, to tear with a frenzy of fingers at his shirt collar. He fell back into the room, the door wide open now, the light from the corridor streaming across the carpet.

"For Christ's sake!" St. John said. "It's a woman!"

Winkler, more observant, more military, sounded just as surprised. "It's Captain Thors!"

● WITNESS

The lights went on, Byngham having hurried to the switch. With their drawn pistols the three men stood unmoving as they observed the attack, as if unable to think of how or why to stop it. With one slim hand the lady held firmly to Daniell's shirt front, and he seemed unable to break loose. With her free hand she struck at his head with a fierce and abashing vigor.

Kilburn, ungripped and unwatched, moved from his chair and quickly put on his pants. Then he hurried to the struggling man and woman and briskly pulled them apart. Just as he got some space between them, Captain Thors let fly with a roundhouse slap at the general's face, half catching him on the jaw. The room shook with the cracking sound of it.

"All right, Captain," Kilburn said. "What's the meaning of this? You've just attacked a superior officer. A lieutenant general in the United States Army. I hope you've got a very good explanation for this—one that will carry some weight when we put this whole matter through channels."

"Yes—what have you to say for yourself?" Byngham's thick brows were joined in a fierce frown.

"Get her out of here!" Daniell stood back, as if expecting the others to carry out his command.

"Wait a minute—are you drunk, Captain?" St. John's tone was very harsh.

"Never mind what *I* am. Why don't you ask General Daniell what *he* is? Whether I've been drinking or not isn't important. A fact is a fact. Go ahead—ask him."

"What's this all about?" Winkler looked at Daniell, as if relieved to ask the question of him rather than the invader.

"That's right. Make him tell you," she said.

Daniell turned to St. John. "General," he said, "make this man sit down. Remember why we are here. First things first."

With the gun, St. John waved the colonel back into his chair.

Daniell's words came more easily now that he had put several feet of distance between himself and the captain.

"We don't want to lose ourselves in a diversion," he said. "And we have no way of knowing the real purpose of this interruption. How closely tied together these two are— Kilburn and our captain here."

She now leaped once more at Daniell, who backed off, throwing up his hands in a primitive defense. Winkler, shoving his gun into his belt, rushed to Daniell's side to help. He grabbed the captain firmly from behind, just as she broke into her brief:

"That's a damned lie! He *knows* it's a lie! He's just try-ing to cover up, that's all. He knows why I'm doing this— it's because I couldn't get anybody to help me, to do some-thing, to get a little justice around here. Colonel Kilburn told me there was nothing he could do, because General Daniell would only be able to talk his way out of it—"

"The lady is obviously hysterical," Daniell said.

"What's she talking about, anyway?" Byngham looked at Daniell.

"That's so, Daniell—what's she talking about?" St. John was impatient. "Let's finish with her—get her out of here so we can move with our own business."

"Yes, make him tell you all about it," the captain said. "Otherwise I'll tell you."

"It should be quite clear to all of us," Daniell said, "that our man is even shrewder than we have already given him credit for. He could not have known that we were going to pick him up tonight. And yet here before us, plain for each of us to see, is his cat's-paw. She is on the verge of breaking up our meeting—of creating a rout among us. Aren't we entitled to ask him some questions about the source of this curious—and, for him, extremely useful—coincidence?"

"That's a lot of crap!" she cried.

"Watch your language, Captain." Winkler, still holding her from behind, spoke firmly.

"Ask him about what he did to me," she said. "Ask him about the rape." She struggled in Winkler's arms, trying to turn around, to make the demand face to face.

"What rape?" St. John said.

"Yes. What do you mean, rape?" Byngham seemed suddenly becalmed by the image.

"Wait a minute, gentlemen," Daniell said. "We must not be panicked at this moment. National security may well hang in the balance—"

"That can wait a few minutes more," Byngham said. "This woman is accusing a general officer of the United States Army. What she's talking about is rape."

"Of course she is," Daniell said. "If you wanted a woman to step into a situation like this, to create maximum confusion among a group of American men, what other charge would you *have* her make against me? Is there any but this one—rape—that would better serve the purposes of an enemy who seeks to evade us?"

"That's right, General. Sneak out of it," she said. "Make it sound like it never happened at all. Or that I attacked *you*. Or that you *had* to do it to save the country. Dream up something. Anything. But you're not going to get away with it."

All of them could hear her breath rising and falling from the bosom that was rising and falling in the arms of General Winkler. Her mouth was unstill, her bobbed hair untidy. Every quality of her exterior person was in a state of completely mobilized and obvious despair. She was too agitated, and they knew her too well—or thought they did—to believe that she was faking.

"You tell us, then," St. John said.

"He came to the Dispensary the other evening. He was supposed to be sick. At least he told me that. He's sick, all right, but not the way he wanted me to think. Nobody is around there at night. So he grabbed me. He attacked me. While I was being a nurse, he was being a criminal. And this is supposed to be a general, a man who's protecting the country from our enemies. What I'm asking right now is, what about *him?* Who's going to protect the country from a man like him? Or at least who's going to protect a woman?"

"She's making a hell of a lot of noise over a pass," St. John said.

"It wasn't a pass. It was rape." The large green eyes trembled with anger.

"This isn't just a woman," Byngham said. "This is a captain. Someone wearing the commissioned uniform of the United States Army."

"She *says* I did it. She *says* she told it to our culprit here. She *says*. Are we going to be turned from a mission by something a woman says?"

"That's right—he's at it again," the captain cried. "If you don't believe me, ask Doctor Bosca. I told him all about it, and he said the same thing as Colonel Kilburn. That I wouldn't stand a chance. The whole Army is going to stick together to see that justice doesn't get done."

"Wait a minute, Captain," Winkler said, as she almost wrested herself loose from him. "That's no way to talk. How do you think they would handle a complaint like yours over *there?*"

"That's not the point at all," Byngham said. "I think we all ought to have a talk with Bosca. Find out if she really did speak to him."

"She undoubtedly did," Daniell said. "That would be an elementary step in the plan. A long and tearful complaint to our dear doctor, to ensure credibility at the denunciation level. And that's what she's on the verge of achieving right now."

"That's another damned lie!" she cried out. "He examined me. He had to clean up the results. It's rape."

"Captain," Daniell said, the tone sorrowful, "you *know* that is the biggest lie of all."

"A lie is a lie," she flung back at him. "And the truth is the truth. Go ahead. Ask Doctor Bosca. I dare you."

In the strained and uneasy silence, a more important event made itself suddenly clear. The armed men were concentrating so much attention on the diversion that they had neglected to watch carefully over the main enemy. Colonel Kilburn had chopped suddenly at the wrist of General St. John, had caught the falling gun in his hand, and now turned it on the others.

"General Daniell—put your gun over there." He nodded

to the sideboard. "And you three officers—please—put yours over there now, too." Then, "You just hold still, Captain." When the guns were at rest, he said, "Now everybody back—away from there. And remember—if I'm what you say I am, I've got nothing to lose right now."

With his free hand, the colonel picked up from the floor his remaining clothes, his eyes on the men.

"Get those guns, Captain," he said, "and follow me."

She did not move.

"What about him? What about what I came for—justice?" The voice wavered, but it was still inflamed.

"O.K. A little justice." With his gun he motioned for Daniell to stand clear of the others. "Now you walk up to him, Captain, and you give him the biggest wallop you know how."

"You'll never get away with it, Kilburn," St. John said. "You can't make a general in this Army stand still for a thing like that. I'll have your ass for this."

"If I'm the man this kangaroo Supreme Court has been claiming I am, then you'll have a lot more than this to knock me for. And if General Daniell is the man I think he is, you might want to get in line right behind her. Now, hit the son of a bitch, Captain."

"No," she said. "That's not enough."

"I can't let you shoot him. Not until we ask him a lot of questions. Now, are you coming with me, or do you want to stay here and plead your case?"

She hesitated.

"Grab the guns and come with me," he said.

At the sideboard she picked them up slowly, one by one, then went to open the door for him.

"We'll finish this later," he announced.

As she closed the door behind them, Daniell's words could be clearly heard: "The cleverest man they've got."

In the corridor, Kilburn made her hurry until they turned the next corner.

"You left out that part about him getting down to business with you, Captain," he said. "You never told me he actually got that far."

"He didn't. The way I told you is the way it really happened."

"Then why did you tell it like that to them?"

"I had to say *some*thing that would make an impression. He kept telling lies, and he was getting away with it. I had to tell one of my own, so they'd know the truth. I don't care about the facts. I know what's right."

● HORN CALL

In the office, before putting the rest of his clothes on, Kilburn called Ramrod on the intercom. Apologized for awakening him. Told him to have the special supplies removed from the closet and stored in the Wranglers' arsenal, in their barracks. Immediately.

Minutes later he was on his way to Dr. Bosca's rooms. The doctor, fully dressed, had been reading.

"They threw a court-martial at me," Kilburn was soon

explaining. He provided details. It was clear that Daniell was, as they had guessed, the hanging judge. The Thors interruption had come exactly in time.

"She broke up the party. Just laying it on the line about what Daniell did to her. The minute she said you'd given her that examination, making a real rape out of it, the wind changed. Things began to blow my way."

"It's nice to hear, Colonel, that there are still people in this country willing to take the word of a doctor. But our Miss Thors, a woman who is able to think on her feet like that, who can toss off a lie so brilliant that it confounds a blue-ribbon panel of professionals—a woman like that is wasted as a nurse. She should be handling diplomacy for some country at least the size of Austria. Do you realize what she has done, Colonel?"

"I don't suppose I'll know until you tell me."

"She—one woman alone—has restructured a situation of international importance. She has grabbed it by its primary equipment, you might say, and reduced it to its elementary human level. Here we are in the middle of a duel between mighty nations for custody of the earth, and she has squeezed the struggle down to its essentials—one man's testicles. That woman, Colonel, understands power."

"No. I didn't realize that," Kilburn said.

"But it's true. Do you know that if the hormones of Henry the Eighth had not broken ranks for Anne Boleyn, then you and I might be having this conversation in Spanish? Because it was that, my friend, that caused him, eventually, to want a divorce. And *that* caused his break with the pope. And *that*, in turn, gave England open season on what had formerly been a Spanish preserve, the Western Hemisphere."

"That's a good thing to know, Doctor. But meanwhile, I'm telling you something in plain English. I'd like you to act from now on as if what she said was true."

"But of course, my dear Colonel. I have no doubt that they will ask me, those dearly beloved men of action. I will spare them none of the horrendous details. The lacerations of the most intimate flesh, the ruptures corporeal and spiritual, the impotent weeping of the frail victim, and in the sacred vessel itself, of course, a full head of the brutal oppressor's perceptible steam. Leave it to me, Colonel—all the important notes in this mightiest of American horn calls will be individually sounded. By the time I am halfway through my diagnosis, nothing less than a public impaling will satisfy those men."

"That's exactly the feeling I want. I have to smoke out that cagey son of a bitch, and the only way I can do it now, fast, is to isolate him from the others."

"Naturally, Colonel. And I will be happy to do my professional share. We must cure the national patient of this local infection."

"Thanks. I'll see you tomorrow, Doctor. Start talking early."

● REASONS

When Kilburn turned the knob of his door and pushed only a few inches, what he saw made him back away instantly. The lights were on in his quarters, and he knew he had earlier turned them off.

"Come in, please." The words came from well inside the room. He was not surprised to recognize the voice.

He had made up his mind to carry a gun until the thing was settled. Feeling the weight and bulk of the .45 that he pulled from his belt, he was reminded of the pleasure he would feel if he could hold at this very moment that Russian pistol, trophy of the night assault in the john. But it was inside.

He stepped out of any likely line of fire and kicked the door wide.

Daniell was seated beside the card table that served as a desk. He was smoking a cigarette.

"I thought I might have to wait all night, Colonel," he said. "I've been keeping the latchstring out for you."

"What do you want?" He closed the door.

"You won't need the gun. I'm not armed."

"With a man like you, General, I'd like to be as comfortable as possible."

"As you wish. But please sit down. Put yourself at ease. We have things to talk about."

"Sure." Kilburn sat in a corner of the sofa. He placed the gun on the end table, not far from his elbow.

"I'd like to discuss a deal with you, Colonel. If you have no objection."

"I'm listening."

"As I see the situation, it's that most unfortunate of results, a dead heat. Not a clear-cut victory for your side or mine, and not even a mutually beneficial compromise. Just a vexing tie."

"Just which *is* your side, General? You've got a big record in our Army. And now you start throwing curves all over the place. Just between you and me and the tape recorder, what happened?"

"Colonel, if you really believe in the record you speak of, then you must not insult my intelligence. There is neither bug nor tape equipment here. You know it and I know it. As to the other, it may be hard to explain to you—without seeming to insult *your* intelligence. But, to enliven the minutes of this meeting, I shall try. You understand, of course, that any attempt by you to quote me I will immediately denounce as a black and perhaps mutinous lie."

"Sure."

"I would throw the considerable weight of my service, my rank, and my personal associations at you. An old Greek proverb I commend to your attention, Colonel: 'When you attack the king, you must kill him.' And in this case, as between you and me, I am of course the king."

"O.K. So why did you do it?"

"Quite a few reasons. Any single one of them, I suppose, might seem trivial, even eccentric. But throw them all into the scale, Kilburn, and they add up. At least for someone like me."

"What were they?"

"Let's assume I said, for one thing, that I consider American cooking a desecration. Would you find that convincing? No. That I think European cooking—almost any national cuisine—to be far more imaginative, tasty, conducive to an expansiveness of the spirit as well as the palate. That would mean nothing to a hamburger-and-coffee type like yourself, Colonel, would it?"

"Probably not."

"And it wasn't really money, actually. Their pay scales,

while handsome, could never compensate for the privileges and living allowances permitted a lieutenant general of our own Army. Especially in my branch of the service. The opportunity for free enterprise within the elastic boundaries of a secret and unquestioned budget borders on the flagrant, Colonel. But perhaps you are too honest to understand such things."

"Perhaps."

"Would you offer me some brandy, Colonel? To smooth the progress of our chat?"

"Help yourself. You know where it is."

Daniell rose and went to the sideboard. He continued to talk as he prepared his drink and then returned to his chair.

"It wasn't ideology, certainly, because I think theirs is at least as archaic as our own—if we have one. In fact, theirs is even less civilized, I would say, by some standards. But anyway, you mustn't think of me as one of their steeped-in-cosmoline, straight-from-the-factory fanatics, someone with two large steel ball bearings where his eyes ought to be."

"All right."

"Was it power?" Reflective puff of smoke from the cigarette. Pause. "Not in the conventional sense. After all, in view of my position in our own Army, how much, really, could they have offered me in the way of rank to exceed that? But even if they had, it would only have bored me. And that, I suppose—"

"What about women?" Kilburn said.

Daniell's smile was almost benign.

"What a charming thing to say, Colonel. What a wonderful asset you must be to an old-fashioned Christmas dinner for the whole family." He sighed, as if looking back across the years to some smooth and gentle time far beyond the sweaty, rock-strewn present. "It must be marvelous to be able to still think, seriously, of a man throwing up a world for one other person—in this case, of course, female."

"What about that London thing? The reason you're here? That's no secret."

"And it wasn't meant to be, Colonel. It went according to plan. It was designed to achieve maximum internal concern. How else could I possibly manipulate matters so as to be assigned to the Ranch?"

"Why didn't they send a younger man?"

"It was far easier to get in at the top. Besides, have a thought for me, Kilburn. Those hot-eyed kids, so full of high ideals and low cunning, they have all the fun. Spread it around, I say."

"What about that pass you made at Captain Thors? Was that just part of some plan too?"

"Exactly, Colonel. I already knew all I could hope to find out about this place—all that I needed to know. My mission was a complete success. The Ranch, I had discovered, pristine, expensive, and topmost secret of the mightiest of powers, is only a gilded cage for a few overwrought and overage birds of paradise that have lost their voices, their plumage, and much of their brains—if they ever had that. Under any intelligent social system, such men would be programed for euthanasia. They would be put out of their and the national misery in a neater, more sensible and inexpensive manner. One can accept functional reasons for a Fort Knox, for burying gold in the ground, but to confuse men like Wadlow, Byngham, and the rest with some major national asset is to bring up the kind of thinking that only reinforces me in my original decision. You are a very lucky man, Colonel. It has never been a duty or a necessity of yours to spend much time listening to the conversation of American leaders."

"I'm listening to one right now."

"Congratulations. You have just scored a point—as they would say at an exciting high-school debate."

"You were telling me why you tried to jump Captain Thors."

"Yes, I was. When I discovered the secret of all this complicated machinery—to keep a pack of military zeroes in a state of overindulged nonbeing—it was time for me to transmit the message. And that, I discovered, was the most difficult part of my assignment. It was far easier to get in than it was to get out. I decided to do the one thing that might get me sent out of here—under a cloud, perhaps, but sent out nevertheless. And I had to get out somehow, if I was to contact one of my people."

" 'My people'?"

"I didn't know you were such a connoisseur of syntax, Colonel. For the moment, or at least for the purposes of this discussion, I feel safe in using that construction. Try not to let it bother you. You and I have more important things to consider. In any case, attempted rape was apparently not provocative enough (to anyone but the Captain, that is) to get me flown out of here for moral, military, or whatever reasons. Official American attitudes about rape would seem to be taking on a traditional European tone. I therefore had to think of something else."

"Why did you attack that Wrangler? How could that help you?"

"It could cause official concern. And that was absolutely

necessary, since I'd missed killing you. And I'm sorry about *that*, Colonel. I'm sure you understand there was nothing personal in it. But all these touches, in addition to putting away a psychopathic fossil like Wadlow, they were necessary to the composition. Only when these things, or at least a few of them, could be seen as creating a pattern of disaster, might I hope that the Guests would be transferred out of harm's way. Away from here. Once they were in transit, in almost any direction, the seal would be broken and I could then make appropriate contact. You see, Colonel, if only your attitude toward rape had not been so horribly modern—if you could have been decently appalled by it—then much of this violence would have been unnecessary. So my conscience is actually quite clear. *You* are largely responsible for much of what has happened. A thought for the future, Colonel: the mature man learns from his mistakes. Next time, take rape a little more seriously."

"You never did tell me the big reason they got you to turn around. If it wasn't money, power, women, some party line, then what was the big idea?"

"The big idea, Colonel, so big, in fact, that your mind may have some problem encompassing it, is the one indispensable challenge to the really civilized man—the assault on the final redoubt of boredom. In a life in which all is not merely possible, or even probable, but in most cases unavoidable, it is not easy to feel a sense of really deep and fulfilling arousal. Some of us yearn for the ultimate challenge to those ultimate qualities which make the difference between a man as nature intended him, and men as fabricated in multimillion-unit lots. All political factions—democracy, communism, or whatever—they represent a 'we.' An artist, which in a way I have the pretension to consider myself, is always an 'I.' Unlike the rest of the population, who love to sing songs and shout slogans about the beauty of marching arm in arm into some new dawn, we fellows are scared witless by the prospect of climbing into a Waring Blendor with the rest of the crowd. We can't even get along with each other, when you get right down to it. Each of us is in business for himself. At heart, I suppose, I'm really an anarchist."

"You mean that if *they* had some outsize secret—we couldn't figure it out—and it was burning a big hole in some of *our* projections, then you might still be working for us?"

"Unquestionably, my dear fellow. When a man gets to my age, he requires a real challenge even more desperately than when he's a looser-limbed, looser-minded fellow like yourself. Otherwise I just might wind up in a place like this one as a *real* patient. I suppose the basic failure is in appropriate opportunity of a certain kind for the citizen approaching his 'golden years.' I'm sure you're familiar with the ritual argument, Colonel."

"I've heard it. Actually, General, I have the feeling I've heard everything."

"Good. Then we can go on to the real reason I called this meeting."

"Sure."

"I'm prepared to make a deal with you. You let me leave here on the next plane—I would suggest a medical explanation. It can be some suitably mysterious complaint with which Doctor Bosca, despite his professional wisdom, is powerless to deal. In return for that, you achieve a measure of official serenity here. Trouble-free repose. Or at least no less than is customary in this de luxe wind tunnel."

"Is that it? The whole deal?"

"Yes. And a handsome one it is for you, too. You will have wiped the slate clean of the enemy."

"How do I write it up in my report? How do I explain, for instance, about Secretary Wadlow? He's got three bullet holes in him. Do you want me to spell him out as a slow suicide?"

"We mustn't strain the official grasp of probability. And I wasn't merely theorizing, earlier, when I threw out those remarks about selective euthanasia. It's really only a delayed form of eugenics. We select one of the Guests, put him away discreetly with one or two bullets, and then invent an appropriate scenario about two Napoleons warring for custody of the only available Alp. I assure you it will be very convincing. I would recommend Byngham as the victim. He has bored me the most during my stay here. But you might prefer a more obvious moral dropout, like Cadetti. It would be even easier for you, then, to revel in the social benefit of the occasion."

"Wadlow has been missed already. You probably saw to that. None of the Guests would believe your kind of story about Byngham or Cadetti if we knocked either one of them over. Especially after that trial."

"Colonel, you are talking about what is believed by a handful of men, each one of them a resident here for some deviation from the national cerebral norm. Are you suggesting that the collective opinion of a wardful of established lunatics, even at *their* level of eminence, would count more than the orderly and precise evaluation of a highly regarded and on-the-line colonel in Counterintelligence? Reality is only what you officially say it is, Colonel. We both know that. Contradiction of what you say will be stamped appropriately—fantasy, insanity, irrationality, gossip, or even Commie talk."

"Well, suppose you're right about that part of it. Who's going to put Byngham or Cadetti away for us?"

"Only a detail, Kilburn. I'll be happy to take care of it personally. It will present no real problem."

"You'd need a gun, of course."

"Yes. At the moment, none of my own are available."

Kilburn said nothing. The gray eyes appeared to be studying the neat beauty of what the general was constructing.

"As simple as that," Daniell said. "Everyone profits that way. The ideal resolution of any disagreement among reasonable men."

"But actually, General, the profit for your crowd is a little more. Isn't it? When you fly away they're going to know something they never knew before. What you'll tell them about the Ranch. That they can stop worrying about it."

"Yes. And you and yours can in turn stop worrying about the consequences of our worrying about it."

"But does that really make us even, General? One of the big reasons for a place like this, for all the security around here, is to keep your guys from knowing what's going on. To keep you off balance. To keep you thinking something bigger—or at least different from what it is—is going on here. To keep your men and functions busy with trying to figure it out. And as long as you don't have that figuring to do any more, that makes your team a few points ahead, doesn't it?"

"No doubt about it, Colonel. But that will be our little secret. It will not be as if you have passed along the keys to four or five nuclear submarine bases. It will be only an inert fact, at best, that we permit to leave here—one that has been merely lying around up here in Idaho, inactive, in a state of negative usefulness."

"No." Kilburn shook his head.

For a moment, Daniell hesitated.

"Always an interesting word," he said. "What shall I attach to it—my description of this place? Or some other item in our discussion?"

"No deal."

"Why not, Colonel?"

"Two reasons. One, it wouldn't be right."

"Let's not get involved in a debate on morality, Colonel. You and I are both too grown-up for that. We don't have principles. They're much too expensive for a world like this one. We have interests. What's the other reason?"

"I just don't like to see a prick get away with murder."

Daniell puffed a thick cloud of cigarette smoke to the ceiling. "Well, Kilburn," he said, "I have to admit you are certainly consistent. You really are a very old-fashioned fellow, and I can only wish you the best of luck with these virtues. But tell me, what happens now? Are you going to denounce me to your superiors? Demand a court-martial for me? Watch my friends and fellow professionals—all in grades considerably higher than your own, of course— join in my defense? Do you imagine for one moment, Colonel, that a house painter will be permitted to publicly scrawl a mustache on an El Greco? If you believe that, then you don't belong in a trade so defiantly labeled Intelligence. We need our heroes more than ever now, when so much of reality has failed us. Only the product of the human imagination has real value these days, Kilburn. That was implicit in what I told you about my reasons for turning around. The press and TV, those blind Homers who work up the dreams of the country, have ground their imagination to the bone to invest me with very special qualities. Just so we could have one more hero—someone to do the job the average fellow doesn't have the stomach or other equipment for. That's the whole point of having heroes, Kilburn. And now you want to hack me loose from the niche where I've been so carefully placed. They'll never let you do it."

"Most of the time, General, you've been telling me I was outranked by the crowd no matter *what* they did. Then, a minute ago, you were putting me in charge of reality around here. Now I'm demoted again. What happened?"

"*I* happened, Colonel. As an ally I can help you to make history for yourself. As an enemy, I will send you to disaster. Remember, unlike the others I am in full possession of all my faculties. And even more to the point, I am especially trained in the sculpture of public opinion. I'll ignore the fact that you don't have a shred of evidence. But even if you had an open-and-shut legal case, it would be uphill all the way for you. And if you succeeded, it would be worse—you would never be forgiven by the press, by any superior officer, or by any churchgoing American citizen. You would have been a very bad boy, Kilburn—you would have been caught relieving yourself in the lagoon at the Lincoln Memorial. Is that what you want?"

"No. It isn't."

"Well, what happens now, then?"

"Wait and see."

"You surprise me, Colonel. You have a flair for the cryptic."

"I also have a gun, and a few other things."

"Yes. And a dead body somewhere about. How do you expect to explain that one to Washington?"

"I'll think of something, General, now that you've told me how. I'll imagine it, then pin a label on it, and that's the way it'll be."

"Congratulations. I had no idea you were such a quick study."

Daniell rose and went to the door.

"If you change your mind," he said, "please do not hesitate to call me."

● THE KNOWLEDGE OF EVIL

Sergeant Yost never ate his meals at the same table as Captain Thors. To do so, he had suggested to her, would be to violate certain laws of logic. How would it be if a police chief was seen frequently enjoying himself at table with a Mafia don? Would not people begin to ask questions? And the answers to such questions, no matter how smoothly contrived, would arouse a suspicion. And suspicion was the mother of investigation. It might even be the grandmother of indictment. It was therefore best for her to continue eating her meals alone, at her own little corner table, the one that bore the burned-in-the-wood sign *Dietitian.*

At one of the smaller tables, he ate breakfast alone. As usual, he had scrambled eggs with smoked sausage, two flapjacks, orange juice, toast, and coffee. After that, the best part of all, the lazy cigarette. He had puffed halfway through it when he realized that Dr. Bosca, at the next table with Admiral Byngham, was giving some kind of seminar on rape. Sergeant Yost never ceased to marvel at the kinds of material that could seem to erupt so casually from a book-lined European mind. This one, anyway. He could hear the voice humming smoothly over the subject, low and sure.

"Throughout history," he heard the doctor say, "we find society stringing barbed wire around certain areas of human expression. Certain fringe aspects of romance are tabooed by the lawmakers. Otherwise, all the library paste that keeps a nation together may begin to melt. So there are the most forbidding judgments against willful violation of the horizontally permissible. The seduction of the young? Very bad. Perversion? The same. Forms of personal affirmation which might be all right in some obviously decaying culture like France are frowned on for the neighborhood. You are a well-traveled man, Admiral, so I need not bore you with examples. But worst of all, of course, is rape. Because there a sin is committed that goes far beyond that of consenting adults who may thumb their noses, in bed, at the mores of the community. There, the very foundation stone of society is attacked—private property—the right of the citizen to call something his own, and so—"

"You examined her thoroughly, Doctor?" The admiral's tone was hard.

"No question about it. I don't care to go once more into the unfortunate medical details. But think back to what I told you about the lesions along the tract; the bruised perineum; the distinct discoloration of Bartholin's gland, as if the most brutal force had been brought to bear. I can assure you, Admiral, an experience like that, such a barbarous invasion of the sanctuary, will take the heart out of the average woman, to say nothing of the more obvious effects. What General Daniell did is more than shameful. It is a sin against the American spirit. I have, as a medical man, seen the results of abominable acts in many countries. 'Man's inhumanity to man,' et cetera. And woman too. But here, Admiral, we live in a condition of government that would make the Athenian Republic cringe with envy, if only they could train their binoculars on us from across the centuries. And what do we find? In the very heartland of that democracy, here at the Ranch?"

"What?"

"Right here, Admiral, a man who poses as a paragon of the American virtues chooses to play ruthless commissar to one other human being, against her will. Democracy is a compact among peoples which implies the consent of the majority. And as between one man and one woman, a single vote cannot constitute such a majority. I have seen the results of that overriding decision by General Daniell, I have seen it on the person of Captain Thors, just as clearly as millions were able to see the results of what Mr. Hitler did to Madame Poland."

The doctor was still talking when Yost rose from the table.

On his way to the office, a part of his mind stood off, like a court reporter, calmly noting the tumult of thoughts in the main arena. A disorder of interior sounds, pressures, demands, was providing a churning steam of energy that pressed him in the direction of an inexorable verdict. There were some things that society had no right, no business even trying, to forbid. The jury jumbling and crying about in his mind had already turned in its decree: General Darwin I-Am-Above-the-Law Daniell would have to pay for what he had done. And it didn't matter what the consequences were likely to be. Even if the doctor could be persuaded to give testimony at the eventual court-martial, a mere sergeant would never be excused for taking the law into his own hands like that. What were laws for if not to be obeyed, even by those who mean to make a vocation of them? And as for Daniell, what good was a law if it didn't work to put a fence around *everybody* in a matter as crucially important as rape? How could it be respected if it was designed to cover everybody but carried hidden in its text an invisible but functional clause that began "except—"? The minute you did a thing like that, you punched a hole in the idea of all men being equal under the law. Right now he would attend to the exception of General Daniell.

Colonel Kilburn had not yet come into the office, and the sergeant was glad of that. The sheriff just might smell something about the way the sergeant was acting, and then he might throw an order, or even a punch, just to keep the sergeant from doing something he might later be sorry for.

In the file drawer, alongside the office automatic, there were four additional guns. He did not wonder how they had got there. But he noticed that one of them, small, sleek and foreign-looking, was nonregulation. Because it seemed more ready to the hand, he picked it from among the others. He saw that it was loaded, slid it into the pocket of his pants, and walked from the office.

Only briefly was he touched by the thought of final verdict. His mind was feeling too much the joy of running free, beyond the niggardly constraints of law and covenant. He was on the way to do something that, regardless of any future penalty, was now so totally rewarding that he could feel a rich and warming torrent of rightness surging through him. And along with that was the homelier warmth at the thought of Susan. It was so like her to protect him. She had not told him the whole story because she had been afraid that he might do something foolish.

● LAST WORDS

There was, for all the Guests, an hour or so after breakfast, before class, when they could make their varieties of peace with nature. He knew that General Daniell, for this reason, would probably be in his quarters by now.

He knocked twice.

When the door opened, the general did not appear surprised to see who it was.

"Yes, Sergeant?"

"I have a message for you, sir," he said.

"What is it?"

"It's official." The words came from him as if automatically, the product of some alert interior machinery. "I'd better tell you inside. Where it's soundproof." That message too seemed devised by some part of his brain that was doing its own thinking, far in advance of anything the sergeant had outlined for himself.

The door opened wider, and when it was shut behind him, he withdrew the gun from his pocket.

"This is the message, General," he said. "You took something that didn't belong to you. Now you're going to pay for it. Just like anybody else who steps out of line and gets caught."

"Wait a minute, Sergeant—what is this all about? Does Colonel Kilburn really believe he can resolve our little problem by sending a gunman in here? Is that it? He's talked you into violating the firmest administration procedures—ordered you to kill a lieutenant general of our own Army. Is that it? And you, Sergeant, without any thought for your own oath, your own career, are going to play zombie to his commands. Is that it?"

"No. It's all my own idea. He doesn't even know about it."

"What is this all about, then, Sergeant? Put that gun away. We'll sit down, you and I, and we'll talk this over man to man, without regard for rank or uniform."

"I don't want to talk about it. I don't want to hear any explanations about it. I just want to kill you."

"But why, Sergeant? At least tell me that."

"Because of what you did to Miss Thors."

"What I did to Miss Thors? You come at me with a gun because of *that?*"

"She's my wife."

"Your *wife?*"

The general's features were contorted, the outline of an internal drama. Incomprehension was struggling with disbelief.

"Anyway, General," the sergeant said, "here's the rest of the message: Fuck you!" He fired two shots. Almost instantly, a gratifying red blur began to spread over that portion of the tan shirt under which the heart should be. The body fell awkwardly to the floor, sounding out a brief expiration of air. Only the most poetic mind could interpret it as the soul's melody, a sigh. In his going, the general left no distinctive visiting card suitable to his station, no winged final words to gild the moment for schoolboys and librarians.

The sergeant put the gun back in his pocket and turned to the door. But in that moment he was struck by how very easily he had managed matters so far. Consequences that only moments ago were too timid to assert themselves were now pounding noisily at his mind. Not only good-by to Susie, to the law, to the Army, but in a thoroughly disheartening way, to life itself.

Already a team of instinctive attorneys were engaged in working out his defense. He surveyed the rooms, looking for the obligatory bugs, but could find none. That did not surprise him, because he could not really expect to find them so quickly. But General Daniell had been a master of the Intelligence arts. So it was not improbable that *he* had found and deactivated the transmitters. More, it was logical to think of him doing that. Therefore it might not even be necessary for the sergeant to somehow get access to those tapes, at Message Center, and erase the record of the morning's event. His skin tingled from the sudden hope.

But then he was struck down by a point that had escaped him while he searched for the bugs. A loose end stuck out of the situation, and it was long enough to hang him: Susie had been to see Colonel Kilburn about General Daniell's attack. And she had no doubt told him the true story of the rape, not just the cover story she had palmed off on her own husband. To Colonel Kilburn, the killer and the motive would be only too clear.

Judgment. There would, after all, be payment for breaking the law. He felt cast down with a sudden and frightening reality. The brief assurance that he might, quite easily, be able to get away with it, had been a dreamland idea. The mind's unrest had been stilled. But now, with sudden awareness of what Colonel Kilburn knew, there came the guarantee of punishment. The loss of the earlier innocence was demoralizing.

His mind clattered with the sounds and sights of a chaotic documentary movie: *Death of a Hero*. Visions of trial, headline, public uproar.

But the private hell was the worst. Through every single minute of his life, beginning very soon, a rock-bound solitary confinement. Not only had he committed the worst of all Army crimes, the killing of a superior officer, but more, he had assassinated a celebrated and unreplaceable unit in the control panel of American security.

He went to the door, opened it carefully, and looked out. No one was around. He hurried back to the office.

Colonel Kilburn was not there, so, before placing the gun back in the drawer, he had time to remove the shells. In the bathroom, he watched as they flushed away. Then he sat down at his desk to do some thinking. But he was aware of only a hodgepodge of thoughts in the service of memory and wish, images that wore the disguise of thinking. He did not regret what he had done. He regretted only that he had not given sufficient study, in advance, to how he might get away with it.

He wondered how long it would be before someone found the body.

● THE ORDEAL OF THE FACT

If the brain is "that organ with which we think that we think," then for Sergeant Yost it had whirred to a stop. Or perhaps it had simply been drowned in the surge of feelings that swelled through him. He knew he could not be thinking, because there was not a single essential point now presented by his mind that could have passed muster with that stern and anonymous editor back there at the Phoenix Academy of Law and the Juridical Sciences. It was always the same man who marked his papers, he knew, because the handwriting, with the detached t-bars and the billowing loops, was unmistakable.

Anyway, at the moment he was in the worst condition that could be suffered by a man who had to do some real thinking. He was filled with feelings—the enemies of argument. He was a walking example of why no lawyer should plead for himself, why it meant having a fool for a client. But as he strode up the corridor toward the kitchen only one thing seemed to matter.

He wanted to tell Susan everything as soon as possible. His mind had junked the earlier movie for a fresh one. Because the way the Army was likely to feel about what he had done, there was every reason to expect that, once apprehended, he would sink from sight. The interests of national security would be invoked at once to serve the needs of those who would make a lesson of the man who dared to frag a general.

All those black tomorrows were to be endured.

He thought once more of the sacrifice made by his wife,

hiding from him the degree of General Daniell's crime. What could he expect from a stone-faced panel of field-grade officers, when his counsel invoked the Unwritten Law at that court-martial?

SUMMARY:

In view of the fact that rape is not really rape in time of war, or certainly under critical field conditions; and since the character of the Ranch was such as to call into being an atmosphere of special national crisis which must have been the moral equivalent of war (the prosecuting officer would be bound to bring that one up) —THEN, how seriously could that charge of rape be taken by a panel of seasoned officers? Especially when they were anxious to discourage the killing of one of their own for *any* reason? And even though the victim of the rape had worn a U.S. Army uniform, did that necessarily make the assault on her more criminal? No. BECAUSE—the prosecutor would leap without fail onto exactly this important point—the woman, for reasons of her own, had forfeited her right to official, or legal, or even decent consideration. (*Remember, gentlemen, this officer, so called, had no compunction about violating her oath to the Army—she withheld from her superiors the fact of her dishonorable marriage to the confessed killer, Sergeant Yost.*)

Anyway, it was bound to be one of the quickest fake trials since those Russians organized their Ministry of Justice.

And all this his wife had tried to prevent by keeping from him the one glaring fact that she must have known would cause it all. How could he ever convey to her the richness of gratitude and love he felt for her concern for him? A lifetime would not do it. And certainly not the kind of lifetime he was about to face. But before that there was an immediacy to his feelings, an arousal of demand, a swelling assertion of longing for her that could be soothed only with that ineffable—and probably final—Yes.

She stood at the broad, waist-high counter, her back to him. She was telling the assisting Wrangler that he had already prepared enough string beans.

"Captain—could I speak to you for a minute?"

She turned at the sound of his voice. There was compression around her lids and brows, a sense of curiosity. He had never come into the kitchen like this before. He could read that in her face.

"Only a minute," he said. And because the lean, browned Wrangler was still within hearing distance, he beckoned to her to come toward him, to walk as he was walking, off to a private corner of the kitchen. Sounds of ironware and murmurs.

"What is it, Sergeant?" she said, as soon as they were beyond the others' hearing.

"I have to tell you something." He tried to keep his face bland, but it was not easy. He knew that it told her he was living through some kind of clamorous happening.

"What is it?" Her voice was suddenly lower.

"I don't want to tell you here. I'm going to my room. You come by there in three minutes. It's important. I have to see you."

"It's really *that* important?"

She looked startled, of course. It was unheard of for him to make a request like this during duty hours. And to *his* room? But then, how could she know what he had done only moments before, to deserve the right to make such a demand of her?

He nodded.

"All right. In three minutes, then." She turned and went back to the pile of green beans that had been left on the counter.

The sergeant moved off.

When he answered her quick and quiet knock, he was already half undressed, his profile a billboard of v·sible intent.

"For God's sake," she said, "is *this* what you call d me out of the kitchen for?"

"I don't want to make a debate out of it, Susan," he said. "I just want to climb all over you, inside of you, every-thing—"

"Now? Right now?" She stood only a few feet from the door, as if she couldn't wait to turn and leave him there, with his tongue hanging out, as it were. She did not under-stand. But then, how could she?

"I know all about it, Susie," he said. "About you and General Daniell."

"You've known about it for a couple of days. And you call me out of the kitchen just to talk about it again, like this?"

"I don't want to talk about it—*you* do. I want to make love. Besides, I know the part of it you didn't tell me. About his raping you. The doctor was telling somebody about it in the Dining Room this morning."

"That's a lie, Norm. All he did was what I told you he did."

"He's a doctor. Why would he lie about it?"

"Because he thought he was telling the truth, that's why."

She hurried through some of the highlights of the night before. Her assault on General Daniell's quarters. The wild and sudden charge she had made against him when she discovered him surrounded and supported by his peers. Colonel Kilburn on display in shorts alone. The confusing melodrama of guns, and other things unexplained. "But what I told them wasn't true. It was something I *had* to tell them. I was drinking, Norm. I *had* to say something that would make them take me seriously, to get them to listen. Doctor Bosca probably heard it from someone who was there. So he's telling it to people as if it's actually a fact."

He had never heard a more ridiculous cover story in his life. She would never make a good lawyer, a good Intelligence operative, or anything else, for that matter, that required a sensible capacity for organizing the facts. But she was doing it all to keep him from feeling bad, and that of course outweighed every other consideration. He was lucky, glad, overwhelmed to be married to a woman like that.

"Look, Susie," he said, "I don't want to waste any more time talking about it. Start taking off your clothes while I wrap this up. Doctor Bosca wasn't talking just about what he heard. He was giving out medical details. He examined you right after it happened. Nobody told him what Daniell did to you. He was telling what he saw, the internal bruises —and you should have told me about that, so I could at least have been a little more gentle—"

"Norm." She said it to interrupt him, making no move to undress. "What do I have to do, or say, to convince you that it never happened? Do you want to go with me to the doctor sometime today and get the facts from him? The real facts?"

"O.K.," he said. "Then let's get it over with. If we have this hanging over us for the rest of our lives, then every time we get near a bed, we'll only talk." The rest of our lives. He thought he had done very well to keep the bitterness out of his voice. "Let's go talk to him right now."

"Have you gone crazy? He's in class. We can't break up his schedule just to ask him a thing like this. Besides, now that I think of it, I don't believe it's such a good idea to ask him. He'll know we're married then. Is that what you want?"

The old story of the inept witness. Trap him in one lie and he moves effortlessly into another. Each time getting himself deeper and deeper into the unequivocal glue of the facts.

"Susie," he said, "first you tell me Doctor Bosca can settle it all for us. Then you tell me you don't want him to settle it all for us. What in hell am I supposed to believe now? I don't give a damn any more who knows we're married. Kilburn probably knows it already. So it doesn't matter any more who else knows it." He began to put on the things he had earlier removed, almost angry with her for this foolish and transparent lying. It was only the goodness of her intent that kept him from exploding at her. She was obviously struggling to keep from him the pain of the irrevocable final fact of rape. He went to the door. "Let's get it over with. Let's go."

When this difference of opinion—now almost irrelevant —was resolved, he would be able to tell her about how he had dealt with General Daniell.

She looked at him for a moment longer, as if to measure precisely the intensity of his will.

"All right, Norm." Her voice was quiet.

He opened the door for her, and then for the first time, as if neither of them any longer gave a damn, they walked up the corridor together.

● PROFESSIONALS

Once again, as a precaution of the night, he had braced a chair against the door and on the chair had balanced a lamp.

In the morning he was up early, and within ten minutes he was rapping on Ramrod's door.

Kilburn wasted no time telling the story. Ramrod, as so often, listened with a special stillness, his eyelids low, as if watching carefully to see that no one in the world tried to violate some private radar pattern of acceptable behavior.

"I'm breaking security to put it on the table, Major. Because right now I need every ally I can get."

"Why don't we do it by the book? Pick up the son of a bitch and throw charges at him. Ship him out of here on a rocket. They know how to pump a creep like that in Washington."

All the qualities of ultimate resolution that are normally attributed to time and miracle are by some people attributed to their headquarters.

"Can't. He hasn't left us any margin," Kilburn said. "No clues, no hints, no evidence that would stand up. It would be my word against his. When's the last time you heard of a colonel laying out a three-star general?"

"Then what's our move?"

"I don't know yet. He's bound to try something new

soon. But what he really wants is to get out of here, so it's the one thing we can't let happen. No matter what he does."

"With all he's done already, including stabbing one of my men, we're just supposed to sit here and wait?"

"Remember, I can't even tell a good lie yet about what happened to Wadlow. We have to catch Daniell cold. Otherwise he screams to his pals. When he hollers 'frame-up' all over Washington, I can sing good-by to that star—and to a lot of other things."

"So, with all he knows, and all he's done, we're just going to talk, while he's figuring out how to get away with it?"

"What would you do?"

"Blast him."

"This isn't Pleiku, and he's not just some brownie we're talking about who's been getting into our poobs. We're dealing with somebody special. What would you do if you had proof the president was a Commie, but it wasn't the kind of proof you could get anyone to believe—would you shoot him too?"

"I sure would."

"No matter what else happened?"

"No matter what else happened. I'm a soldier. You're a soldier. When there's nothing else to do, you do what you think is best, no matter how the cards are stacked."

"Do you realize what this could mean, if we did what you're practically saying?"

"Do you realize what it could mean if we didn't?"

"Major, you're talking about murder."

"I am like hell. I'm talking about national security. Capital punishment. Battlefield justice. I'm talking about a lot of things, but not a single one of them is murder."

"And how do we explain it when they ask us what happened?"

"One shot in the head—a fake suicide—and we hardly have to think at all."

"Probably. Most of the thinking will come from having to explain Wadlow, anyway."

"That can come later. This guy is now. I feel very personal about him."

"So do I. I never felt so personal about a guy in my life."

They knew that General Daniell would be at breakfast, and decided to wait, to give him time to return to his quarters. They smoked two cigarettes each, talking of nasty situations they had shared, and then went by separate routes to Daniell's room. Ramrod walked more slowly, to permit Kilburn first crack at the door.

They stood over the body for an instant in silence. Then Ramrod asked his question, for the record:

"You didn't do this last night, did you? Just between you and me?"

"No. I'm just as surprised as you are."

"It looks like somebody was real mad at him."

"We've got a few suspects, if I think about it."

"Well, anyway, it saves us a big problem."

"No. Just because somebody else did it, that doesn't prove that you or I didn't. It could still mean my ass."

"It's too bad he couldn't get himself shot in the head, instead of the chest."

"Yes. If you got a sleeping bag, could you get this thing over to the meat room? Leave it there for a while? It'll have to leave on the afternoon plane, with the other one."

There could of course be no more waiting.

"Sure. You think you can come up with something by then?"

"I don't know. But I'm going to give it a hell of a try."

After Ramrod left, Kilburn set himself to thinking. He had several hours, yet, before the helicopter. So he had exactly that much time to think up a buyable explanation.

Could Captain Thors have killed him?

No.

Daniell had only made a crude pass at her. Women didn't shoot three-star generals for a thing like that, not even in silent movies.

He was facing a real problem now. In its own way, it was as big as the original one.

He would wait in his office until class was over, and then speak to Bosca. The doctor might have some ideas. Meanwhile, he wondered, where had the gun come from? General St. John, that strong-arm lunatic? No. Could it be one of the Wranglers, picking up the scent on Daniell and getting back at him for that knifing? Impossible. He flipped through his memory trying to find some time when he had been in quite this bad a situation. Never.

● CONSULTATION

Dr. Bosca had meant to take the class, that morning, on yet another campaign through the merits of true belief. A wise one was best, of course, especially if it could be objectively validated, but for achieving results, almost any deeply felt belief would serve. It was the universal solvent that could drain the sludge from the machinery that moved the world. It was the magic that relieved man from the perils of thinking, of imagination, of fret and worry. It dispersed the inner demons that lay in ambush along the path to achievement and repose. The Greeks, of course, had allowed rationalism to the few, while encouraging religion for the many. A wise society, if one made the usual allowances for infanticide, human sacrifice, a frivolous theology, a war over a woman, and other foolishness. (Class discussion.)

Discarded.

He would have to improvise, now, a lecture more fitting to the needs of the occasion. A rape had not only been attempted, but it had been committed. He would fill the classroom air with material likely to stir up the students about the enormity of General Daniell's act. And even though that act had not really taken place, well, that tied in rather neatly, Dr. Bosca thought, with the original lesson plan. By the time he was finished with the students this morning, he was sure he could have them committed to the belief— despite anything General Daniell might claim to the contrary—that rape had been done. There wasn't a fact in the world that could hold up against the feeling he was about to set afire.

Daniell was not in class, but the doctor was not surprised. There were sure to be other evidences of his elusiveness in the time before some decision would be made.

On the blackboard the doctor spelled out in large letters the topic for the day:

SEX AND POWER

There had been much talking among the men when he entered the room. They continued to mutter, now and then, as he moved into the subject:

ITEM:

Just because a man becomes important, powerful, great, we must not forget that he carries along with him, to this high place, all the interior baggage that entitles him to the label *human being*.

ITEM:

A president of the French Republic, late in the last century, while entertaining a lady visitor one afternoon in a room of the Elysée Palace, was persuaded by her responses to such unbearable spiritual heights that he could no longer sufficiently maintain the discretion appropriate to the leader of a major world power. Locked against her, he died, his fingers so clenched in her hair as to fix her head in a politically awkward position. Her scream, which brought the guards on the run, was carefully deleted from history, along with the visit itself, in the interests of more important French concerns. Had the president committed an antisocial act? No, the doctor said. The will of both parties was no doubt in at least preliminary agreement.

ITEM:

Early in our century, a lady picketed the White House with a sign that demanded justice for her daughter. The Chief Executive had sired the child, she claimed, during a romantic moment in the coatroom of the Senate Office Building. Was this rape? No, because the lady herself professed as often and in as many ways as possible that it had resulted from the mysterious workings of a shared love.

ITEM:

A great prime minister of Britain, scholars are aware, was in the habit of absenting himself from duller meetings of his cabinet in order to spend twenty minutes or so in unusual office procedures with one of the more attractive secretaries. Was this rape? Probably not. Even those who may touch at power only from below may yet enjoy the privilege.

Power has no sex, the doctor pointed out, after a few brief and instructive facts about Catherine the Great. It was equally true, he noted, that one human being crying out alone against the evils of power was usually impotent. *Unless,* and this was an important point, the victim chose to bring his (in the immediate context, more likely, *her*) arguments before the world in a democracy. Because that was what democracy was for—to bring about a truly equal franchise for every citizen, up to and including the rights of the boudoir.

Dr. Bosca was gratified to see, as he touched on the luminous points of this area, that the class had fallen silent. It was giving him all its attention. He took relish from the easy statement that in a wonderful country like America, only here, probably, could it be truly said that even in bed the man was not necessarily always on top. Because democracy demanded its fee everywhere in our society.

The doctor was about to set forth some examples, to work his way in easy stages through the kind of scholarship most likely to intensify feeling about General Daniell, when the door swung open.

"I'm sorry to break in like this, Doctor." It was Sergeant Yost. "I wonder if I could speak to you for a minute —out here in the hall?"

"Certainly, Sergeant."

He stepped into the corridor, saw Captain Thors, and nodded agreeably to her.

The sergeant shut the door, closing the three of them away from the class.

"This morning, Doctor," he said, "at breakfast, I heard you telling Admiral Byngham that Captain Thors had been raped by General Daniell. Is that true?"

"Yes. Quite true. I did tell him that."

"Did you tell him," the captain asked, her expression severe, "that you performed an examination on me?"

"I did," the doctor said, trying to look and sound as coolly clinical as possible. He reached for the doorknob and turned it. Casually, he pressed the door open about a foot. "I think it is important that the facts should be known." He raised his voice just enough. "No useful purpose is served, Captain Thors," he said, looking at her almost in tender reprimand, "by pretending that the ravagings of your person were less vile than we know them to have been." He looked then at Sergeant Yost. "Please excuse me. The class is waiting."

As he shut the door behind him, he puffed a contented billow of smoke into the room. It was amazing how all the careful calculations of logical thought could be so casually scrapped and rewritten by that always unexpected intruder in the house of probability—coincidence.

● **KINDNESSES TO CLIO**

On the intercom, the colonel asked Dr. Bosca to come to the office when his class was finished. Waiting, he wondered where the sergeant could be. Yost knew enough by now to be included in the discussion, and he just might be a help.

The doctor made himself comfortable on the couch. Kilburn told of discovering that Daniell had been shot.

"Ha!" The almost-black eyes went wide with sudden interest.

"That's right. And now I'll tell you something else." He ran through a summary of his discussion with Daniell the night before.

"So now," he concluded, "I'm like some priest who knows the one thing the cops don't know—I got it in the confessional and can't tell them. Except that here they wouldn't believe it. Any more than they'd believe he shot Wadlow. And I don't even know who knocked him over. I have to think of a story to fit that one, on top of everything else. That's what I have to talk to you about, Doctor. This isn't just a bunch of facts I'm up against. I'm facing a lot of psychology that's flying around in here."

"Delighted, Colonel. I can help you right off with the easiest part of our problem—the identity of the killer. Sergeant Yost."

"Oh?"

"He came to me with Miss Thors to find out if it was true that I had examined her for rape. I explained that I had, and that she had been most grievously assaulted. All this according to our agreed-upon scenario. Since he had come to me in class, I was careful to see that others received the benefit of my medical report."

"Well, *she* knows it wasn't rape. She must have told him that. Why would he go on thinking it?"

"Ah, Colonel, there we wander off into poetry, politics, romance. True lunacy. What a man chooses to believe is not always what he should believe. For most of history, men chose to believe that the earth was flat. Was that a fact? Americans choose to believe that their country has a most-favored-nation arrangement with God. Is that a fact? To both questions reality answers No. An unfact often does noble work, permitting man to go about his business with more calm, more grace. Anyway, for whatever mysterious reason, Sergeant Yost believed. I have no doubt of it. His table, at breakfast, was only a few feet from the one at which I was feeding the horrors of the rape, according to plan, to our blabbermouth in residence, Admiral Byngham. I had no idea the sergeant would react so dramatically."

"She's his wife. They got married before they came out here. It's a secret."

"Well, in any case, he cannot be permitted to have killed General Daniell. The fact does not suit our purposes."

"Why not?"

"The stakes are too high for mere honesty. How do you think it would look to the world if it heard that a wizard of cosmic Intelligence functions had been brought down in a situation that any suburban milkman would have the good sense to arrange with discretion? It would mean that our leaders were not really gods. That they were only temporary immortals. That they were practically human. The public must not be afflicted with such disheartening news. And as for the all-highest in the Pentagon, they would like it even less. What is the point of all that eminence if you have to think that even some unhappy clerk can push you from Olympus? Believe me, Colonel, it is always easier to accept the wildest kind of explanation than to face the fact that you may be casually dispensable."

"You're telling me, then, that as far as Sergeant Yost is concerned, it couldn't have happened that way?"

"Exactly. I do not claim that, with dogged persistence, the sergeant could not eventually make his admission stick, even against the firmest official opposition. But the results for you, my dear Colonel, would be somewhat worse than exasperating. There would be far too much official rage to be expended on a mere sergeant. You are the one they would see as the betrayer. Daniell is one of their own, and you allowed a classless churl to destroy him. When a god is struck down, people are usually very unhappy if someone of appropriate rank is not punished. Congratulations, Colonel. You are on your way to achieving a form of negative greatness. That is, unless we can find some way to exclude Sergeant Yost from the story."

"He just might exclude himself. If we say nothing, he may figure he's gotten away with it. Assuming that, can we come up with something?"

"It is only a matter of removing the dissonances from the original score. With a little ingenuity we should be able to provide the kind of lullaby you can sleep to."

"The helicopter gets here around five. Can we compose it by then?"

"The French Revolution got 'The Marseillaise' exactly in time to use it. We should be able to do no worse. Now, we have, still, Mr. Wadlow with us? He has not been sent out?"

"He's in the meat house. He'll have to go on the plane with Daniell. So you'd better make a duet out of that thing you're composing."

"Wonderful, Colonel." The doctor blew out much smoke. "I have not had such a challenging assignment since the

Italian government threatened to defrock me—professionally, I mean—for conduct beyond the call of medical duty."

"I'd like to send them up in that plane together, and then crash it. That would tie it up. If I could figure out what they were doing in it, and what to do about the pilot."

"The principle is sound, Colonel. Whatever happened to them was the result of a joint experience. That not only relieves us of the need to think of two separate stories but has the wholesome virtue of making both deaths more believable."

"How do you figure that?"

"It is the Law of Inverse Digestibility—a fact not of physics but of life. The larger the story that must be swallowed, the easier it is for most people to do so. Mr. Hitler understood it well. And even the Bible tells us that a man may strain at a gnat but swallow a camel. So it is only a matter of finding the proper formula."

"When?"

"We're coming to it, little by little, Colonel." A long puff at the dark-brown cigarette. "Here we have two men, each in his own way an American icon. We start with that. We have therefore a responsibility to the nation. Nothing we decide may be permitted to diminish their divine stature. Icons are extremely scarce, and we cannot defraud the American people of any of the very few they are still able to clutch to their bosom. That excludes any possibility of exposing General Daniell as an agent."

"I saw that one coming. But I can live with it."

"He will serve no practical purpose for the enemy. We might as well use him in the way that best serves our own. In death he may give the country far more as a martyr than he was able to give the other side as an agent."

"You're giving me the editorial. How about that tune you were going to work up?"

"Of course. Now Secretary Wadlow, I recall, had three separate wounds. How many bullets for Daniell?"

"I don't know. More than one."

"Well, then—is it possible for a man to secure a pistol on these premises if he really put his mind to it?"

"Daniell did. Not only that, he broke into the gun closet with some of the Guests. They all had guns for a while."

"Those events never happened, Colonel."

"You're right. Sloppy security."

"We will deal with that detail later. But as for our two bodies, I think it best if we provide a scene instantly understandable to the audience we are addressing—not only your superiors, but the American people themselves. If *they* approve of what has happened, then official approval will not be far behind."

"What happened?"

"A shoot-out—two solitary men facing each other on a lonely afternoon, in this far corner of America."

"I always liked that movie," Kilburn said. "But what's it doing in here?"

"I will reconstruct the facts for you, exactly as they happened: Secretary Wadlow, a man who has given much to the American dream, was obsessed with the idea that General Daniell was a foreign agent. He kept his secret from everyone but me, confiding his concern in moments of professional intimacy. I will be able to swear to all this in convincing detail: paranoidal homicidal schizophrenia—the usual. We are on firm ground here. The secretary was dispatched to us originally because of an uneasy relationship with reality. The tendency to believe, therefore, in the collapse of a once noble and inspiring mind, will be all too logical, I can assure you."

"Fine. Now tell me how he did it."

"Is there a weapon, perhaps, in this office?"

Kilburn went to the file cabinet and removed a .45 from the drawer.

"Good," the doctor said. "Then, as we recall it, Wadlow must have seen it during a visit here. When he decided, with that wreckage of a steel-trap mind, to perform this final service for history, he came to your office, caused you to leave for a moment on some pretext, and used your absence to good effect. Because you're a fine security officer, you noticed within minutes that the gun had been stolen. Two and two are put together. You rush off to Wadlow's rooms and find he is not there. Sensing a psychiatric problem, you call me. I hurry with you immediately to General Daniell's rooms, where we find both bodies on the floor. A gun fight has occurred, in the homely and familiar frontier tradition. Mr. Wadlow was obviously let into the room by his unwitting victim. After the first shots, victim was able to wrench murder weapon from hand of unstrung assailant and fire several shots before falling to his final rest. Stranger things, and more unbelievable, have happened in history, Colonel, and people believe them only because they happened. From now on, this happened."

"I'm afraid it didn't and it won't. The bullets in the bodies won't match. They're probably from different guns."

"No one will discover that. Secretary Wadlow was a Christian Scientist. They shrink from autopsy. And I, in my own report of this matter, will emphasize the secretary's fears that anyone should ever tamper with the holy envelope of flesh. It will be made clear that I gave him a doctor's promise that, should he pass on here, no crude medical weapon would invade his person. Your people in Washington would not violate such a sanction. And even if they should, what alternative thesis could they offer to match the symmetry, the smooth believability of ours? They are not in the business of establishing truth. That is for real-estate appraisers, philosophers, and loan officers in banks. Your superiors will want to produce a maximum dividend from the available materials. We are helping them to achieve this. They may choose to edit the story for popular consumption, but ours is the story they will believe."

"What about the Guests? They've already missed Wadlow."

"That only proves he had broken from the reservation, had suddenly turned outlaw. One more small strand of fact to help tie more securely this very neat package of ours. And after what they know of Daniell's odious treatment of their nurse and dietitian, they will see this as the vengeance of God himself."

If a sigh could convey not only relief, but also a sense of pleased admiration, then the colonel's did exactly that.

The door came open, and Sergeant Yost walked slowly into the office.

"Colonel," he said, "I'm turning myself in. I just shot General Daniell."

"What proof do you have of that?" But the doctor's calm question was buried under the colonel's brusque, "What do you mean, you just shot him?"

"I shot him, that's all. For raping Captain Thors. My wife."

"You could not have shot him, Sergeant," Bosca said. "I was talking to him only a few moments ago."

"It couldn't have been General Daniell." Yost shook his head. "I shot him over half an hour ago. In his room. I left him on the floor."

Kilburn rose.

"You wait here, Doctor," he said. "Maybe we can settle this right now." He turned to Yost. "You come with me."

They walked in silence through the corridors till they reached Daniell's quarters. When there was no answer to his knock, the colonel used his master key to open the door. The room was bare.

"Well, Sergeant," Kilburn said, "where's your victim?"

"I don't know, Colonel. But I shot him. I know I shot him. Twice, right in the chest. He was dead when I left him. I don't know what's happened since then. I had a good reason. She's my wife. I don't care what happens now."

"Well, you're going to be a lawyer, Sergeant. Can you tell me how we can have a murder when you can't even find the body?"

The sergeant pointed to a small, kidney-shaped stain in the carpet. "There's some proof," he said. "Blood."

Kilburn shook his head slowly. "No it isn't. It's wine. I did that myself in here, last night."

"Well, I know what I did," Yost said. "I don't know what somebody else did. I left it lying right here, Colonel. I swear."

"Lots of people swear to lots of things, Yost. I don't know what your game is, but you come with me right now. There's at least one thing we can straighten out for you."

Back at the office, he said, "Tell the sergeant about that rape story, Doctor."

"Well, Mr. Yost," Bosca said, "you will have to forgive me for the authority with which I answered a certain question this morning. And for letting you overhear what I told Admiral Byngham. I did not know at either time the depth of your concern in this matter. Colonel Kilburn and I, for reasons that are classified, had devised a plan to smoke a certain party into the open. The story of the rape was a complete fabrication. A necessary lie, you might say. I am truly sorry."

"Then it's even worse," the sergeant said. "Because then I killed an innocent man."

"If you shot him, what gun did you use?" the colonel said.

Yost went to the file drawer and took out the Beretta. "This one."

The colonel took it from him, broke open the chamber, examined the contents with a glance, and looked back at the sergeant.

"I don't see any empty shells in here," he said.

"I threw them down the toilet."

"Only a guilty man would do a thing like that, Sergeant." The doctor's tone was patient and instructive. "But you came here and confessed. Why would you bother to hide clues if you were going to make a clean breast of it?"

"I guess, when I did it, I wasn't sure what I was going to do."

"Well," Kilburn said, "you claim you shot someone, and we go to find the body, and it's not there. Then we look at the gun, and there's no sign it's been used. What do you think you're trying to get away with, Sergeant? Would you mind telling me what you're up to? That's an order."

"Smell the gun, Colonel. You can tell it's just been fired."

Kilburn put his nose to the chamber and breathed deeply.

"I don't smell a thing." He handed the gun to the doctor. "You try it."

"I can smell nothing," Bosca said. "For the past few days I have had a severe cold."

"All right, then, Sergeant," the colonel said. "I don't want to hear any more cock and bull from you about killing. And you're not to discuss it with anyone else, either. Anyone. Meanwhile you're confined to quarters until further notice."

"May I suggest, Colonel," Bosca said, "that the sergeant discuss with Miss Thors an appropriate arrangement about his meals and other matters?"

"O.K." Kilburn nodded to Yost. "That you can do. Just remember what I said about keeping security on this one. All the way." The scowl was official.

"Yes, sir."

With the closing of the door, the colonel spoke.

"This gun is Daniell's—the one he used on Wadlow. That makes it easier for us."

"Not just for us, Colonel."

"Do you think we convinced him?"

"It does not matter. He sees now that despite what he knows, he may have trouble getting his world to believe it. His conscience may yield to this reality. So, in effect, what he knows becomes invalid. The earth, we might say, remains flat, even though he has proved to his own satisfaction that it is actually round. Organized error has once more triumphed over disorganized fact."

"We still have another fact we have to score a win over," Kilburn said. "He helped me to move Wadlow to the meat room."

"I have been thinking of exactly that." The doctor puffed out a long, slow sigh of cigarette smoke. "But even the truth may have its uses for us."

"How?"

"You and I will visit the sergeant this afternoon. We shall reveal to him what actually happened. It will be a sacred national trust we share with him. We will tell it to him not merely as a noncommissioned officer of Intelligence, who must keep this secret for the good of the country, but we shall appeal to an even higher motive—the professional confidence of a man who will soon become a lawyer. His killing of Daniell was an unknowing act of patriotism—but it cannot be admitted as a fact. His trained legal mind will see the point of that immediately."

"And if he tries to go pure on us? If he squeals?"

"Highly unlikely, Colonel. But should it happen, he can be brought to earth easily enough by the revelation in suitable context of a few psychiatric details: he consulted me a number of times. He told me of voices, of visions, of lapses of memory. The usual. But I can assure you, my friend, our Sergeant Yost, with a wife and a brand-new career to think about, is not ready to play Prometheus, to bring down fire from the gods. He will soon find persuasive reasons to share our view of the facts. In a way, it will serve as a kind of on-the-job training for him as a lawyer."

"And what about the reason they sent me here? How do I wrap that up?"

"That is the simplest part of all. The report that an enemy agent had infiltrated here was obviously in error. Even Intelligence makes mistakes, I have heard, Colonel. Daniell will not rise from the grave to prove you a liar."

"And what about those stunts—the cigars, the liquor, the other things?"

"Daniell's work. Done out of boredom. He boasted of them to me, in his last session."

"And he stabbed that Wrangler, too, because he was bored? You thinking of trying that one on anybody?"

"No. You believe that resulted from some personal grudge. Your friend Ramrod may help you there, if he wishes. Anyway, it is unlikely to be repeated."

"You really think we can get away with all this?"

"Unmistakably. We are the only ones in possession of the facts. They are therefore whatever we choose to reveal them to be. National epics are composed from just such private monopolies. Clio, the muse of history, has always required man's assistance to do her job properly. We have only to present our story with a straight face. No extraneous details. When in doubt, we cannot recall. The people to whom we tell our facts will be in the market for exactly these. Never fear, Colonel. For this great work you will go on to even greater glories. You will have proved yourself to your superiors. They will see you as worthy of being, in time— perhaps even a short time—one of themselves."

"What about you? What's going to happen with you after all this? Are you going to keep wasting your time here —governess to a crowd like this? If we get away with it, you really ought to be Chief of Staff."

"I have more important work than that," he said. "I am writing a book. The Guests are my raw material. Such guinea pigs are unprecedented in the history of science. When the result of my work is eventually cast upon the waters, a few people will know a few more facts. Real facts. That will be my reward. Do you know that Sigmund Freud's greatest single book sold exactly six hundred copies in its first eight years?"

"No. I haven't bought a copy yet."

"But a fact exists, my friend, even when the world ignores it."

"Well, you and I have a new way to look at that one, I guess."

"And another fact, Colonel—I think it would be wise to get Sergeant Yost and his lady out of here as soon as possible. Would it present difficulties to have them transferred?"

"I can probably arrange to have them both posted somewhere else."

"Good. As pleasant a place as possible, then. It might make for special problems if he were to continue in this tight little world of ours while sharing an important secret of his superiors. The toxic possibilities are less if he is in isolation somewhere, so to speak."

Colonel Kilburn sighed.

"I don't know if all this will pay off, but at least, the way it sounds, we could make a run for it." He put out his hand and Bosca took it. "I want to thank you, Doctor," he said. "You just might have done me worlds of good."

"And myself too, Colonel."

"Call me Sam."

● BELIEVERS

Before he began class that afternoon, Dr. Bosca called Mr. Cadetti over to him. Medical concern was expressed about the student's curious pallor.

Did he feel a special pain of any kind?

Of course. There was that "golf ball" in his liver.

Well, in view of the flesh tones of the moment, the telltale hang of the submaxillary, it might be well to stay on the safe side.

Mr. Cadetti went happily off to his rooms.

Teacher began with a discussion of Joan of Arc. For the first minutes he had difficulties with General St. John. The general had special insights on how the sainted leader's military tactics might have been improved at Orléans. But the doctor was finally able to silence him. There were aspects of her career, he pointed out, which, while bordering on the province of psychiatry, should have special interest for all leaders of men. She believed in something, and because she believed most powerfully, she was able to communicate this belief to other men. And so, in concert with her, they marched together and France was saved. Moral: it was dangerous to approach certain facts with a jeweler's eyeglass.

ITEM:

It was well known that the lyrics of the national anthem were virtually unsingable. That they lacked the simplicity and drive of other national chants. That the music was borrowed from an old English drinking song. And yet, despite such disadvantages, it worked. All true Americans were convinced that it was the best song in the world.

ITEM:

It was the motto of the Texas Rangers that "A little man can always beat a big man, if he just keeps coming." To keep coming, you had to believe in something that went beyond the visible facts.

ITEM:

The True Church, holding dominion in the West for almost two thousand years, was based on certain evidences that would be inadmissible at a well-run court-martial. But to poke and pry at such details was only a form of nit-picking. The bumblebee did not care that mathematicians had proved its wingspread inadequate to lift its body mass off the ground. It flew nevertheless. And so the flight of the one true religion, like so many others, has been powered by a sound psychological axiom: to those who believe, all is possible.

The class was asked to name a single notable mountain that had been moved by nonbelievers.

None.

Most of the glory in the history of the world had been achieved by men who had visions, dreams, faith in their star. Belief was a form of energy, and no man or nation could become great without it. The world may yield itself to many suitors, but least happily to those who approach it only with verifiable facts. People like that were fit only to live behind desks.

"And so, gentlemen," he said, "if we believe in something hard enough and lovingly enough, then, regardless of the opinion an engineer may have of it, it becomes for us a working fact. We will now address ourselves to what purpose can be most usefully served by the facts we may have, or the beliefs we may choose to have, in the matter of the absence of Secretary Wadlow. And also our General Daniell. Question: Is it not true that a graceful myth can sometimes be far more valuable to a people than an ugly fact? Answer: Unmistakably. And so, for the good of his country and his time, the lips of the wise and heroic leader will, with the knowledge of certain facts, remain sealed."

Details and discussion followed, and it was one of the more exciting classes, they all agreed. There was much for each student to ponder. Later, in the sauna, they talked among themselves and came to the conclusion that Dr. Bosca was one of the most thoughtful and perceptive men any of them had ever met, among civilians.

That night, listening to the tapes with Colonel Kilburn, the doctor nodded amiably through the cigarette smoke, as the recorded voices chatted away about the inherent good sense in Teacher's little talk on the "Napoleons of Silence."

● THE TRUTH (SEMIOFFICIAL)

Only the briefest and most bare account was released from Washington. The first speculations appeared in print almost immediately, followed by a gush of inspired guesses made available through reliable source, informed circle, and other anonymous founts. And when official corroboration was sought from those who were in a position not only to know but also to purvey what they knew, there was only the most frigid of refusals to explain.

For nine days the newspapers and the American air shouted of the catastrophic plane crash (sabotage? fog? human or mechanical error? other?) as the bodies lay in state. Queries about pilot, plane, and crew were deflected with the maximum-security response of "No comment." Even though the site of the crash remained unrevealed, judicious guessing placed it somewhere in the Southeast (Fort Benning? Cape Kennedy?) But in the nightmare of speculation, gossip, and uneasy rumor, one fact stood out clearly. A severe blow had been dealt that firm and unwobbling international equilibrium to which reasonable men had given the name "peace." Washington was considering appropriate new measures.

Secretary Wadlow was not a military man, but he had, in his junior year at college, been an active member of ROTC. This fact, among others, was noted in the executive order that permitted him to be buried in Arlington Cemetery, alongside General Daniell. The ceremony was discreet but affecting. After the more formal speeches, a few terse words of farewell were spoken by "a Colonel Kilburn, believed to be a close friend of both men." Posthumous awards were buried with the caskets, as a lone bugler sounded taps.

● TOWARD THE FUTURE

Although the new assignment was only a few hours from Phoenix, Sergeant Yost was in no great hurry. He waited. It was some weeks after his wife had finished redecorating their off-the-base apartment that he felt ready. At that time he included, in one of his papers on Cross-Examination, a note of inquiry: now that he was nearing the end of the course, and since he expected to be in Phoenix on a forthcoming afternoon, would it be possible for him to visit the Academy?

The reply was cool. It did not welcome, but it did not reject.

He felt disappointed as he stood across the street from the two-story frame building. The flaking brown paint added to the general air of seediness. He had not been prepared for quite this obvious absence of visible stability. It would have been a good deal closer to his idea of the fitness of things if the place had been built of granite, or at least of brick.

He was even more uneasy, on entering the lobby, to discover that the school did not occupy the entire building. It was located on the top floor, and there it laid claim only to four rooms.

When he met the mysterious gentleman—elderly, lean, palsied, with the look of a secret lush—who corrected all his papers, he thought better of his original idea, which was to invite the man out for a drink. After a few casual remarks, the exchange of sober legal precepts, the sergeant descended the stairs and drove home.

"You know, Susie," he said, "I wouldn't have minded so much if it only looked a little better. A little more solid. So a guy could have some faith in the school, at least. But it looked like the kind of a place where everybody expects it to be raided any minute. The way they operate there, like it's undercover, you get the feeling they think they're doing something illegal."

"Listen, Norm," she said, "don't worry so much. It's accredited, so what do you care what it looks like? I'll bet Abraham Lincoln's law school didn't look so marvelous, either. The important thing is that you get the degree. After that, what you *do* with it is the only thing that matters. Nobody's going to care where it came from if you make a nice noise with it every time you swing it in court."

Her words cheered him.

"I can hardly wait to get started on it," he said. "Meanwhile, you sound just like Doctor Bosca. That's the kind of thing he'd be throwing out every once in a while."